HERMIONE LEE

Evernight Teen ®

www.evernightteen.com

ISBN: 978-0-3695-1129-4

Cover Artist: Jay Aheer

Editor: Stephanie Marrie

HERMIONE LEE

DEDICATION

To Blake Alb, Denise Sawicki, and Darrell Sawicki, three of the loveliest people I've ever met. You changed my life and made me a better person, and I'll always be grateful to have known you.

ACKNOWLEDGEMENTS

Thank you to Stacey Adderley and Stephanie Marrie from Evernight Teen for making my novel the best it can be. I'm grateful for your help and am honored to work with you two. A huge thank you to my beta readers—Cheryl Peña and Shine Wang, for your honest feedback. Last but not least, thank you to my family and writer friends—Blake Alb, Candice Lisle, Darrell Sawicki, Denise Sawicki, Gloria Lakritz, Julie Parker, Lee Ann Sontheimer Murphy, and Tonya Staufer—for being a part of my journey. Finally, thank you to every reader who picked up a copy of *Stars, Clouds, and Shadows*. I hope this novel takes you on an emotional rollercoaster and leaves a profound impression on you. Please note that the angels and devils in the story are not religious or associated with any religion. Enjoy the ride and the surprises along the way!

HERMIONE LEE

STARS, CLOUDS, AND SHADOWS

Hermione Lee

Copyright © 2025

A rose by any other name would smell as sweet.

—William Shakespeare, *Romeo and Juliet*

HERMIONE LEE

Preface

They had instructed her to assassinate him. But in the end, she couldn't. Her family and her clan imposed their expectations on her, but he was the only boy who loved her for who she was. How could she betray someone who had stolen her heart, who had become a fragment of her soul? To eliminate him would mean destroying an indispensable part of herself. She would never be complete again.

"I'm sorry," Evangelina whispered, to herself, to him, and to her fellow angels. She was about to make a decision that would change her life forever.

HERMIONE LEE

Chapter One

Innocent
(Evangelina)

"What? Murder him?"

Numb with shock, Evangelina Leclair stared at her father. Were her ears deceiving her? True, her clan held a grudge against the devils for ages, but killing one of them? The angels hadn't been that extreme before. They never were.

Her father Milton glared at her, decisiveness etched upon every inch of his face. "You will do as I say," he ordered. "Why?" Evangelina burst out foolishly. "Why kill him? Why stoop to that level? We're angels. Not vigilantes. Why should we kill them just because they threatened us? How does that make us any better than they are?"

Her father's eyes flashed with anger. She had touched a nerve. Fifty-three years old with a hot temper, he never tolerated disobedience. "Evangelina Leclair, am I not making myself clear?"

Evangelina pursed her lips. Contradicting him was one thing, but following his absurd and unwise plan could lead to the demise of their entire angelic clan. The devils had been their enemies for centuries, and they had slayed countless angels during battles. Yet indignant as she was, she would never take an innocent life and use their ongoing rivalry as an excuse.

Her father rose to his feet, hands on his hips. "Let me make this clear. You are to murder a devil by the name of Diome Lenoir, a junior in Horizon High, a human high school. Approach him, befriend him, and eliminate him after lowering his guard. This is an order, not a plea."

"He did nothing wrong!" Evangelina countered, rising to her feet. "He's innocent! Just like the thousands of angels in our clan!"

"Evangelina, do not talk back to your father!" her mother Golda snapped. "This is for the best."

Evangelina turned to her. "The best? Murdering someone for the greater good?" She shook her head, unable to follow their logic. "What if it was someone from our tribe? What if the devils killed an angel and advertised it a deed 'for the greater good?' If we want to end all battles, we should reason with the devils instead."

"They have no reason," her father retorted. "They're the cruelest, most malevolent beings imaginable. Those evil creatures started more than half of the battles in history. Nasty, chaos-loving monsters they are."

"But what difference does it make if we—if I—kill Diome Lenoir? The rivalry won't end. Nothing will change."

"One devil down. And the more devils dead, the better."

Evangelina sighed. "Dad, he's innocent. He's just like me, just a teenager, but only from a different clan. Why target him?"

He glared at her. "Innocent? The devils are all guilty."

"Not him," Evangelina insisted. "And not the thousands of babies and teenagers in the devil clan. They don't deserve this at all."

"Well, switch sides and join the devils if you think so highly of them!" her father thundered, his cheeks paling in fury. "If you have a shred of self-respect left, I expect you to obey me and kill that devil. Fail to do so, and there will be consequences."

And with that, he stood up and breezed out of the living room while a dazed, disoriented Evangelina remained rooted to the spot.

****

As she shuffled back to her room that night, Evangelina had a sinister premonition: her erratic heartbeat pounding in her ears. The origin of the hatred between angels and devils was a tale older than time, yet it had a profound impact on their lives for centuries. Evangelina stared out of the white-framed window in her bedroom at the ocean of churning clouds below. Stars sprinkled the vast universe, dotting it like glitter on black velvet. It was a charming sight to behold, even more so at twilight. Their house was built on the clouds, or to be precise, among the clouds. All angels resided in the Land of Heavenly Dreams, high above the world humans called home, and even higher above the burning bowels where the devils dwelled. It was ironic, how their rivalry thrived despite how far away from each other the two clans lived. The angels and devils had always been enemies, but Evangelina didn't understand why her father was so dead set on having her murder a teenage devil out of the blue. Was it because he was an easy target, a mere student in a human high school?

With a sigh, Evangelina flopped down on her bed, pulled the fluffy cloud-woven blankets to her chest, and analyzed the reason why she had defied her father that afternoon. He'd been so furious at her disobedience that he refused to speak to her for the rest of the day, yet she had a valid reason to disobey him. His plan was ridiculous. They were angels, not assassins. Just because the devils killed their people didn't mean it was acceptable for them to pay their enemies back with bloodshed. That would only result in a vicious cycle of misunderstanding, discrimination, and rivalry. However, what bothered her the most was leaving her comfort zone and descending into the human world just to approach a devil and murder him. Evangelina had no idea what humans were like, but her mother could coach her on that the subject. Golda, like some angels, had chosen to get a proper education in a proper human school. Evangelina, on the other hand, had been shielded from the humans' culture since birth. She was oblivious to many things they deemed normal, and she dreaded the possibility of accidentally exposing their existence to her human classmates. Evangelina would no doubt end up banished from their clan in that unfortunate case.

A few of the devils also learned from the humans, as evidenced by the little information she knew about Diome Lenoir. All the devils were surnamed Lenoir, while all the angels were surnamed Leclair, since they were both clans rather than races. *Diome's just like my mother,* thought Evangelina. Like her, he must be an aspiring inventor who dreamed of making life more convenient for those living in magical realms by studying in human schools and learning their technology and culture. It was all thanks to those inventors that there were malls, hotels, and libraries in the heavenly towns, and beds, bathrooms, and kitchens in their magical realm. The only thing the angels didn't need was light, as they were granted the ability to summon light as necessary. All they had to do was to channel their energy by pointing at a candle, and it would glow brighter than a lightbulb. The angels could determine their light's color, shape, and heat, and at the same time could to extinguish it.

Those were gifts Evangelina had been born with, gifts she cherished even though many angels took them for granted. The devils were blessed—or rather, cursed—with the flair of summoning darkness. Their powers brought destruction and death. The mere notion sent a frisson crawling down her spine. The notion of approaching and then killing one of the devils terrified her more than anything else.

Yet most curious about her future was interacting with the humans. It was hard to imagine there lived a group of people that could neither channel the light nor harness the darkness, yet considered themselves "normal." None of the angels dared to venture into the human world for longer than a day, not even Evangelina's parents, for risking their exposure would spell disaster for their entire clan. The humans might hunt them down or put them in science labs and examine them.

The young angels attended school too, where the teachers—all angels—taught them English, math, history, geography, and human studies, always finding a way to instill the ideology that devils were evil and that the angels would prevail over them one day. Education in the Land of Heavenly Dreams was a form of brainwashing.

Evangelina wondered what school in the human world was like. What would she learn? She also wondered about Diome Lenoir, and whether he knew he was targeted by the angels. It was ironic. The humans regarded angels as celestial beings, the epitome of pureness and kindness. Yet she knew better than anyone else that the angels were simply a bunch of vigilantes who were no better than their underground enemies. The devils killed angels with their dark magic, while the angels retaliated by blinding them with light and murdering them with incandescent, white-hot sparks. The angels were no saints, yet every angel sought a reason to harm the devils, to prove themself superior to them. The devils wasted no effort in doing the same, launching attacks and invasions on the Land of Heavenly Dreams from time to time. It was cruel and perverse, but there was nothing Evangelina could do. Their rivalry was like a mountain, unmovable, significant, and impactful.

Again, Evangelina's mind drifted to Diome Lenoir. What was he like? What could he be doing at this moment? Might he figure out his fate?

But that was impossible. His fate rested with her, and she had a decision to make.

Go to sleep, Evangelina, she reminded herself. Taking one last glance at the confetti of constellations outside the window, she dipped and swirled into her dreamscapes, painting a thousand possible versions of the future.

****

Too soon, a week passed. The time had come for Evangelina to make her descent. The angels were accustomed to wearing long, flowing robes, but sometimes they dressed in human clothes. Evangelina had plenty of shirts, pants, skirts, and dresses in her wardrobe, so getting ready for human school wasn't a huge challenge.

Evangelina took off her thick, feathery wings and set them on her bed, grateful that angels were born with removable wings. She headed into the bathroom and splashed her face with the cool water, then dried it with a fluffy white towel. With a thick mane of platinum-blonde waves and clear, pale blue eyes, she was the envy of many angels. She, however, didn't obsess over her appearance. Unlike the vain girls she knew, Evangelina believed a kind heart mattered a thousand times more than an attractive face. Sometimes the most important things in life were invisible to the naked eye.

Evangelina donned a white shirt with ruffles on the front, picked up a dark blue skirt, and pressed it to her frame in front of her elliptical mirror. She hoped she could fit in with the other students, not because she was a conformist, but because she had a genuine interest in humans and wanted to befriend them.

Her mother popped into the bathroom. "Hurry up, sweetie. You're going to be late."

"All right. I'm coming."

Evangelina stepped into a pair of black loafers and grabbed her bag. With a heart full of anxiety and excitement, she dashed down the stairs.

"Good morning. Have you got your wings ready?" her father asked before sipping a steaming cup of coffee at the breakfast table.

"Oh, they're still in my room." Evangelina raced up the stairs, taking two at a time.

She put on her wings, shrugged, and flew back downstairs. "School ends at four, right?"

"At Horizon High, yes. Don't forget your breakfast. And remember to bring your human money."

The angels sold magical food—cloud cakes, stardust cupcakes, and moonlight milkshakes to the humans. Any angel about to embark on a trip to the human world could exchange their currency for human money in the Bank of Heavenly Dreams.

Her father entered the kitchen and returned with a small lunchbox filled with baked bread and sliced apples.

"Thank you, Dad," whispered Evangelina. Ever since the argument about murdering Diome, the two of them spoke little.

Although Evangelina made no attempt to contradict her father's order, she hadn't conceded. Perhaps he would change his mind soon. She could try talking sense into her father in a few weeks, hopefully when he had forgotten about their earlier argument. Or if that didn't work, she could convince Diome to transfer to another school. Then she would have a reason to fail her mission, and her father wouldn't blame her.

What would she do after her descent? Would she obey her father's commands or would she succumb to her conscience? Evangelina had never killed anyone or anything before, not even an insect. Yet she had no intention of enduring her father's wrath. He hated the devils with every fiber of his being, for his parents—Evangelina's grandmother and grandfather—both died in one of the innumerable invasions the devils had initiated. Her father could disown her should she refuse to comply with his orders. He'd always had a fiery temper, but never had he stormed out of the room with intense indignation burning in his pupils as he had that afternoon. Testing his patience would no doubt be foolish and reckless.

"I'm going to school." Evangelina waved to her parents. "Goodbye."

She stepped outside and inhaled the fresh, clean morning air. Their house, like all the other angels', was built on one of the many floating islands high above the clouds. Mint-green grass and tiny pink, yellow, orange, and blue tulips blanketed the lawn outside her home. She could make out the faraway islands in the distance, some obscured by light swirls of mist, others vivid with bright blossoms and rippling fields of verdant grass.

The sky was a lovely, spotless azure today. There was not a single cloud in sight. Below her lay a swirling ocean of clouds, white, gray, and every hue in between, separating their land from the human world. Evangelina beamed. The clouds were different every day, but she could appreciate the beauty in every form they took. Living in the clouds was truly amazing. She couldn't believe there were humans down there, miles below her, oblivious to the marvels dwelling in the clouds. The humans couldn't have known about their culture and the vibrant hills on the floating islands. Evangelina's mother had told her about the humans and their greed. They had ravaged countless forests and destroyed innumerable lands for their obsession with gold. Yet despite that, she believed not all humans were like that. It was wrong to stereotype a group of people and impose the crimes of a certain few on them, just because they were all humans. She still wanted to befriend her new classmates and find out more about them.

Reaching the end of the cobblestone path outside her house, Evangelina took a leap and dove down. She shrugged her shoulders, spreading her wings. The clouds hung low, much lower than usual, and she smiled at the idea of how many mysteries they veiled. Of course, she had been to the human world before, but those were brief visits, no longer than three hours. This time, she would be there for seven hours.

Evangelina passed the thick film of clouds, or rather, they passed her, enveloping her figure in a moist blanket of white fog. She liked how the soft clouds feathered against her face. Although they were no more than wisps of mist, they beautified everything they covered.

Soaring through the clouds was therapeutic. The soft, constant hum of the wind, the cool, calming air, and the blossoms of cloudy mists and misty clouds that adorned the pure blue skies made a wonderful multi-sensory experience.

Veiled by the clouds, Evangelina spotted a small green meadow way down below. Horizon Park. That was the park her parents had instructed her to land on. The east side was separated from the rest of the park by a patch of trees, a haunted forest according to rumors. Very few humans came to the east part of Horizon Park, which made it an ideal destination for her descent. She couldn't afford to be exposed.

Evangelina approached the field as she gathered speed and lowered her body, dipping down and preparing for her great dive. When she was ready, she made an almost vertical nosedive, pulling up when the ground was only ten feet from her face. Then, she let her shoulders sag and succumbed to gravity. Her feet hit solid ground in a matter of moments. She tapped twice on both shoulders and let her wings drop. Scanning the area to check if anyone was watching, she shrank her wings by tapping on the iridescent feather buried among the fluffy white ones. After stuffing the shrunken wings into a small pocket in her school bag, she took out her map and studied the crisscrossing roads.

"Horizon Street," she muttered. "On the other side of the park."

Turning around, she spotted a tall blue-bricked building. A golden plaque hung on the front, flaunting the words *Horizon High*.

Evangelina smiled. Her day was going well.

"Not off to a bad start, huh?" she murmured to herself as she headed for her new school.

The closer she got, the more worried she became, however. What if the teachers made her introduce herself? It was October, and the new term had already begun. Her parents had told the administration office she was homeschooled. Perhaps she could fabricate a convincing story about the fun subjects her parents invented and taught her. Evangelina tried to brainstorm, but her mind, crammed with possible versions of her first day of school, refused to cooperate.

She wondered what her course schedule would be like and whether she would share any classes with Diome Lenoir. Perhaps they had no classes together. In that case, she would have a reason not to get acquainted with him.

But even so, her father would make her find a way to approach him. Approaching him didn't mean she had to do the deed, though. She could befriend him and warn him against her father's evil plan, beg him to transfer to another school, and lie to her father. She never told lies, for she couldn't cope with the overwhelming guilt, but a lie was a small price to pay if it meant she could spare an innocent life.

The school gates were tall and ornate, reminding Evangelina of the palaces she read of in storybooks. Schools were palaces of knowledge. That realization rendered the edifice before her more sublime than ever.

A steady stream of students poured through the doors, and Evangelina joined them. They were interesting, she noticed. Some had pale skin while others had darker complexions. Unlike the angels, their hair came in different colors: red, orange, blond, black, brown, and every color in between. Many of them turned to stare at her as she passed them. Her stomach knotted itself.

"Is that a new kid?" a boy with dark skin asked a girl with red pigtails.

"Might be. I don't remember her from any of my classes."

"Her hair is almost white. And she's so tall and pretty."

Evangelina sighed with relief. They hadn't figured out her identity. They were simply attracted to her appearance. Making her way up the front steps of the school, she hurried to the administration office, head bowed and shoulders hunched, hoping to draw as little attention as possible.

The school was a labyrinth, much larger than the angels' school she attended. Evangelina cursed the map.

"Sorry, do you know where the administration

office is?" she asked a dark-skinned girl with black plaits.

"Over there." The girl pointed to the end of the corridor. "Last room on the right."

Evangelina beamed. "Thank you."

She hurried to the office and pushed the wooden door open. "Excuse me, is Mr. Bryant here?" she asked the nearest teacher, a bald man with glasses. Mr. Bryant was the teacher in charge of new students, as her parents had informed her.

"I am Mr. Bryant. You're Evangelina Leclair, the new student in eleventh grade, I suppose? How do you do?"

Evangelina giggled in a fruitless attempt to disguise her nervousness. "A bit anxious, to be honest. I've never been to a real school before."

She was being truthful, but not entirely. Her main concern was that someone would figure out what she was. However, there was no way she could tell Mr. Bryant her worries.

"Don't be afraid, Evangelina," chirped Mr. Bryant with a friendly grin. "The kids here are nicer than the ones in Redwood High, the school I worked in last year. You'll like everyone here, I promise. Here's your course schedule, by the way." He handed her a timetable. "Your first class is homeroom in room 104, and your second class is history in Room 301."

"And my homeroom teacher is?"

"Mrs. Hoover."

"Got it, thank you."

Evangelina found her homeroom, a corner classroom that overlooked the town of Horizon through a tall floor-length window. Curious, she gazed up at the clouds. No sight of any floating islands. Human civilization was quite similar to the angels, except that their land wasn't split into thousands of small floating islands.

Taking a seat in the last row, Evangelina studied her timetable. Her mind drifted to Diome, her target. She made a bet with herself whether he would be in her homeroom or not.

More and more kids filed in. She studied them. People-watching was rather interesting: guessing their backstories, wondering about their lives, and imagining what it was like to be them. What were they thinking? Not many of them had noticed her, thanks to the seat she had chosen.

Mrs. Hoover, a pretty lady with caramel-colored skin and braided hair, entered the classroom. Her eyes found Evangelina's, and she nodded at her.

"Well, we're joined by a new classmate today," she announced, flashing an impeccable smile at Evangelina. "Evangelina Leclair, welcome to Horizon High."

The kids twisted around in their seats to stare at Evangelina, whose blood boiled in her cheeks. A torrent of hushed murmurs erupted among the other students. Whatever they whispered about, Evangelina didn't want to know.

"Would you like to introduce yourself?" Mrs. Hoover asked.

"Yes, ma'am. So, uh, good morning, everyone. I've been homeschooled ever since I was five. Horizon High is a lovely school, and I look forward to learning more here."

She cringed at the awkwardness, wishing she could jump into a hole. What was she saying? Evangelina contemplated whether it was possible to die from shame. She sounded like a robot who had rehearsed her lines too well.

"Nice to hear that, Evangelina. What do you like

to do in your free time? Any hobbies?"

Soaring through the clouds and navigating the floating islands, Evangelina thought, suppressing a smile as she imagined the teacher's reaction at her insane reply.

Just then, a figure emerged in the doorway, seizing her attention. He was a boy about her height, with fluffy raven hair, wild eyebrows, and dark gray eyes. Dressed in black from head to toe, he had on a leather jacket, black jeans, and a skull necklace.

He was handsome in a way Evangelina never imagined she would appreciate but was inexplicably drawn to. There was arrogance in his eyes. An aura of darkness traced his figure.

Mrs. Hoover's gaze followed Evangelina's to the doorway, and she noticed the boy. "Ah, I thought you were still stuck in the traffic jam on Horizon Street," she joked. "Glad you made it here just in time, Diome."

Evangelina's mind came to a screeching halt. *Diome? Not ... Diome Lenoir?*

Chapter Two

Not in a Thousand Years
(Diome)

The moment Diome Lenoir saw her, he was mesmerized.

How could anyone possess such beauty, such grace? She was incredible. He took the seat beside hers, nodding a quick greeting. His heart raced already.

Mrs. Hoover asked the new girl about her family and hometown, but Diome was too focused on her beauty to listen. To be precise, it wasn't her beauty alone that attracted him. Her soft yet firm voice, her serene demeanor, and her confidence differentiated her from the others. Her face was devoid of makeup, baring her stunning features: long eyelashes, eyes like pale blue sapphires, thin eyebrows the perfect shade of brown, and coral red lips. Many of the boys were eyeing her too, but she didn't pay them much attention.

"Thank you, Evangelina," continued Mrs. Hoover. "Now, everyone, the school has asked me to inform you that ... "

Diome focused on his geography textbook, pretending to develop an interest in the map of the human world. He rested his head on his chin, swept his bangs to the right, and snuck a glance at Evangelina through the screen of hair. She was minding her own business, doodling a cloud on a piece of paper—her course schedule. Instead of texting on her phone, taking pictures of herself, or reapplying her makeup, she was lost in a realm of her creations. She was a white lily among a sea of garish blossoms with a natural charm that spoke volumes.

Clouds. Something in Diome's mind clicked. Could it be? Might she be an angel? Like most of them, her hair was blonde, almost white, and her azure eyes surpassed that of the bluest sky. *But how was that possible?* An angel in a human school. How high were the chances of that happening?

But just because it was unlikely didn't mean it was impossible. He himself was a devil from the Burning Bowels, for instance. The humans knew nothing about their existence. None of the kids suspected he was a supernatural creature. But under the raven hair, dark clothes, and human flesh, he had burgundy blood—devil blood—coursing through his veins.

There was a common misunderstanding among the humans that all devils were evil, while all angels were kind. Diome, his family, and his fellow devils were born with the gift of harnessing the darkness. He could summon puffs of black smoke, extinguish flames with a snap of his fingers, and destroy objects with hellfire. Unlike the dainty flames angels lit, the devils' cursed fire melted candles in an instant and ruined everything consumed by the blazes. Diome had always considered it unfair that "devil" had the word "evil" in it. Like a self-fulfilling prophecy for new devil babies, it was as if they were destined to dwell in the darkness.

Depressed. That was the only word Diome associated with himself. Every now and then, he found himself trapped in a bottomless pit of sadness. He resented himself, everything about him, and especially his identity as a devil. How was it fair that angels had a natural affinity for light when devils were the ones despised and connected with darkness? As much as he knew about human culture, they worshipped angels and shunned devils in many religions. But in reality, neither side was better. The angels and devils had a long history of hatred. Whenever they fought, both sides sustained great losses. Far from pacifists or virtuous guardians of the light, they too initiated invasions in the Burning Bowels and ambushed the devils. An enmity as old as time, Diome knew both sides were to blame. Equally guilty, nothing gave anyone—devil or angel—a reason to kill. Such disrespect for life was appalling. Diome remembered the shock when he first learned of their rivalry with the angels at the age of five. Whenever the topic arose, his parents become almost unrecognizable, overcome with a sizzling desire to eradicate every single angel in the Land of Heavenly Dreams. Growing up, he learned nothing was constant—he could be breathing his last on any day. Having survived countless invasions, he had witnessed intense battles of light, darkness, and flames. He witnessed devils die before him while he was utterly powerless, unable to save them and stop the raging chaos in the Burning Bowels. That was where his depression stemmed from, he supposed. The sense of helplessness that plagued him all the time, trailing behind him like a kite's tail. Before the deep, bottomless hatred both clans had accumulated over the course of history, Diome stood weak, small, and feeble, more vulnerable than he would have liked to admit.

****

At lunchtime, Diome took his usual spot at the corner table. He had no friends, and although he was always polite to anyone who approached him, he never revealed more about himself than necessary. In their eyes, he was the weird loner who couldn't fit into the crowd but wasn't mean to anyone either. Perhaps some of them deemed him haughty or arrogant, for he never socialized with them unless the teachers made them work in groups. Yet under that aloof exterior, he was timid and terrified.

He chewed on his vegetable and chicken breast salad, wondering how Horizon High could churn out such rubbery and flavorless meat. Were all school lunches that horrible? The slices of cabbage and lettuce were bitter. The tomato was so sour it made him frown.

Glancing up at the clock, he caught sight of a tall figure with long, platinum-blonde hair at the entrance of the cafeteria. Evangelina.

For a moment, Diome contemplated whether he should invite her to his table. It was empty, with plenty of space to accommodate more than a few people. But would she accept his offer? Plus, what if he let slip of his true identity? He didn't want to frighten her away.

A girl with curly brown hair and a fuzzy blue sweater approached Evangelina. "Hi, Evangelina. I'm Camille Barton. You're in my math class, I remember. Do you need a place to sit? What about joining me and my friend Merilee Summers?"

Evangelina smiled. "I'd love to. Thanks."

Diome's heart sank. He had let his insecurities get the best of him again. Sighing, he devoted his attention to the salad again, though his appetite had dwindled.

Fifth period—art—came after lunchtime. Mr. Paterson, the art teacher, never cared whether the kids turned in their projects on time or not. Rumor had it that he gave everyone in his class an A no matter how lousily they performed. Since he was so laid-back, everyone took advantage of him and never paid attention to him in class.

Diome got out his history textbook and flipped through it, oblivious of Mr. Paterson's long, boring drawl about paper crafts. He enjoyed learning about the humans' culture and all sorts of historical events; however, they often perplexed him. The rivalry between the various ethnic groups was something he found inconceivable—to wit, the Holocaust, the Cultural Revolution, and the Cambodian Genocide. They were all humans, weren't they? Both the perpetrators and the victims. Why torment each other so? It made less sense to him than the hatred between the devils and angels.

There was a commotion from the other end of the classroom. Diome, who had been cramming the names of the prominent world leaders during World War II into his head, glanced up. A throng of boys had gathered by the table beside his. He caught a glimpse of Evangelina's hair among the crowd. Mr. Paterson, engrossed in whatever was on his computer screen, was unaware of the cacophony in the classroom.

Curious, Diome approached them.

"I should take her to the infirmary," Warren declared.

"No, you already helped her carry her books to her locker this morning!" another boy cut in.

"I didn't! She rejected my help in the end."

Diome peered over Evangelina's shoulder and caught her pressing a handkerchief to her hand. She removed it and dabbed at the cut with a tissue. To Diome's utmost astonishment, her blood was white. Before he could inspect it, she taped the tissue to her gash.

Flabbergasted, Diome struggled to process what he had witnessed. It couldn't be. A glance at the immaculate tissue on her hand answered his question. There wasn't a speck of crimson on the white fabric.

Evangelina was an angel.

The sudden realization shook Diome. She had almost exposed the angels' existence to the others, but fortunately, the boys surrounding her were so engrossed in their argument they paid no attention to her blood. Some of them had even started wrestling, attracting more bystanders.

"I want to!" Warren shouted.

"You've had your fun," growled Norman. "Last time Sarah Brookes came, you escorted her to her homeroom and—"

"That's last time!" Warren yelled, punching his arm. "This time, I—"

"Excuse me." Evangelina stood up abruptly and skirted around the boys. "I'd like to go alone."

Like a weightless shadow, she glided over to Mr. Paterson, informed him of what had happened, and exited the art classroom. The boys, who had ended their fight, returned to their seats grumbling, while many girls glared at Evangelina's retreating figure, jealousy shooting from their eyes like arrows.

What an independent spirit, thought Diome. She didn't like being pampered like a princess or relying on others. He walked back to his table and gazed at the words and pictures. For some reason, they blurred into a meaningless blob of colors. All he could think of was Evangelina, how different she was from all the girls he knew. Like a pristine white lotus, she rose tall and proud, the other flowers paling in comparison. Her purity was unrivaled. It carried a certain hint of detachment. Ethereal and otherworldly, she didn't belong in the mundane human world. She was a divine creature that had descended from the skies.

Now that Diome came to think of it, wasn't it true? Evangelina was an angel who hailed from the Land of Heavenly Dreams. A serious realization struck him, and his spirit plummeted. Evangelina and her clan of angels were the devils' enemies. Even though Diome didn't care what she was or where she came from, they would never have a future together. It was impossible. Their families wouldn't approve of it.

Diome rested his head in his arms, suddenly overcome by a tide of frustration. It was as if he had woken up from a beautiful dream, and all the wonderful possibilities he had entertained vanished. As much as he adored Evangelina, their fates were written in the stars even before they were born. They could never fall in love, much less maintain a cordial friendship—that was, as long as his identity was exposed. Diome could choose not to reveal what he was, but if he wished to become more than friends with her, there would come a day when he would have to unravel his façade. In fairy tales, the prince still loved Cinderella no matter how humble her status. But if the genders were reversed, and the stakes were higher, would it still be the same? Diome could not expect her to accept him the way he was. His people had murdered millions—or, he shuddered at the likelihood of a possible higher death toll—of angels. How could he be foolish enough to imagine she would love him after learning of his background?

The merry bell announced the beginning of recess. Diome rose to his feet, grabbed his book bag, and left with a heart heavier than ever.

On the way to his next class, geography, he passed the infirmary and spotted Evangelina sitting by the nurse, who was talking on the phone.

"Excuse me," Evangelina's friend Camille cut in. Merilee soon followed. Diome stepped aside to let the two girls pass.

"Evangelina, are you all right?" Merilee asked.

"I'm fine. Just hurt my finger during art class."

"Paper cut?" Camille asked.

"A pair of scissors. It's not serious, though."

"Let me see."

Outside, Diome held his breath.

"How come it's white?" Camille asked.

"Someone spilled white paint on my finger," Evangelina lied. Diome sighed with relief. He heard Camille murmur a reply but wasn't close enough to hear her clearly. Gazing at the three of them through the doorway, he debated with himself whether he should approach Evangelina and show his concern for her. But still, he couldn't bring himself to enter the infirmary. He feared rejection, but more than that, he feared if she welcomed his arrival and befriended him, he would grow attached to her. And once they formed a bond—be it platonic or romantic, he would never in an eternity find the courage to come clean about his identity. Part of him deemed himself unworthy of her affection, for she was an angel, a creature high above in the skies. There was a rift between them that nothing could bridge, both literally and metaphorically.

Diome thought of his favorite play *Romeo and Juliet* by William Shakespeare, his favorite playwright in the human world. The two star-crossed lovers had a relationship strong enough to move mountains, but their romance was destined to end up in ashes, for the Montagues and the Capulets had let rivalry blind them. They were too immersed in their hatred for each other to realize how much pressure the animosity between the two clans had imbued in young Romeo and Juliet. When they discovered truth of their forbidden love, it was too late. They couldn't reverse the tragedy, and the lovers could only reunite after death.

Therefore, Diome concluded that love wasn't as powerful as people claimed. Yes, it could save lives and change hearts. But in this case, everything was insurmountable. There were too many hurdles he had to jump over, too many barriers to break through. He had not an inkling what Evangelina thought of him, and whether she even knew of his existence.

Or was he being too pessimistic? Should he have more faith in love, or at least attempt to confess his crush on her? It was love at first sight. A deep part of him knew that the same way he knew his name. But then again, how could Diome summon the courage to approach her when he had never been brave enough to face himself?

****

The sun shone among the clouds that afternoon, but that, if anything, depressed Diome further. Everything, from the vibrant daisies and wildflowers to the emerald-green trees, appeared to delight in his plight.

Diome headed into town, about to return home. At the end of the town was a cliff, and at the bottom of the cliff was a magical cave invisible to the human eye. It was the entrance to the Burning Bowels, home to an entire world of devils. Deep underground, they built their homes above the lake of lava, which the devils were immune to. It was a lightless, joyless place in which clocks were the only reminders of the time passing above the ground.

As he ambled by Cassie's Flower Shop, as per his usual route, he spotted a graceful figure hovering by the roses.

"Evangelina," he called before he could convince himself otherwise.

She turned around. His heart skipped a beat when her big blue eyes met his. "Diome," she replied, nodding in greeting.

Something warm and fuzzy stirred in Diome when she uttered his name. "You remember me?"

"From homeroom, yes."

"We also have the same art class," Diome reminded her. "How's your finger, by the way?"

Evangelina averted his eyes and grew pale. In most cases, that would've indicated fear, but Diome knew

33

since she had white blood, this could only mean she was flustered. "I didn't know you found out."

Diome resisted an urge to laugh. "Are you kidding? With all that commotion around you, how could I not?"

Evangelina bit her lip, stooping down to examine a white rose. "I didn't like that attention at all. It made me so uncomfortable, how they swarmed around me and even fought to 'escort' me to the infirmary. Kind of disrespectful too. It's as if they're trying to make my decisions for me. They didn't even bother to ask me what I thought and whether I wanted to be escorted. I was right there, and in case they hadn't noticed, I have legs. Surely I can walk myself to the infirmary."

"They just wanted your attention, I guess." Diome shrugged.

"Why would they?"

Diome tried to lighten the mood. "Let's see. Because you're pretty?" Evangelina smiled. "Why, thank you."

"You say that as if my words hold any weight."

"Yes, they mean more to me than you think they do. I wish the guys were more mature, though."

A spell of silence fell upon them before Diome broke it.

"You like roses, don't you? Have you been to Cassie's before?"

Evangelina shook her head. "My first time. First day in this town. It's called Horizon, I think?"

"Yes. I hope you like it here. Where do you live?"

Diome knew the answer already, but he didn't want to reveal he knew what she was.

"I live in the neighboring town."

"Which one?" Diome asked, wondering what witty answers she would concoct to avoid telling the truth.

Evangelina didn't reply. Instead, she devoted her attention to a pink rose. "Do you like flowers?"

"Not really," Diome replied. "But I think they're pretty."

"If you were a flower, what would you be?" Evangelina asked.

"A black petunia."

Evangelina studied him, a mixture of amusement and curiosity in her eyes. "Interesting. You seem to have an obsession with black."

"Some people are destined to walk in the darkness," Diome replied.

"Spoken like a tortured artist," Evangelina remarked. "Like something Van Gogh would say."

"You know him?" Diome asked. She had only been in school for a few hours. How could she have learned so much?

"I read about him in a book in the library," Evangelina replied. "He lived a tragic life. Epic, but tragic."

Diome nodded. "I like his works. Many of them were inspired by nature. Sad he died at thirty-seven, though. He committed suicide because he had depression. He's not the only great artist who took his own life, though. Sylvia Plath and Ernest Hemingway too. A huge pity. They were great writers."

Evangelina sighed. "Makes me wonder if behind everything beautiful lies a sad story. Check out the roses here. They're all lovely, but without the thorns, would a rose still be a rose? Similarly, if Van Gogh hadn't had a hard life, would he still be known as the famous painter?"

Diome was taken aback at her insightfulness. Evangelina was much wiser than anyone he had known. Her words reminded him of *Romeo and Juliet*. Far from blessed, their love story had been melancholic and tear-jerking. But wasn't that one of the reasons it was a popular play? Tales with happy endings were soothing to read, but way too bland and unreal. Reality was much more complicated. Without the thorns along the way, Romeo and Juliet's romance wouldn't have touched so many hearts.

"You're saying that imperfection is a form of perfection." Diome was pleased with himself for managing a reply that didn't expose his stupidity.

Evangelina nodded. "That's true. Utter perfection isn't real. I prefer pretty leaves with a tiny hole, white clouds with a tint of gray, and stars neither too dim nor bright. Sometimes flaws can highlight the rawness and reality of things and bring out their beauty instead."

Diome marveled at the truth in her words. There was only one small problem in her theory—she herself was perfect, and yet she was the epitome of beauty.

"I'll have to be back home before 4:30," Evangelina said. "See you."

Diome waved at her, hoping the angel would never walk away from his life. The iridescent sunlight doused Evangelina with its radiant beams. The streets of Horizon were stunning, but even more so when her elegant figure traveled along the road. He had known her for only a few hours, but she had set his heart aflame. Before today, he thought "love at first sight" was impossible. However, Evangelina shattered any doubts he had about the theory. Like a key that led him through doors to the unknown, she had aroused alien emotions within him: obsession, passion, and confusion for the unfamiliar. Yet warm sensations flowing through him tugged at his heartstrings. This was love, wasn't it?

****

Donning his black, leathery wings, Diome

reached the cliff. Making sure nobody was spying on him, he leapt off and made a dive. Currents of cold air brushed his cheeks as he ventured downward. Seeking the mouth of the cave, he delved into the darkness as he zoomed in. The blackness wrapped around him like a blanket.

Forward, forward, and forward. The tunnel wound its way down, reaching, carving, winding into the center of the Earth. Diome had to navigate his way through the darkness carefully, so that he wouldn't collide with the hard, stony walls when making his descent.

At last, he sighted the ocean of lava unfurling below him. He lifted his head, flapped his wings, and glided above the sizzling, orange sea, searching for his home among the houses that lined both sides of it. The scorching color burned into his eyes, as did the heat, but nevertheless, he was used to the unpleasant conditions of the Burning Bowels.

"Hello, Diome."

He glanced up and spotted Lenora, one of his neighbors hovering a few feet above him. She fluttered beside him. Her long, fiery hair and the folds of her black robe flapped behind her like the sail of a ship on a blustery day.

"Good day at school?" she asked with a flirtatious wink. A year his junior, she was infatuated with him, but he didn't reciprocate her feelings.

"It was all right," Diome replied, not wanting to converse with her more than necessary.

"I wish I could go to a human school too," Lenora gushed.

"If you aspire to be an inventor, you can," Diome replied.

"I want to be a warrior and kill tons of angels in future battles. The devils will worship me as a hero."

Lenora had a smug expression as she declared her determination. It kindled a flame of indignation in Diome. So what if her family were extremists and supremacists, devils who believed every angel deserved a punishment worse than death? Blinded by hatred, she had no morals, like ninety-nine percent of the dumb devils he knew.

The presidents of the angels, Albert Leclair, and the president of the devils, Ebony Lenoir, had been advocating for peace and voicing their hopes the enmity would cease. Yet neither of them dared to take severe measures and enact a law that prohibited their people from harming each other. The Land of Heavenly Dreams and the Burning Bowels were both democratic nations and held presidential elections every six years. Both presidents understood they would lose support from the extremists if they jailed the angels and devils who initiated battles.

Useless politicians, thought Diome. Male or female, devil or angel, they only took their own benefits into consideration, never the greater good for the future.

"What's wrong?" Lenora asked, noticing the frown on Diome's face.

"Nothing," he lied. He was unwilling to confess his frustration and disappointment at how some devils made eradicating all angels the ambition of their lives, as if such a cruel, callous act of genocide was something worthy of a century's glory.

Diome arrived at his home, a red-bricked house with towering walls and three floors. He made a touchdown on the roof.

"Can I come in with you?" asked Lenora, anticipation gleaming in her eyes.

"Not today, sorry. I'm not feeling very well today. Maybe next time."

It was an excuse to drive her away, but Diome didn't feel guilty. She may have been his admirer, but that didn't change the fact her family had corrupted her. Diome couldn't befriend anyone who favored bloodlust and shunned peace.

Lenora nodded. "All right. Good day."

And with a leap, she flew away, vanishing into the distance.

****

"Mom, Dad, I'm home," Diome called.

"Killed any angels today, son?" his mother Dolores asked. "One of them tried to invade our Burning Bowels today and fell into the lava lake."

"Some of our folks spotted him and tore off his wings during their fight," his father Erik added. "The lowly scum got fried to a crisp. Serves him right."

As selfish as it sounded, Diome hoped with every fiber of his being the fallen angel was no relative or acquaintance of Evangelina's. He retreated into his room and sat down. Like the other kids in Horizon High, he had a cell phone, but unlike them, he wasn't addicted to it. He purchased the cell phone simply because he didn't want to stand out among the kids. It was bizarre for an eleventh grader not to own one of those cool gadgets they couldn't stop obsessing over. The devils in the Burning Bowels had learned much from the humans. They too had toilets, water pipes, and supermarkets. However, they didn't have Internet connections, so it would be impossible to use his phone at home.

In his spare time, Diome devoted himself to writing plays. He had been working on one about a fantasy world in which angels and devils co-existed in peace and harmony. His English teacher Mrs. Armstrong would call it a work of utopian literature. Diome lamented that it would forever be a dream, an unfulfilled illusion. Restoring peace between the two sides was more impossible than freezing the Burning Bowels.

Diome knew he should tackle his history and geography homework, but not now. Instead, he lay on his bed, contemplating Evangelina. Not in a thousand years would he meet another angel who possessed her charm, who rivaled her in grace. So beautiful, wise, and innocent. What was she doing at this moment, way up high in the Land of Heavenly Dreams? Had he performed all right in her presence today?

He wished he had the power of telepathy. If only he knew what Evangelina thought of him, if only he knew how much more it would take to win her over. He desired to be hers as much as he craved she would be his. He pictured himself kissing Evangelina on a fluffy cloud, soft but not quite as tender as her lips.

If only the devils and angels would listen to reason and quell their hatred for each other. If only fortune would smile upon him one day. If only he and Evangelina stood a chance together as a couple. If only, if only.

Chapter Three

A Series of Occurrences
(Evangelina)

After her first weekend, Evangelina looked forward to the next five days of school. She adored her new friends Camille and Merilee. Most of the kids in school seemed to like her, beaming at her when passing her in the hallways. The students at Horizon High were indeed as kind as Mr. Bryant had claimed. However, Evangelina wished she could reveal more about herself to them.

Many boys flirted with her in the hallways, winking at her and flashing smiles whenever she walked by. She nodded at them in response, a calm, collected nod that meant nothing more than a polite gesture of greeting. Of course, she wasn't romantically into any of them, but she didn't want to be rude either. She knew they were smitten by her beauty, by the aura of mystery that enveloped her figure. Yet Evangelina wished she didn't have to keep her mask on at all times. For the first time, she wanted to be human, to fit in, to be accepted and not be treated like a mystery.

Because her parents demanded she return to the Land of Heavenly Dreams no later than 4:30 p.m., Evangelina couldn't have dinner with her friends or hang out with them for longer than an hour. A quick trip to the ice cream parlor or the Horizon Library was all she could squeeze in. Still, she was grateful to have made new friends in Horizon High.

"I don't think it's fair that some people don't have to wear makeup to look pretty," Camille groaned.

Evangelina had met her and Merilee on her way to school after leaving Horizon Park. The air was cold and moist, a light fog veiling everything in the distance. It was a good day to descend from the clouds without being discovered.

"You're just jealous of Evangelina because she doesn't need any eyeshadow or lipstick," remarked Merilee, rebraiding her shoulder-length hair. She was dressed in a red checkered shirt and blue jeans, which had a casual charm.

Camille beamed at Evangelina, admiring her lacy purple dress. "Oh, of course. Who wouldn't be?"

Evangelina smiled. Truth be told, she thought wearing makeup was vain. Why were people so scared to let their true selves shine? Part of herself examined this notion. Camille had two cheeks full of acne and an explosion of brown curls no hair gel could tame. Yet Evangelina had been gifted with a silky waterfall of platinum-blonde hair and perfect skin free of blemishes. Judging her friends for wearing makeup sounded rather insensitive, for Evangelina's flawless features made her outshine even the most beautiful girls in the eleventh grade. To people who deemed themselves imperfect, it was easier for others to advocate the importance of loving oneself.

"Camille, Evangelina, any plans after school today?" Merilee asked.

Evangelina shook her head. "No. Why are you asking?"

"My brother told me there's a new café around a block away from Horizon High. It just opened yesterday. Say, could we have a girl's night out?"

Evangelina sighed. "I'd love that, but you know my parents are really strict. I have to be home before 4:30."

Camille pouted. "Crap. Why? Are they scared you'll get kidnapped?"

"Tell them you'll be with us," Merilee joined in. "We'll protect you in case anything happens. I've got a black belt in karate!"

Evangelina gave her an appreciative smile. "I'll stay until four o'clock, ladies. How's that?"

"All right, I guess," conceded Camille. "At least we have an hour. Might be able to blow through some homework at least."

Evangelina liked Camille and Merilee because they were different from the other kids. They weren't obsessed with being popular or interested in gossiping about others. The two of them were far from conspicuous—they weren't nerds, jocks, or socialites, and they didn't fit in with any crowd. Neither too beautiful or too clever, they were the kind of people who slipped by unnoticed. However, they were kind, easygoing, and down-to-earth.

Yet despite the joy of befriending them, Evangelina hadn't forgotten why she came to Horizon High. She had been observing Diome Lenoir from afar in classes or hallways. He was introverted and seldom raised his hand in class. Perhaps she imagined it, but he seemed scared of her. Whenever their gazes met, he would avert his eyes almost instantly. Evangelina wondered whether he had figured out what she was.

The trio entered the school lobby and came across the locker hall. It was 7:50 a.m., and throngs of noisy students were standing by their lockers and chatting. The hubbub of voices carried a thousand snippets of random conversations.

"Camille, Merilee," began Evangelina, an idea dawning on her mind. "Do you two happen to know anything about Diome Lenoir?"

Merilee blushed and giggled. "Who doesn't know him?"

"Dark, brooding, and handsome," gushed Camille. "Do you like him, Evangelina? Why are you asking about him?"

Because my parents instructed me to kill him. "He's very mysterious."

Merilee nodded. "True that. He never hangs out with the other kids. I think he's depressed sometimes, to be honest."

"I wonder why," Camille mused. "It's like he's got a dark secret weighing on him."

Pity for Diome rose in Evangelina like a wave. Being a devil must be difficult for him. She could only imagine how much hatred for the angels his family had imbued in him, the same way her parents force-fed her negative information about the devils.

"Ever talked to him before?" she asked her friends.

"He was my partner in biology," replied Merilee. "He was very quiet most of the time. Like he was afraid to open his mouth."

"Maybe he's a vampire," surmised Camille. "Or some supernatural creature."

Camille has no idea how right she is. Diome wasn't human, and that must be the reason he acted so aloof at all times.

"Read too many paranormal romance novels, haven't you?" Merilee chuckled.

"It's fun to believe in things like that," Camille answered. "Adds some zest to our boring school life."

"Is school that bad?" Evangelina asked. "I quite like it."

"Well, classes are boring, but you got to admit there's some fun stuff too," Merilee half-agreed.

When Camille rolled her eyes, Merilee added, "Cheer up. The Halloween Dance is coming soon."

"There's a Halloween Dance?" Evangelina's eyes widened. "In our school?"

"Yes. In the gym," Merilee answered. "We had it last year too, but I had to go visit my grandpa in the hospital, so I missed it. Looking forward to the dance this year, though!"

Camille grinned. "Awesome, there's something cool in store for us. When's the dance?"

"October 30th, next Friday."

"Next Friday?" Evangelina asked. "How come I didn't know this earlier?"

"The dance committee had some problems with the event, and many people weren't sure whether there would even be a dance this year or not," Merilee clarified. "But I guess they sorted things out in the end. They announced the date yesterday. Everyone's pairing up and scrambling to find a date now."

"Do you need a date to go?" Evangelina asked.

Camille shook her head. "Not last year. Anyone who's willing to cough up the admission fee—five bucks—can go. They have nice snacks, and I definitely recommend you go."

"I'll consider it," Evangelina promised her.

At that moment, the bell for class rang.

"See you two at lunch," Evangelina chirped, gathering her books and stuffing the rest into her locker. Camille and Merilee had the same homeroom, so they waved goodbye to her and hurried upstairs.

Evangelina reviewed her textbooks in homeroom, but she couldn't focus. From the corner of her eye, she caught Diome Lenoir staring at her. Determined not to stare back, she read her algebra textbook.

Was he interested in her? Why was he staring in

her direction? Had he—Evangelina's heart skipped a beat at that possibility—found out what she was?

The tiny numbers and symbols blurred before Evangelina's unfocused eyes. She could no longer feign interest in her reading material. Letting her mind wander, she recalled her father's order. Had Diome any way of knowing her parents' plan to murder him? His fate rested with her. Although Evangelina had no intention of murdering him, she feared her father would kill him if she failed to take action soon. The only way to save Diome was to warn him about the vengeful angels and ask him to leave Horizon High. Then, she could lie to her parents and tell them she had eliminated him, when in fact, she had spared his life.

Evangelina was delighted that she had the second period free. She had forgotten that amid the excitement of meeting Camille and Merilee on her way to school, and then she was so occupied with worrying about Diome that she had forgotten about her free period. Walking to her locker, she opened it, got out her copy of *Romeo and Juliet*, which they were reading for English, and stuffed it into her bag.

"Excuse me, you dropped this earlier," began someone who sounded familiar.

Evangelina turned and noticed Diome standing by her locker. He was clad in his favorite black leather jacket, faded gray jeans, and ankle-length boots.

"Oh, hi there. It's you."

Diome nodded. "You left your algebra book in the classroom."

"Thanks." Evangelina smiled. "I guess I'd better not delay you. You probably have class soon."

"I have the second period free, in fact."

"Really? That's nice," Evangelina replied.

"What are you reading?" Diome asked, leaning

closer to get a peek at her book.

"*Romeo and Juliet*. For English class. Have you read it before? The blurb interests me."

Diome's gaze softened. "It's a poignant romance. I've read it before. My favorite play."

"I can't wait to start it," gushed Evangelina. "I love my new classes. I've never learned anything like these before. By the way, want to go take a walk on the campus?"

Evangelina was trying to earn Diome's trust. Sooner or later, she would have to come clean about her identity, tell him her parents had sent her to the human world to murder him, and beg him to leave Horizon High.

Diome nodded. "Sounds good."

The two of them ambled outdoors, and along the way, hundreds of jealous glares stabbed Evangelina like a hailstorm of arrows.

"How long have you been in Horizon High?" Evangelina asked.

"I enrolled in tenth grade."

Evangelina wondered when he started school in the human world, what he learned from the humans, and why he was interested in the humans' culture.

"You were homeschooled before?" Diome asked, slowing his stride.

"Yes. My parents thought they shouldn't deny me a chance to have some high school experiences like regular kids, though, which is why they sent me to Horizon High."

"I can't believe you like it here," muttered Diome, shaking his head.

"I can't believe almost everyone hates school," Evangelina replied.

"You're definitely special, that's for sure,"

remarked Diome.

What did he mean by that? Diome had a pensive expression, as if he was worlds away from her. Did he know more than he was willing to reveal? Might he know who she was? Evangelina combed her mind, but she had never done anything magical, anything that suggested the possibility she wasn't human. How could he have known?

"In what way am I special?" Evangelina asked carefully.

Diome didn't speak, but Evangelina could have sworn she saw a slight flush of crimson creep into his cheeks.

"Sorry, I must go now. I haven't finished my science homework yet, and I have science for fourth period."

Evangelina suppressed the urge to smile. "Goodbye, then. Good luck on finishing your homework."

Diome nodded and breezed away, heading back into the school building. Evangelina watched his retreating figure grow smaller and smaller and disappear when he rounded a corner. There was something about him that Evangelina found intriguing. Tall and enigmatic, he held an endless fountain of mysteries. Yet there was a subtle melancholy about him. Like an exotic creature trapped in a cage, he didn't belong in Horizon High. However, as much as Evangelina had to keep her distance to protect him, she hoped he would stay forever. She would delay her confession for a day longer, if only to have Diome stay in her school for a day longer.

Evangelina shook her head and smiled in spite of herself. Was she falling for him? To love Diome, someone her tribe antagonized, someone she was ordered to murder ... The thought was absurd, like a cheesy drama. But if the peculiar, overwhelming curiosity bubbling in her wasn't infatuation for Diome, what was it?

****

The next few periods flew by, and soon, the last bell chimed. Evangelina met up with Camille and Merilee, her mind swirling with square roots, chromosomes, facts about the regency era, and William Shakespeare's bibliography. Although she had trouble catching up with science, she loved her classes.

"Do you have a favorite subject?" Merilee asked Evangelina as they left the gates.

"English, I guess. History is also fun."

"Are you reading Shakespeare in English?" Camille asked. "I have Ms. Brown for English, and she's making us read *A Midsummer's Night Dream*. Silly play, in my not-so-humble opinion."

"I'm in Mr. Hughes' class. We're working on *Romeo and Juliet*," replied Evangelina.

"Aww, I'd trade books with you in a heartbeat," groaned Camille.

"We're studying *As You Like It* in our English class," Merilee rejoined the conversation. "I think it's kind of a pointless play, though. Contemporary novels and poems are much superior to the oldies."

"Really? I thought you wanted to be an English literature professor." Camille regarded her with surprise.

Merilee shrugged. "And who said English literature professors must have a profound love for the classics? No, thank you. I'm going to promote the beauty of modern novels and show my students how lucky they are to be living in the twenty-first century, showered with plenty of high-quality literature. Check out those cool fantasy romance novels they keep publishing each year. I mean, I can't be the only romantasy lover out there, right? Anyway, do you guys have any homework?"

Camille smiled. "No, not much. Just finish reading the first scene of act one."

"That's nice. I've got to read the first act—" A thought popped into Evangelina's mind. "Wait a moment." She rummaged through her bag. "Oh no, I left my copy of *Romeo and Juliet* in the classroom."

"Your English classroom?" Merilee asked. "I can go get it for you."

"No, it's fine, I'll go get it. I'll join you two later."

Evangelina headed back into her classroom, retrieved her book, and rushed into the nearest elevator.

"Wait!" someone shouted.

Evangelina held the doors, only to see Diome hurry into the elevator.

"Oh, it's you again. Say, why do we keep running into each other?" She shot him a mischievous grin.

Diome shrugged. "Do you believe in fate?"

Evangelina hit the button marked first floor, and the doors closed. She took a moment to process his words, and when comprehension dawned on her, she almost gasped. "What do you mean?"

"Like, some encounters are destined. Every time you meet someone, fate is pulling the strings and willing you together. Some inexplicable things are written in the stars. Serendipitous."

"Oh dear, 1 pity whoever gets that word in a spelling bee," quipped Evangelina, masking her nervousness and garnering a giggle from Diome. Her heart fluttered at an incredible speed. Growing dizzy, she leaned against the mirrored wall, struggling to maintain her composure.

The elevator jolted to a stop, but the doors didn't open.

"What's wrong with it?" Diome asked, his smile melting.

"We're on the second floor," Evangelina noticed.

"What's going on?" Diome edged closer to the elevator doors and peered out. "What? No way! We're stuck between the second and third floor!"

"And the elevator isn't working?"

Evangelina pressed the emergency button.

Silence.

"Help!" shouted Diome, pounding the doors. "Help!"

"Can anyone hear us?" Evangelina screeched. "We're in the elevator!"

Diome frowned and sighed. "I don't think anyone will hear us. This is the side elevator, not the main elevator."

Evangelina sat down on the linoleum floor. "What do we do? I've never been trapped in an elevator before."

Diome whipped out his phone. "Don't panic, I'll call for help." He tapped on the screen a few times and cursed. "What the—? My battery's dead!"

Evangelina pummeled her fist on her knee. "This can't go on! When will they find us here?"

Diome sat down next to her. "No idea. The nearby classrooms are all empty. Everyone's in the other side of the school, since it's after-school club time. And most of the teachers are either stuck in meetings or have left school."

"And the custodian?" Evangelina asked.

Diome pursed his lips. "She's sick today. Didn't see her at all."

Evangelina groaned. "Oh, great. Is this serendipity's fault?"

Diome chuckled. "Maybe. Or karma. The jury is

out, I guess.".

"How are you in the mood for joking when we're trapped here?" Evangelina asked, dismayed.

"It's not that we can do anything, is it? Do you have your phone, by the way? Perhaps you can call for help."

Evangelina fixed her gaze on the floor, developing a sudden interest in a crumpled note in a corner. "I-I don't have a phone."

Diome's eyes widened. "You don't have a phone?"

"No. Well, I guess we have to wait this out. Bizarre, isn't it? It's as if the elevator suddenly had a mind of its own. I swear I'll never take an elevator again. Does this happen often?"

Diome shook his head. "Rarely. Let's talk about other things to take our minds off this. Do you have any siblings?"

Evangelina shook her head. "I'm an only child."

"Same. Only son here. Where do you live?"

The gears in Evangelina's mind spun to concoct an answer. "Um, two blocks away from school."

"Oh, by Berry Bakery?"

"That's it," Evangelina lied. She couldn't reveal the truth of her living in the clouds.

Diome devoted his attention to his silver skull bracelet.

"That's interesting." Evangelina scooted closer to inspect it. "You like skulls a lot? You sure have a gothy sense of fashion."

"You noticed!" Diome exclaimed. "I thought nobody would."

"I quite like those skulls, to be honest. Perfect for a Halloween costume."

"There's a Halloween dance next week. Did you

know that?"

Evangelina held her breath. "My friends told me, yes. Do you guys have dances often? I thought school was all about studying."

"Far from that, in fact. Many football tournaments, basketball games, formal dances, and fun events like that. I'm not into any of them, though."

"Not surprised, since you're an introvert," Evangelina remarked.

"And you're an extrovert, I assume?"

"Depends on who I'm talking to," Evangelina replied.

"How do you like it here in Horizon High? You accustomed to everything here?" Diome asked.

"Oh, it's a decent school," replied Evangelina. "I like it very much. Wish I came earlier. I also made some friends."

A flash of longing took over Diome's gaze. "Friends." He sighed. "I could never make any. I don't fit in with the others."

Evangelina tilted her head. "In what way?"

"In every way. We don't listen to the same music or watch the same movies. I'm more interested in exploring new places than sports."

"Exploring new places?"

"Caves and mountains, yes. They're sublime. What about you? Do you have any hobbies?"

"Although I haven't sewn anything before, I'd really love to be a fashion designer. I like drawing sketches of pretty clothes."

"Did you design the purple dress you're wearing? It's beautiful on you."

Evangelina blushed. "If only I could design something like it. Thank you."

"Don't forget the little people like me when you

become famous one day," Diome quipped.

"I promise I won't," replied Evangelina to humor him. "I've never seen such a wealth of expressions on your face before, by the way. I thought you were a gothy, depressed loner, but you can be quite a chatterbox."

"I'm glad I didn't leave a lousy impression on you," admitted Diome. "I guess today's elevator adventure wasn't all bad, huh?"

"No. We both made a new friend." Evangelina smiled.

Just then, the elevator rose, and the doors opened.

"Evangelina!" Merilee cried. She, Camille, and the school nurse Mrs. Evans stood outside.

"Are you all right? We were so worried!" Camille said.

"I'm fine," Evangelina reassured them.

Mrs. Evans turned to Diome. "And you, Diome?"

"I'm all right, ma'am," he replied.

"What happened?" Merilee asked.

"I stepped into the elevator after getting my book from the classroom, and Diome joined me. The elevator suddenly had a mind of its own, though, and it wouldn't budge. We were stuck between the second and third floor for a long while. Then the elevator moved upward and the doors finally opened."

Camille bit her lip. "We thought something happened to you. Merilee and I ran back to school and searched all the floors, but we didn't see or hear you. Honestly, we thought you were murdered!"

"Don't worry," Evangelina assured them. "It's all over. Just a broken elevator."

"That was a close call, Miss Leclair," Mrs. Evans remarked, frowning. "I'll have to report this to the custodian. We were lucky nobody was injured today. Now, you four better go home before your parents start worrying about your safety. Off you go."

"Thanks, Mrs. Evans. Good night."

"What's the time now?" Evangelina asked Camille and Merilee when they left school. Diome had parted ways with them at the entrance and headed downtown.

"It's 4:30," answered Camille.

"It's 4:30?" Evangelina gasped. "I have to go home now, sorry. My parents won't be happy that I'm late."

"Sorry about that. Hope they don't grill you too bad," fretted Merilee. "I'll keep my fingers crossed for you."

"Me too," added Camille. "Good luck."

Evangelina thanked and bade them farewell. On her flight back to the Land of Heavenly Dreams, she pondered today's events. How did Diome feel about her? He had managed to do something nobody else had—capture her heart. As unbelievable as it was, Evangelina was in love with him. They had only had three conversations, but she felt inexplicably connected to him for some reasons. Their souls were tethered together by something no reason or logic could explain.

The gold and pink clouds around her grew softer and rosier. The world, a blissful blur of ethereal colors, had no edges. A smile lifted the corners of her lips. Was this what being in love felt like? She had no experience to draw from. Therefore, she had no idea. All she knew was that she felt lighter than a feather, like a balloon filled with joy. When she closed her eyes, she imagined Diome's figure and heard his deep, enigmatic voice. Tender yet thrilling emotions accompanied his presence.

Evangelina knew she shouldn't fall in love with him. No, she was ordered to murder him. But she couldn't help it. Her sense and logic told her it was wrong, yet her heart believed otherwise. Every fiber of her being, every ounce of her soul was deeply enamored with Diome Lenoir. She yearned to be his best friend, or even better, more than friends with him. It was something reason couldn't explain. Something invisible and intangible had touched her heart, and yet none of the words she knew could articulate the kaleidoscope of sensations flowing through her mind and cascading through her veins like a merry river. This was love, blooming and thriving in her. This was love, a vibrant blossom flourishing in a dark abyss. This was love, a candle burning in a storm, unwavering and inextinguishable. So what if the angels and devils were rivals? What if her father demanded she kill Diome? Her parents couldn't manipulate her mind. She loved Diome, and it was none of their business. Furthermore, she was a living, breathing individual, not an extension of her parents. She had no obligation to eliminate an innocent devil. Sometimes melancholic and pensive, Diome was someone Evangelina felt an unexplainable desire to protect. She wanted to guard him from the harms of both his and her kind. Their tribes would be determined to keep them apart, but her love for him was stronger than any rivalry.

Diome was a victim of his fellow devils. He spoke little and appeared rather standoffish. He didn't have any friends, that much was evident. She hoped by extending a hand of friendship to him, she could lessen his loneliness.

All of a sudden, it occurred to Evangelina how alike angels and devils were. If angels represented the light and devils symbolized darkness, there was only a fine line between the two. Anyone could be one or the other, or both at the same time. In the angels' eyes, the devils were to blame for everything, but to the devils, the angels were the malevolent ones. And since everyone was the hero of their story, nobody felt a semblance of remorse when the two sides went to battle. They were all vigilantes fighting for dominance over the other, struggling to enforce their definition of justice on the world and those around them.

Evangelina's parents had instructed her to murder Diome, who had committed no wrongdoings. Pure and innocent, he was exactly the way anyone would picture an angel. Evangelina could not bring herself to harm him, for he posed no threat to her, and on the contrary, was lonesome and depressed. If she obeyed her parents' orders and slayed him, she would stoop lower than a devil, not literally but metaphorically. She was the only angel she knew who had a conscience, and she would do anything within her power to protect Diome.

****

"You're late," Evangelina's father snapped as she returned. He was sitting at the table in the dining room, glaring at her. As an architect, he worked from home and sketched blueprints for new buildings all day long.

"I'm sorry," Evangelina whimpered. "I was trapped in the school elevator. It broke down, and I was left alone in it for an hour." She wasn't foolish enough to bring up Diome and upset her father.

Her father raised his eyebrows. "Really? Are you all right, then?"

Evangelina nodded.

"At least you're fine now. Speaking of school, I was going to ask whether you have spoken to the devil boy. You do remember why you're in Horizon High, don't you?"

Evangelina froze. Her heart pounded in her ears, and her chest was heavier than before. "Yes, I've spoken to Diome. Once or twice."

She prayed her father would cease his questioning, but alas, her prayers proved in vain.

"Good. Have you earned his trust, then? When will you murder him?"

"I ... I'm not comfortable with the idea of killing someone—"

"He's not someone. He's a devil! And that's not murder you're committing. You're doing everyone a favor. The world would be a much better place without those nasty creatures."

"He hasn't done anything wrong," insisted Evangelina. "Believe it or not, he's been polite and friendly to me, and—"

Her father stood up abruptly. "It's a trap, you fool! You listen to me right now, Evangelina Leclair! You will do as I say and kill that devil. Or else—"

"Or else what? Or else you'll disown me?" Evangelina retorted. A sudden bout of courage and recklessness had seized her.

"What's going on?"

A figure with blonde curls emerged at the stairwell. Her mother. Evangelina groaned inwardly. If there was anyone who would take his side, it would be her.

"Your rebel of a daughter was just arguing with me," her father growled, hands on hips. "She thinks she's too noble to be an assassin."

Evangelina's mother drew out a long sigh. "Evangelina, dear, what's gotten into you?"

"I don't want to kill Diome Lenoir," Evangelina insisted. "It's wrong."

"Wrong!" shouted her father. "Golda, I can't deal with her anymore. You talk some sense into this little traitor! Somehow she's taking that devil's side and refusing to kill—"

"You keep calling Diome a threat, but in reality, we're the ones threatening his life!" Evangelina cried. "He's a teenager like me. He did nothing wrong. How can you justify—?"

"He's a devil!" Her mother joined the quarrel. "Evangelina, what's wrong with you?"

"What's wrong with me? Nothing's wrong. What's wrong with you two?"

Her father's face was burning with wrath. Her mother's lips were pinched into a line, her furious eyes sharper than blades. For a fleeting moment, Evangelina thought she detected disappointment in their faces. They appeared wounded by her words. However, Evangelina couldn't yield to them. She prized her morals and principles over anything else.

"Go to your room," her mother ordered through gritted teeth. "*Now*. And no dinner tonight unless you apologize to me and your father. We didn't raise you to become an ungrateful, backstabbing brat."

Without a word, Evangelina turned on her heels and stomped up the stairs. She would never apologize, for she hadn't done anything wrong. It was insane, comical almost, for her mother to associate her with ungratefulness when they were the ones forcing her to betray her beliefs. She was sixteen, no longer a child. And whether they liked it or not, she would make them accept the fact she would never kill Diome.

Of course, Evangelina could lie to them, claiming she had killed Diome when in fact, she had spared his life, like the hunter in the fairy tale *Snow White*. A tide of disappointment for her parents flooded her. She had much higher expectations for them, and she had hoped better from them.

No matter what they believed, though, Evangelina would stand her ground. For too long a time, the angels and devils had been strengthening their rivalry with cruel invasions and countless brawls. Evangelina swore to herself she would shatter it and end the vicious cycle of revenge.

****

The next day was a huge improvement, thanks to Camille and Merilee. They insisted that Evangelina go with them to pick their costumes for the Halloween dance. Camille was going with her boyfriend, Joey O'Brien. Even though Merilee was single, she enjoyed tagging along with them. Evangelina wasn't obsessed with fine outfits, but a Halloween dance was a special occasion she was willing to dress up for.

"I'm there for the food!" Merilee squealed, bouncing on the balls of her feet as they headed downtown after school.

"How come you don't ever get fat?" Camille whined with a hilarious pout.

"Good genes," Merilee replied, lifting her chin and giggling. "Evangelina, do you have a date?"

Evangelina shook her head. "You two are my dates," she quipped.

Merilee smiled. "What an honor! Will your parents let you come? It starts at six in the evening."

"They've given up on me," answered Evangelina.

Camille's eyes widened. "You must be kidding."

"Why would I?"

Evangelina wasn't lying. Yesterday after the argument, her father stormed into her room and told her they would never impose any curfews on her, and she was free to go home anytime. Evangelina felt a modicum of guilt for shouting at her parents, but part of her felt they deserved a lecture. They were being unfair, prejudiced, and unreasonable.

"Well, no offense, but you don't look too sad

about it," Merilee remarked.

"I'm not sad at all. You see, we had a quarrel yesterday. They were trying to force me to do something insane."

"What was it?" Camille asked.

But fortunately, Evangelina was spared the necessity of answering as the town loomed over them. The colorful buildings, cutesy awnings outside the doors and windows, and the vibrant displays of clothes and food were something she'd never seen before. They passed a bakery, a Chinese restaurant, a shop with clothes for toddlers, another that sold baby supplies, a café, and a bookstore. Evangelina marveled at the rainbow of colors, at the joy and enthusiasm gushing from every corner of the cozy little town. It was marvelous, how the humans had built the gorgeous little shops brick by brick, step by step, colored and decorated everything, and formed an adorable town. Like a vibrant spectrum dancing before her eyes, the beauty was breathtaking. Evangelina had never seen anything like that in the Land of Heavenly Dreams. There were thousands, perhaps millions of floating islands, one or two shops or houses on each. It was impossible to see two shops, let alone hundreds of them, aligned in such close proximity.

"We're here," announced Merilee, pushing open the glass door to a boutique.

Camille squealed upon passing the racks of dresses, while Evangelina took a moment to appreciate the glittering rows of outfits.

"Like it?" Merilee asked.

"Wow," was all Evangelina could manage. "This is incredible."

"I'm not sure what I want to dress up as." Merilee sifted through the gowns. "Something cute. Maybe a ladybug or a bumblebee. What about you, Evangelina?"

"Something dark," she replied. "It's Halloween, after all. A devil would be interesting."

"Yeah, I'll get you a pair of horns to suit your dress," Merilee offered. "I like this one. Tea-length. The yellow and black stripes are really unique. Have you seen a bumblebee with red hair, by the way? I should dye my hair black, don't you think?"

"You would look splendid the way you are," Evangelina replied.

Meanwhile, Camille had taken an interest in a sparkly pink jumpsuit and put it on.

"How do I look?" she asked, grinning.

"Pretty in pink," Merilee answered. "It's a Halloween dance, you know. What are you supposed to be?"

"Let's see ... What about myself?"

The three of them laughed and agreed it was a witty idea.

"Merilee says she wants to dress up as a bee." Evangelina giggled. "What do you think about that, Camille?"

Camille stroked her chin. "Creative idea. She'd need a stinger. I could make one with aluminum foil."

"Like an antenna," Merilee replied. "Evangelina wants to be a devil."

Camille's eyebrows lifted. "Oh, a devil? Interesting. I thought you would want to be an angel instead. Your hair color's really light. You'd look good in white."

Evangelina smiled, acknowledging the irony. She *was* an angel in reality, an angel who, for once, wanted to take advantage of the Halloween dance and be a devil.

"Angels aren't scary enough," she replied. "Devils are more mysterious."

"Well, bees aren't scary either," Merilee pointed

out. "They produce honey." Twirling before the mirror, she watched her skirts billow around her like a fan. She was happier with her dress than a bumblebee in a field of flowers.

"Bees have stingers," Evangelina reminded her. "I don't think there's anything scary about Camille though."

Camille laughed. "Be glad you haven't seen my scary side! You will when my little sister Camilla messes with my makeup kit and paints a mural on the house walls with my eyeshadow!"

"What a talented young artist," Evangelina joked. "You inspired her potential."

"Yeah, of course. I'm going to go with this pink sequin jumpsuit here. Merilee's clearly in love with her bee dress. Check out the outfits there. What's your favorite color?"

Evangelina browsed through them, admiring each design. "I was thinking of going with black."

She rummaged through the black gowns while Camille proceeded to checkout and Merilee headed for the dressing rooms. Many of them were slim and form-fitting, while others were puffier with fuller skirts. Evangelina sought a dress somewhere between the two extremes, voluminous yet not overly extravagant or flamboyant. She tried on a black sheath gown dotted with sequins, another with silver geometry patterns, and another adorned with yards of lace, but none of them suited her taste.

"What about this one?" Camille suggested, handing Evangelina a fluffy gown dotted with milky pearls and sparkling rhinestones. She scrutinized it and smoothed the countless layers of ruffles that cascaded down like undulating waves shining on a midnight ocean. It had a sweetheart neckline and off-the-shoulder sleeves adorned with a ring of black fur.

"It's lovely," Evangelina gushed. "I'll try it on for a bit."

When she laced it on and gazed into the mirror, she couldn't believe the person in it was herself. The dress shone like a luminous pearl, transforming her into a gothic angel. Providing a shocking contrast to her splash of platinum-blonde hair, it gleamed black and bright, as if light and darkness had reconciled and decided to thrive together.

"Amazing," breathed Merilee, who abandoned her interest in her yellow eyeshadow the moment Evangelina stepped out of her dressing room.

Evangelina beamed, satisfied with her new treasure. "This is the one." She checked her purse, but discovered, with a pang of astonishment, that she forgot to bring her human money.

"Oh no," she moaned. "I forgot to bring my hum—I mean, my money."

"We can lend you some," Camille offered, getting out her wallet as she made her way to the checkout counter. "Just pay us half the price back."

"What, really?"

"Ninety dollars plus who knows how much for tax ... Shoot, I'm five bucks short. Merilee, help me."

"Here you go." Merilee slapped a five-dollar-bill onto her hand.

Evangelina blushed. She had only known them for a week and a half, but they treated her like a bosom friend. Camille and Merilee were much kinder to her than they needed to be.

"Thank you two so much." Evangelina was flustered by their generosity.

Camille winked. "Hey, what are friends for?"

****

The day of the Halloween dance arrived, and the

three of them gathered at Camille's house after school. They went to a Malaysian restaurant and had dinner— spring rolls and flat noodles. Joey O'Brien, dashing in his maroon vampire tuxedo, joined them. Evangelina and Merilee made fun of the lovebirds until they blushed redder than the roses on Camille's corsage.

As Evangelina sipped her delicious coconut juice, listening to Camille and Joey's conversation about universities, she reminded herself of how fortunate she was to have them. It would be a magical night with her friends. To many others, it was ordinary, mundane even. But to her, nothing mattered more than creating precious memories with her human friends. The humans led such carefree lives. None of them had to worry about being slain by devils or ordered to murder anyone. She couldn't become one of them, but tonight, she could pretend she was no different from them—a regular human uninvolved in epic, centuries-long rivalries.

When they finished their meal, all four of them departed for the Halloween dance. Evangelina had never been to an event quite like it. All the angels would have a debutante ball when they reached seventeen. Evangelina was still sixteen.

The venue was decorated in gothic hues, tall, spidery candelabras with tall ivory candles and blazing orange flames. A pleasant tang of jasmine wafted from nowhere, teasing Evangelina's nose. The atmosphere was dark and mysterious. It was impossible to tell they were in the school gymnasium.

"Look at the refreshments!" Merilee announced, pointing at the long table of grape punches, tiny sandwiches, cherry-topped cakes, and jellybeans. She glided over the table and began piling the finger food on her plate. With her yellow-and-black antenna headband and her organza wings (made by her little brother Mike), her costume was perfect.

Evangelina burst out laughing as Merilee devoured her snacks. "How strange to see people gobbling up food like wolves in a semi-formal event."

Merilee rolled her eyes. "Oh, loosen up, Evangelina. You sound like my mom!"

"Fine, fine, I'm just joking, you know. Who cares about any rules? Let's pig out!"

"Yeah, it's not as if we have dates to please."

Evangelina shrugged and poured herself as glass of grape punch. "I wouldn't want to please my date if I had one. If he likes me for who I am, he won't mind how I act. What's with all the people-pleasing stuff?"

Images of her parents flashed in her mind. They had reconciled and were back on speaking terms last night, though neither side had apologized. It was nice of them to remove her curfew for the dance, which meant she was allowed to return as late as she wished.

She watched Camille and Joey waltz. They kissed whenever they leaned close. Under the romantic, atmospheric lights, a magical aura filled the air. The dance committee did a magnificent job decorating the venue. All the lights were turned off. The whole gymnasium was lit by a buttery yellow glow issuing from the elaborate lamp posts that lined the walls. Black, burgundy, and violet roses and Jack-o-lanterns with sinister grins adorned the refreshments table. Someone had placed a fog machine by the back door, and white mist glided in the air in a thousand dreamy tendrils like gossamer ribbons with long tails. It reminded her of her home above the clouds. Everything felt surreal, the lights, the soft music, the ambient hues. If her feet weren't planted firmly on the floor, she would have mistaken her surroundings for a dreamscape.

"Evangelina?"

She turned and discovered Diome standing three feet away from her. Clad in a blinding white suit and feathery wings, he had dressed up as an angel.

"Diome!" Evangelina greeted him with a laugh. She was grateful for the semi-darkness, for it was the perfect mask for her blushing face. Her heart was racing at a speed she didn't know was possible, and a torrent of lightheadedness swept over her mind.

"We meet again."

"Indeed. You're an angel, I guess?"

A smile flitted across Diome's face. "Yes. And I see that you're a dark creature with horns."

"A devil," Evangelina corrected him.

"No, devils have wings. You're not wearing any."

"Really?" Evangelina asked, feigning astonishment. She knew devils also had wings, but she chose an inaccurate portrayal on purpose so that Diome wouldn't suspect she knew what real devils looked like.

Diome nodded. "I bet."

"How do you know what real devils look like? Have you seen one?" Evangelina teased him.

"I thought a pair of sheer black wings would complete your look is all. I do like the black horns and the wine red roses in your hair, though."

"Thank you." Evangelina had styled her tresses in a high bun and decorated it with a ring of dark red roses. "Why did you want to dress up as an angel?"

"And why did you want to dress up as a devil?" Diome asked.

"Hey, I asked the question first." Evangelina disguised her nervousness with fake cheeriness.

"A costume party is an opportunity for everyone to realize their innermost dreams through cosplay. For example, people who dream of being a princess would wear puffy ball gowns, while animal lovers might dress up as their favorite animal. I think everyone's costumes more or less reflect their personalities and hopes."

Evangelina blinked. "That's deep. So are you saying you want to be an angel?"

Diome devoted his gaze to his feet. "Sometimes."

The two of them remained silent, watching the merry couples glide and twirl around them as laughter rang in the air. Skeletons, butterflies, princesses, vampires, werewolves, witches, wizards, fairies, elves, mermaids, and trolls danced by, immersed in the revelry. Evangelina pondered Diome's words regarding costumes. She could only imagine how harsh his family must have been on him. Since devils were usually painted the villains in history, often initiating wars and battles, he must have hated his own clan.

Evangelina gazed down at her shimmering black dress, wondering why she had chosen such a costume. If Diome's theory made sense, then part of her longed to become a devil. Why? Was it to rebel against her parents' order? Somewhere in the depths of her soul, she knew the true answer but kept evading it—she wanted to be like Diome. Her costume was a reflection of her unspoken infatuation for him. Unlike the devils and angels blinded by hatred, he had a pure heart. She desired nothing better than to hold his hand and confess her love for him.

Hold his hand ... A mad notion popped into her mind, so bold it frightened even herself. But if she didn't put it to action now, she might never have a chance for the rest of her life.

As the final notes of the previous song slowed to a halt, a few couples left the dance floor. She mustered her determination and cleared her throat.

"Diome," Evangelina started, fighting to keep her voice steady. She extended a hand to him. "May I have the next dance?"

The silence that ensued her words stretched on for an eternity. She knew only a few seconds had passed, but to her, they felt like an hour.

It was surprise, at first, that registered on Diome's face. Then, a smile.

"I'd be honored," he replied with a slight bow.

Relief streamed through Evangelina's veins as a genuine smile bloomed on her face. "Thank you."

The two of them flitted over to the dance floor like fish in a glittering river. Evangelina pictured themselves in the ballroom of a palace, drifting in a sea of gentry. All around them were princes, princesses, dukes, duchesses, and royalty decked out in their finest. She placed a hand on his waist and held the other, wondering if she were the first angel to dance with a devil in history. A family of butterflies fluttered in her stomach as she felt his cold fingers interlock with hers. He rested his other hand on her bare shoulder, sending a shiver through her body. She gathered her courage and gazed into his eyes. They were soulful, almost wistful. Alluring, enchanting, mesmerizing. Like caves that held endless mysteries, they bore into the depths of her soul.

When a slow, melodious, yet somewhat mournful tune played, they began their dance. Like swans on a lake, they glided around each other in perfect sync. She felt as if she were flying, soaring in her dreams and drifting in a wonderland. As she focused on Diome, the lights in the background dimmed. The figures devolved into a blurry bokeh of dreamy circles. Was this how it felt to have eyes for nobody but her significant other? It was surreal, the thrill, the moment, the ambience. She couldn't believe it was real. Countless times, she fantasized what it would be like to date Diome. She hadn't contemplated the idea of inviting him to the dance, for she feared she wouldn't have the bravery to ask him to leave Horizon High if she grew too attached to him. However, there they were now, spinning around each other in a whirlwind of happiness. Neither of them spoke, but no words were necessary.

Evangelina relished every second of their dance, the touch of his skin, the glow of his eyes, and the charm of the ethereal atmosphere. She knew they were Evangelina Leclair and Diome Lenoir, an angel and a devil destined to antagonize each other. But in this perfect moment that would engrave itself in her memory, they were one.

Chapter Four

A Friend to Cherish
(Diome)

An hour had fluttered by since Evangelina invited Diome to dance. He still couldn't believe his fortune. Had he done anything particularly outstanding that earned him such a reward? The beacon of luck was shining on him tonight. Every step, every breath, every moment he spent twirling and spinning with Evangelina had been whimsical. She kindled in his heart an array of emotions—foreign, unfamiliar, but pleasant. He couldn't understand how she had charmed his heart. Never had he felt that way. It was a blend of happiness, excitement, and fear. Dancing with her was like flying—no, more than flying. And it was then when they swung and swayed under the dim lights that Diome realized just how enamored with Evangelina he was. Mesmerizing and breathtaking, she had captured him. Like a black hole, she possessed a gravitational pull on him. He had fallen into a deep pond of profound fondness, so deep that he could never escape. Evangelina had left a veritable angel's mark upon his heart.

They danced the night away, drunk in the hues and melodies, in the sweet perfume and intoxicating merriment. Soon, it was ten o'clock. Many of the couples had left the venue. Evangelina and Diome, though, weren't in a hurry to end their amazing night. Bathing in the glow of the night, the two of them strolled on the school grounds. The moonlit sky cast a gentle silver aura on the lawns, the buildings, and the stone-framed pond, beautifying the landscape.

Never had Diome dared to dream of such a night.

A dance with Evangelina was already too much to expect, but five dances and a nocturnal walk under the moon and stars? Unbelievable.

"You hungry?" Evangelina asked. "I snuck some refreshments out. Here." She handed him a napkin with some tiny sandwiches with bacon, lettuce, and tomato, and a piece of cherry cake wrapped in it.

"Thank you." Diome took the sandwiches. He wasn't expressing his gratitude solely for the snacks. There were so many things he was grateful for—her invitation to dance with him, the incredible memories he had created with her, and everything that happened on this splendid night.

They came across a bench. Evangelina gestured for him to sit down with her. Silence lingered between them—peaceful silence that wrapped around their figures like a comforting blanket. The sequins on her gown winked at Diome. He gazed at her figure, traced by moonlight. Drinking in the blissful present, he did his best to engrave every little sensory detail in his mind, from the coolness of the breeze, the darkness of the night, the mystery of the moonshine, to the calming aura Evangelina's presence brought. He recalled the colors and sounds that passed his eyes and the sensations streaming through his veins like the sun's rays on a cloudless morning. And he came to realize just how blessed he was to be the owner of those precious memories. With a divine, beautiful soul, she was more than a friend.

"I have a question," Diome began. "Why did you invite me to dance with you?"

"Are you saying it should be the other way round? That guys should take the initiative?"

"No, no," Diome clarified, kicking himself inwardly for his poor wording. "I didn't mean that at all."

"Sorry if I sounded judgmental," Evangelina apologized. "I was just confused."

Diome nodded. "What I was saying was, why did you invite *me* out of all the other kids? I'm not the richest, cleverest, fastest, or handsomest guy. My grades are mediocre, and I'm not on any sports team. I'm nothing special."

"You think too little of yourself." A slight smile lurked on Evangelina's lips.

What did she mean by that? Diome didn't dare overthink her words. She was simply offering him courage.

"I came to the ball for the food at first," Diome admitted. "But I never thought we'd have such a memorable night."

"Me too, for the food part," replied Evangelina. "But also, there's a little more than that. I wanted to have some normal high school experiences and memories."

"Of course."

"What fun events does Horizon High have every term?" Evangelina asked. "I'm already looking forward to the next."

"Many sports events. Basketball, football, baseball—"

"Any non-sports events?"

"The prom for the twelfth graders. Horizon High doesn't have that many events, though."

"I'm glad tonight was fun." Evangelina smiled. "My friend Camille came with her boyfriend Joey. My other friend Merilee met up with a cute guy called Allen. I thought I would be the last to find a partner, but then I found you."

"Magical, isn't it? What are the odds of running into the same guy again and again?" Diome teased her. He was more at ease, now that he had witnessed

Evangelina's lighthearted side. At least she regarded him as a friend.

"Very slim, I agree," she answered, studying her fingers.

"How come you don't wear any jewelry?" Diome asked, noticing her bare, slender fingers.

"Spending less time fussing over my appearance gives me more time to focus on the important things. Why aren't you wearing your skull accessories, by the way? Where's Diome and what did you do to him?"

Diome smirked. "You forgot. I'm an angel tonight."

"Ah, that you are. And I'm a devil. Do you think angels and devils exist, by the way?"

Diome's heart skipped a beat. Did she know something? Had he given himself away by accident? He remained quiet for a minute, his mind whirring to generate a wise reply.

"I like to imagine they do," he finally answered.

Evangelina raised her eyebrows. "Why?"

Her tone was genuine, curious, rather than amused or disdainful, which relieved Diome.

"Well, I write plays for fun—"

Evangelina's eyes widened. "You do?"

Perhaps Diome imagined it, but he detected respect in her gaze. "I do, but I haven't finished the one I'm working on right now."

"It's still incredible," she gushed.

"Thanks. I think it's important to keep an open mind when writing plays. Assume anything can happen next. That's why I choose to believe angels and devils exist. So I'll have more room for imagination."

"Interesting," Evangelina remarked. "What's your play about?"

Diome almost blurted out the answer, but he

remembered he had to remain undercover. He couldn't tell her what he was. Part of him felt like a liar, a cheat, a coward for not being brave enough to come clean. However, he had a valid reason not to. He and Evangelina were friends now. What would become of their friendship if she knew what he was?

"Diome, what's your play about?" Evangelina repeated.

"Oh, um ... " Diome scrambled for the right words, but found himself at an utter loss. "Sorry, I'm a bit shy when it comes to sharing my work. Even my parents have no idea what I wrote. It's not that I don't trust you, though. I just ... I'm not very confident when it comes to my play."

It wasn't a lie. He wasn't foolish enough to flaunt his creation in front of his parents. They would be furious if they knew how much he craved peace between the devils and angels.

"I get it," Evangelina consoled him. "We all have our insecurities, I guess."

"There's a common saying called, 'We all have our devils.' Devils are always associated with evil, darkness, and all things unpleasant. What do you think? If devils really exist, would they all be wicked? Religious theories aside, that is. Like, if devils were ordinary creatures like lions, bears, and monkeys, would they be good or bad?"

"There are good lions, bears, and monkeys as well as evil ones. Just like humans. There are great people who influenced the world, and there are criminals, thieves, and rapists too. In other words, kindness and evil is universal. In every town, in every country, on every continent, there are good and bad people. If devils existed, it would be the same—some of them might turn out decent, and some of them might become evil."

"That's an insightful answer," Diome replied. "Say, are you Aristotle, Plato, or Socrates?"

Evangelina laughed. "Neither, but I'm flattered."

With a wide smile on her face, she appeared livelier, more cheerful, more mischievous, like a garden fairy that emerged from a children's book and entered the world. Beautiful, but in a different way than her usual dainty, demure self.

A few more moments transpired before Evangelina spoke again.

"Diome ... Do you ... do you want to know the real reason I invited you to dance with me?" Her tone was prudent, measured, and slightly tense.

"Go on." Diome suddenly grew nervous. Cold sweat seeped from his palms, and he wiped them on his trousers.

"I ... " Evangelina avoided his gaze. "I enjoy your company very much."

She uttered one word at a time, unraveling like a child tearing open a wrapped gift one piece of paper at a time.

"Enjoy? Or more than that?" Diome choked. A moment of silence.

"More than that," Evangelina corrected him. "Oh, how should I say this? I've ... I've never been in a relationship before, but I guess that's because I never met anyone I truly liked ... "

Was this a confession? Diome grinned. His ears, eyes, and senses must be deceiving him. Evangelina *loved* him? Was that what she meant to tell him?

"Are you saying you hated everyone you met before me?" He teased her, emboldened by her courage to express her feelings first.

"Yes, yes—I mean, no, that's not what I ... " Evangelina took a deep breath and tucked a strand of hair behind her ear, blushing.

Diome reached out to hold her hand. "Guess what?"

Evangelina shook her head and focused on her gown's cascading ruffles.

"You're not alone." Diome savored those words as they left his lips.

Evangelina glanced up at him. "Do you mean it?"

Diome nodded firmly. "I do."

A smile bloomed on Evangelina's face, revealing her dimples. Diome could've sworn there were tears in her glossy eyes.

"I can't believe this. It must be a figment of my imagination. I ... Thank you, Diome."

Diome chuckled. "I can't believe this any more than you can. But sometimes, reality can be more incredible than you think. You just have to believe." He noticed Evangelina's smile was gone, replaced by downturned lips. "What's wrong?"

Evangelina shook her head. "We ... Diome, you know I like you. I really do. But we can't ... " She exhaled and turned away. "We can't be together."

The four words crushed him like a boulder. "Why?"

"I'm ... I'm not human," she faltered.

Diome wasn't astonished at her revelation, but rather that she had the courage to come clean first. A sudden thought popped into his mind. Could she have known what he was?

Evangelina's eyes glazed over as if she were trying to make sense of an unexplainable fact. "You weren't shocked when I told you I wasn't human. How did you know?" she whispered.

"That you're an angel? Remember the first day you came to school, and you cut your finger during art class? I noticed your white blood. Nobody else saw it because they were too busy fighting and arguing about who got to take you to the infirmary. But I noticed the cut."

"Ingenious," Evangelina murmured. "You're very observant."

Diome nodded. Anxiety leapt in him like a frog in boiling water. Should he reveal what he was? As he was debating with himself, Evangelina spoke again.

"Diome," she began, her voice gentler than ever. "It doesn't matter who you are and what your family believes. What matters is what you think and what you want to become."

"How did you know I'm a devil?" Now it was Diome's turn to worry whether he had done anything reckless and exposed his identity by accident.

Evangelina closed her eyes. "From the start. I knew from the start. It's not pure coincidence I enrolled in Horizon High. My parents made me come. They somehow knew you were here, and they wanted me to assassinate you."

Diome blinked. "Me? Why did they target me?"

A frown creased Evangelina's forehead. Tears glistened on her eyelashes. "My father said, 'The more devils dead, the better.' I don't know how he found out you were studying here, but when he sees a devil, he ... " Her tears streamed down her cheeks.

Diome brushed the tears away with a thumb, edged closer to her, and wrapped his arms around her.

"I'm sorry," she whispered. "I won't ever hurt you no matter what, but ... I'm scared for you. We can't be together."

"But I love you," Diome murmured, as if that was enough to secure their relationship.

"I love you too," she replied shakily. "Believe me,

I tried to change my parents' minds. However, they wouldn't listen. They insisted I had to kill you. I promised myself I would convince you to transfer and then lie to them, saying that I murdered you. But I can't do it. Driving you away would be like sticking a needle into myself."

Diome held onto her tighter. She was brave, much braver and stronger than she appeared. Respect for Evangelina welled up in him as he once again acknowledged how perfect she was.

"Diome, neither of us deserves this, but I don't want you to upset your parents by ... being with me. They hate us angels, don't they?"

Diome sighed. "They're extremists, yes." He made no attempt to sugarcoat the truth, for he knew empty bubbles of lies were too fragile to stand the test of time. They could shatter anytime at the slightest threat.

"Can we forget who we really are and just be you and me?" Evangelina murmured. "We're not in the Land of Heavenly Dreams or the Burning Bowels now. Just two ordinary high school kids in a regular high school. I'm an angel and you're a devil, but what difference does it make? We all have emotions. We all get hurt and upset."

"True," replied Diome. "Have you finished your book, *Romeo and Juliet*?"

Evangelina nodded. "They're just like us. Lovers whose families are rivals."

"It's my favorite play," Diome told her.

The angels and devils had locked themselves in a cage of hatred, not knowing they held the key that could free themselves from the immense burden of history. And yet, he and Evangelina were sitting next to each other at this moment, nothing to separate them.

"We could date in secret," Evangelina proposed.

"I'll stall my parents."

"For how long? What if they find out we're dating?"

"I'd say a few months. I can tell them I'm trying to earn your trust and planning to murder you when the opportunity presents itself."

"I wish it was a lot easier." Diome sighed. They had barely set foot on their path of love, but already it was paved with thorns.

"But think about it, what's life without a little challenge or two?" Evangelina replied. "Do you remember the first time we spoke, at the flower shop? We talked about roses and thorns."

"And you said, 'Flaws can highlight the rawness and reality of things and bring out their beauty instead,'" Diome recited.

Evangelina blinked, stunned. "Y-you remember my words."

"Of course I do. It's not like I have amnesia, is it?" Diome quipped.

That made Evangelina giggle. "Well, you remembered every word of it. May I ask you something, by the way?"

"Just go ahead. It's totally all right."

"When did you discover ... ?" Evangelina cleared her throat. "Well, when did you find out you were ... you liked me?"

"From the moment I saw you, I knew you were different from the other girls. And that time in art class when those boys were fighting over who gets to escort you to the infirmary, you just stood up and went alone. That was so cool of you. And when we met at that flower shop and had our first conversation, your words left a deep impression on me."

Evangelina smiled. "I'm glad I met you. You

came to the human world because you're an aspiring inventor, right?"

"Gosh, Evangelina, how many things do you know about me that I don't know?" Diome chuckled.

"I'm saying that because my mother is also an inventor. The technology in the Land of Heavenly Clouds is pretty advanced. We have bathrooms, kitchens, libraries, hotels, and water pipes."

"Where do you get the water from?" Diome asked.

"Created the water with our magic. Can devils conjure water?"

"We can. But we're better at summoning darkness. I suppose angels like you have an affinity for light."

Evangelina tapped her palm twice. An orange blossom of flame rose from her skin. She stared at it with unblinking eyes. Diome gasped as the flame yellowed, greened, blued, purpled, pinked, and reddened.

"Wow," he murmured. "Amazing."

"I can create life too, if I want, though I'm not as good at that as the adult angels." Evangelina stooped and picked up a shriveled red rose on the ground by a rose bush. She tapped on it thrice. The blossom lifted its head, and as if reborn, it regained color.

"Beautiful," breathed Diome. He wished he had been gifted the power to resurrect wilted flowers, but on the contrary, his powers could only destroy life.

"What colors do you like?" Evangelina asked. "I'll give you this rose as a little present."

Diome shrugged. "I'd say black but at the same time I don't want you to turn the rose black. Make it your favorite color, then, so I'll be reminded of you whenever I look at it."

Evangelina pressed her right thumb to the hearty

petals, and icy hues of cobalt-blue, azure, turquoise, and apple-green took over the rose. Diome gazed at the swirling palette of blue and green, admiring her masterpiece.

"For you." Evangelina handed him the flower. "Be careful, though. Don't prick your fingers."

"I'm happy you didn't de-thorn it," replied Diome, twirling his lovely souvenir.

"Because like you said on that fateful afternoon, 'Imperfection is a form of perfection.'" Evangelina remembered.

Now it was Diome's turn to marvel at her memory. "You remember every word of it!" Joy bubbled in him like a merry creek, flooding every inch of him.

"Of course I do. It's not like I have amnesia, is it?" Evangelina parroted his earlier reply.

Diome beamed. "I can't create life like you angels, but I'd like to give you something special in return."

Evangelina lifted her eyebrows. "What is it?"

Before the tide of courage in him ebbed, Diome leaned close to Evangelina and kissed her. The moment her soft mouth encountered his, unsettling his equilibrium, he forgot to breathe. His world consisted of only Evangelina. Everything else faded into the background. Evangelina's warmth enveloped him in an aura of comfort, banishing every doubt he had had. His worries evaporated like morning mist, replaced by pure bliss. Filled with delight and relaxation, he felt as though he had been transported to a safe sanctuary where his troubles were worlds away from him. Nothing could ravage the indescribable euphoria that permeated every fiber of his being. He had never kissed anyone before. Not even his parents, for they believed boys should be raised to be tough and therefore deprived him of affection.

When he broke their kiss, Diome was still immersed in the glow of their love.

"If only this night can last forever," he murmured.

"It won't, but our love will," Evangelina assured him.

Diome visualized them as a prince and a princess in a Medieval palace courtyard, their romance shining like the brightest star in the darkest night. With her, they could conquer every obstacle in their way. He wasn't sure why he had such unwavering faith in their romance. Yet his intuition told him that, together, they could become something bigger, braver, better.

****

The next few days went by in a gust of wind. Diome had never been more excited about school. He placed Evangelina's rose on a ceramic vase he purchased from Cassie's Flower Shop—a gorgeous green gradient that faded to white. She told him it wouldn't need any watering, for it thrived on magic. For that, Diome was relieved. Never could he take care of any plants without killing them. As a boy, he had once picked some daisies in Horizon Park, placed them in a tiny vase with water, and brought them back to his bedroom. However, it didn't take a day for them to expire and rot. Either it was because of the infernal conditions in the Burning Bowels, or it was due to the fact their owner was a devil capable of destroying life without even meaning to, or a combination of both possibilities. Therefore, Diome was overjoyed to have a rose—and not just any mundane rose, one that Evangelina made with care and instilled with colors and love. He wouldn't have traded it for a mountain of gold or an ocean of diamonds.

Diome and Evangelina spent many glorious afternoons at various places in Horizon. Often they had an afternoon snack at a random café. Evangelina dared not head home after six in the evening, for she feared suspicions would arise in her parents' minds. However, every second they spent with each other was priceless.

Kind Evangelina introduced Diome to her friends Camille and Merilee, and because of that, Diome had two more new friends. He spoke little with them but enjoyed their presence. School was no longer dull and repetitive. Quite the contrary, every day was a brand-new adventure. He spent innumerable mornings with Evangelina taking walks on the campus, countless afternoons discussing fun facts about the human world while savoring lattes, doughnuts, and ice cream. He also spent numerous evenings dreaming about Evangelina. Her divine countenance, graceful figure, and dreamy voice would weave their way into his nighttime visions like threads of beautiful silk on a mural of embroidered patterns. Every time he recalled her, his heart grew warmer, his footsteps lighter, and his spirits higher. The world grew more saturated, the colors more vivid and the harsh angles toned down. Love made a person view everything in a different light. It made people hopeful, enthusiastic, and optimistic about their futures, rosy and dazzling in equal measure.

A week after the Halloween dance, Diome promised to take Evangelina on a picnic date to the beach. There would only be the two of them, which meant they were free to discuss anything magical without worrying about revealing themselves to the humans.

After school, they bought some chocolate-chip cookies, caramel apples, cupcakes, and sandwiches, and boarded a bus.

"When do you have to get home today?" Evangelina asked, gazing out at the colorful buildings.

"I don't have a curfew. My parents don't care

how late I go home."

"Don't they worry about you?" Evangelina's eyes betrayed concern.

Diome shrugged. "Not much. They think I'm a boy, and boys should run around outside and toughen themselves up."

"You don't agree with them," Evangelina observed.

Diome shook his head. "I wish they would care about me more. Everyone is wired differently. There's no way you can label people like products or group them like farm animals. Everyone is unique in their own way. Just because they think I don't need them doesn't mean it's true on my end."

"Have you talked to them about it?" Evangelina asked.

"I've tried, but they won't listen to me."

"Mine won't when I try to talk sense into them either." Evangelina lowered her volume. "I keep telling them it's wrong to murder devils, but what I think matters less than their beliefs."

The bus slowed to a stop on reaching its final destination. Diome and Evangelina paid their fares, waved goodbye to the driver, and hopped off.

Before them were a few shrubs, bare and brown. It was November now, and the weather was chillier than before. Diome had on a double-breasted coat, while Evangelina had a periwinkle blue scarf and thick, woolly stockings on. Her hair fluttered in the ocean breeze as they made their way past the undergrowth and to the soft, spongy sand. Unfurling in front of them was the infinite ocean, an aquamarine carpet of waves. It kissed the cerulean sky in the far distance, almost meeting the heavens.

"Nice place for a first date," Evangelina beamed.

"I was worried you wouldn't like it," Diome replied. "It's not dinner in a fine restaurant, a cozy homemade lunch, or anything special. Just a beach date."

"Diome, you worry too much." Evangelina took his hand. "It's the thought that counts. And anyway, the beach in Horizon is striking. I'm really happy you brought me here."

Leaning against each other, they tackled their desserts while watching the torrents of tides, white against blue. Like scallops of lace, the waves caressed the sand like a mother stroking her baby's tender skin.

"What's it like in the Land of Heavenly Dreams?" Diome asked, taking a bite of a caramel apple and savoring the combination of sweetness and sourness.

"Tons of floating islands. You can't get anywhere without flying."

"What do the islands look like? "

"Most of them are covered with grass and dotted with flowers. You can see little hills, small waterfalls, and natural ponds. I love watching the stars, clouds, and shadows, and how they change every day."

"Shadows?"

"Among the layered clouds. And the sun and moon."

"Are there roses in the Land of Heavenly Dreams?"

Evangelina bit into a cupcake with chocolate frosting and a cherry on top. "Sure. There are buttercups, daisies, and meadowsweets in every color you can imagine."

"Are there rainbows? Do you get to see shooting stars often?"

"Oh, yes. They're sublime, the landscapes in the Land of Heavenly Dreams."

"I wish I could visit it one day without worrying

about getting killed," lamented Diome. "It sounds terrific. In the Burning Bowels way down underground, we've got a giant sea of lava. The buildings are all red-bricked. Everything there's either red or orange. The colors sizzle in your eyes."

"That doesn't sound very pleasant," remarked Evangelina. "I wish you could come to the Land of Heavenly Dreams. You would love it there."

"I bet I would. It sounds so unbelievable. A world above the clouds. Floating islands with pretty green grass. It's blue up there most of the time, I guess?"

Evangelina nodded. "In the daytime. Believe it or not, I would love to go to the Burning Bowels one day."

Diome stared at her. "You've got to be joking."

Evangelina shook her head. "I swear I'm not. A change of scenery would be interesting."

"If the devils and angels reconcile one day, we might be able to visit each other without worrying about our lives," Diome replied, despite doubting he would live to see that day. They two clans detested each other too much to see reason, much less make peace.

"I want to be hopeful, but it's not up to us." Evangelina sighed. "I'd give anything to live in harmony with the devils."

"So you don't blame the devils for the battles in history?"

"Both sides were wrong. And it won't do us any good to dwell on the death toll and point fingers. Nobody can rewrite history, but we're not as powerless as we think either. We can change now. Because every day, every week, every month, and every year will become history someday. Sadly, the angels and devils are all too dumb to realize this. Everyone's too blinded by hatred to care."

Diome held her hand. "At least we're making a

difference."

"Indeed. Oh, when did our conversation get so heavy? Let's talk about some happier topics."

And as they chatted about school, books, and the wonders of the human world, Diome realized that, for the first time in his life, he wasn't alone in this vast, boundless universe.

Chapter Five
Birthday and Deathday
(Evangelina)

The November mist teased Evangelina's nose. She could inhale the dewy air in her bedroom. It glided in through the window opposite her bed, chilling her room. She wondered whether there was a cold day in the Burning Bowels.

Diome hung out with her every day at school and afterwards. With him, she was the happiest angel in the world. She couldn't believe she had the courage to confess her love for him. Even more unbelievably, he had reciprocated her love. Camille and Merilee made fun of them, calling them the "sunshine girl" and the "brooding boy." Evangelina didn't mind their teasing. She was proud to have Diome. He might not be the most popular kid or the star student, but he was perfect for her.

She found her classes interesting. School in the Land of Heavenly Dreams wasn't half as challenging as Horizon High. She found history, civics, and science more difficult than the others, but nevertheless, she liked learning. Her favorite class was geography. Learning about the famous rivers, mountains, and deserts in the human world was eye-opening. She was relieved her ten years of education in the Land of Heavenly Dreams was useful. In her human studies class back then, the angels learned all about baseball, television, airplanes, shopping malls, and countless technological inventions the humans had created. Therefore, she understood what her friends were talking about when they got excited about sports or exchanged hilarious stories about their family trips.

However, the only person she could confide in

was Diome. Only he knew what secrets lay behind her human garb and ordinary façade. He paid her his full attention and fixed his pretty gray eyes on her whenever she spoke. His gaze was penetrating at times, as if he were staring into the depths of her heart. The best memories they shared were their after-school adventures. Memories of her and Diome lurked in the town library, the café by the school, Horizon Park, and the Italian diner in the town square. She forgot where she was and who she was every time he kissed her. The world's edges and angles softened, and the moment seemed to last forever.

For some reason, Evangelina had never dreamed about what it felt like to be loved. Truth be told, she found the concept rather silly. Who would devote their entire life to another person and give up the freedom and flexibility of being single? But whenever Diome's lips greeted hers, her doubts vanished like mist. With the right person, everything was different. As though Diome's presence was a filter, the world became more saturated, the colors around her grew brighter and rosier.

****

"What are you smiling about, Evangelina?" Auntie Bronwyn asked. She was one of their neighbors who lived on the floating island below them.

"Oh, nothing," Evangelina replied, resuming her sketching. She was thinking about Diome, of course, but she would have to be insane to admit that.

The neighbors were having a gathering in the garden before Evangelina's house. It was a sunny day, the air warmer than an average November morning. They were all clad in flowing white robes and sitting at a round table, sipping their coffee. Angels and devils usually wore robes when they weren't in the human world. The angels favored white outfits, since they were closer to the sun and white robes absorbed less heat. On the other hand, the devils always wore black robes, since their bodies were immune to fire and heat.

"Evangelina's been going to a human school called Horizon High," Evangelina's mother told the neighbors.

"Really? I didn't know that," gasped Uncle Thomas, who lived under their island. "What have you been learning at school?"

"The usual. We study algebra in math, democratic rights in civics, and geography. And we're starting a book called *The Sorrows of Young Werther* in English." Evangelina smiled a little. "Our teacher likes romantic literature. She made us read Shakespeare's *Romeo and Juliet* in October, and now, she's asking us to read this new novel. We're going to write a paper comparing them at the end of the term."

"Fascinating," remarked Uncle Thomas. "But why did you want to study in the human world? I thought you wanted to be a designer."

Evangelina was sketching a black leather jacket, a pad of paper resting on her lap. She had been teaching herself to sew with magic, although she hadn't gotten the hang of it yet.

"There's a devil in her school called Diome Lenoir," Evangelina's father answered. "We want her to kill him."

Evangelina bit her lip, a coil of anger rising in her like steam. Her parents hadn't relented, of course, but neither had she.

"How's your secret mission going, little assassin?" Auntie Bronwyn asked.

When her parents asked her about Diome last night, Evangelina told them she was befriending him and winning his trust before executing the plan. She would lie to them about killing Diome in the end. She would elope with Diome if they found out she was lying. They could move to Canada, Australia, or somewhere in Africa or Asia, where they could begin anew.

"She's doing her best," Evangelina's mother explained. "Trying to befriend that devil for now. Win his trust and then eliminate him."

Uncle Thomas guffawed. "Clever plan! The devils won't even know how he died! They can't blame us for Diome Lenoir's death, can they? There won't be any evidence to link us to him! Who would have thought our brilliant Evangelina was attending his school undercover?"

Evangelina gnashed her teeth and balled her hands into fists. She kept her head down, so they didn't notice the fury written on her face. *How shameless and heartless were they?*

"Be careful and don't blow your cover, little spy," Auntie Bronwyn reminded her.

"I won't," Evangelina replied, erasing a squiggly line on the jacket's sleeve. It took all of her self-control to not lash out at the cruel adults. There they were, discussing the murder of a devil in a distastefully casual attitude.

"How old is she? Sixteen?" Uncle Thomas asked, changing the topic.

"She turns seventeen on November fifteenth," her mother replied. "That's next Saturday."

"Oh, will she be at the debutante ball next month?" Auntie Bronwyn asked. "They welcome seventeen-year-old angels from every family."

Attending a debutante ball was a tradition for young female angels in the Land of Heavenly Dreams, regardless of their families' economic status. Evangelina was surprised when she heard humans had dances like that too. She thought this event only existed in the Land of Heavenly Dreams.

"Of course." Her mother swelled with pride. "She'll be the prettiest angel there."

"Do you think the devils have debutante balls too?" Evangelina asked out of the blue.

The adults halted their conversation and turned to stare at her.

Her father let out a snort of laughter. "I couldn't care less about those devils."

"Same," Uncle Thomas added. "They could burn in the lava ocean and I wouldn't give a damn about them."

"The screaming," drawled Auntie Bronwyn. "It's music. I heard it once when I joined some angels who were launching a surprise attack on those nasty devils. I watched them drop into the lava sea when we destroyed their wings. Even though they're immune to lava, they can drown in it. It's like the humans and their oceans."

What was wrong with those homicidal maniacs? They were decent angels, helpful and friendly to their neighbors, but when the issue of the devils arose, every ounce of their sense and logic evaporated, replaced by extreme perversity and poisonous hatred.

Focusing on her design, Evangelina ignored them. When she perfected her sewing skills, she would make this jacket and surprise Diome with it. She immersed herself in the precious recollections of her and Diome together. He was her secret weapon, she realized. The thought of him lifted her spirits whenever she was down. It was her pride, her honor, her blessing to have him.

A cunning smile curled Evangelina's lips as she glanced up at her parents, Auntie Bronwyn, and Uncle Thomas. None of them knew she was dating Diome. She was proud of her peaceful rebellion, of her nonconformity. The sweet satisfaction empowered her.

Nobody could steal her secret pleasure, for they were all oblivious to the euphoric sensations and blissful dreams Diome brought her. He and she were the only ones wise enough to rise above the mutual hatred their clans harbored for each other. Although they couldn't control the foolish majority, they could choose to be themselves. And neither of them were prepared to yield to their family's expectations and superficial beliefs.

****

"Evangelina!" someone called on her way to school the next day.

Evangelina glanced up and spotted her former classmate, Carol, on an island. She was sitting by a pond, her messy black curls jumbled in a loose bun. Beside her was a lake, a fishing rod in her hands,

"Hey, Carol." Evangelina waved at her and landed on the island. "What brings you here so early?"

"I woke up at four in the morning and flew out," explained Carol. "I'm over the moon."

"Oh? And why is that?" Evangelina asked.

"It's my seventeenth birthday today!" Carol sang. "I got an invitation to the debutante ball next month!"

"Congratulations, and happy birthday!" Evangelina clapped her hands.

"Thanks! I heard you're at a new school in the human world. Are you getting used to it there?"

Evangelina nodded. "Yes, I love it there. I'd better get going, or I'll be late. See you soon!"

Carol smiled and waved goodbye to her.

Evangelina observed the low, flat cloudscape, her thoughts drifting away. Everyone was eager and elated about the debutante ball. But Evangelina wasn't keen on attending. She had Diome already, and she wasn't interested in finding a suitor. Yet she couldn't say no to the ball, for she didn't want her parents to suspect anything.

Making her descent, Evangelina shrunk her wings, folded them, and resumed her journey to school. Could she lie to them and tell them she was dating a human classmate in Horizon High? Some of the angels married humans and brought them to the Land of Heavenly Dreams. Her cover story could collapse at the slightest bit of scrutiny, though, for when her parents started prodding her for details, she might not be able to answer all of their questions and remember every little thing she fabricated. No, that wouldn't do.

"Boo!" someone behind her burst out.

Evangelina jumped about a foot in the air.

Camille and Merilee clutched their stomachs, doubling over in a fit of giggles.

Evangelina gave them each a mock punch on the arm. "You're lucky I didn't have a heart attack. Or else you two will have to pay my medical bills!"

Merilee grinned. "Sorry, couldn't resist it. You were so deep in thought that we couldn't miss this great opportunity to scare you."

Evangelina rolled her eyes and laughed. "How old are you two? Still jump-scaring people like little kids? I'll get you two back next time, you mark my words."

"What were you thinking about earlier? Diome?" Camille asked.

"No," Evangelina replied. "I was thinking about the book we read in English. *The Sorrows of Young Werther.*"

"A sad story for sure. To die for love is romantic, isn't it?" Camille gushed.

"I wish someone would die for me," swooned Merilee. "I bet Diome would risk his life for you, Evangelina. You're the lucky duck among us."

Merilee and her boyfriend Allen had broken up a

few days ago. It was a peaceful breakup, though, and they remained friends.

"I want Diome to live and not die for me," Evangelina replied. "What we feel when we're alive matters the most. It doesn't matter how we die, but how we live. Dying is only an instant, but living takes years. I'd rather have a lifetime's happy memories with him."

Camille and Merilee blinked. "How practical," remarked Camille.

"That's an interesting concept," Merilee added. "I've never thought of it that way. You must love Diome very much."

"I do," answered Evangelina.

"To the extent you would take a knife for him?" Camille asked.

Evangelina pondered over the topic. Moments ago, she had eloquently criticized the romance in sacrificing one's life for another, but Camille's words rendered her speechless. There was no question how she would react if Diome's life was in danger. She would protect him without hesitation. It had nothing to do with chivalry or valor. She just couldn't stand the thought of losing him. The notion of his eyes dulling, his face paling, and his pulse silencing was too much to bear.

Camille's eyes rounded. "What? You'd do it?"

Evangelina nodded. "I would. But let's face it, how high are the chances of that happening?"

Very high. Camille and Merilee had no clue how much danger she and Diome were in.

"You don't want him to die for you, but you want to die for him," continued Camille. "Yes, very logical."

"I'd prefer it if neither of us died, thank you very much," Evangelina answered. "Why do you love tragedies so much? What's gotten into you lately?"

Camille smiled and ignored her question. "I just

like teasing you about your sweetheart. What do you love about him? No offense, but he doesn't appear to be very gallant or sporty. He's a good guy, of course, but I'm curious what about him intrigues you. Diome was super quiet before you came. He never socialized with anyone, and really, we thought he'd be the last kid in Horizon High to get a girlfriend. I'm dying to know how you charmed the dark, gothy boy."

Evangelina lapsed into a spell of silence. What did she love about Diome? She hadn't given it much thought before Camille brought up the question. He wasn't very humorous, nor was he outgoing and outspoken. Nevertheless, she was comfortable around him. And even if she wasn't romantically involved with him, their fates were intertwined like two vines. One couldn't help but marvel at the innumerable connections they shared. He was a devil and she was an angel, but they were both pacifists born in a family of supremacists. They disliked and disdained their parents' beliefs and weren't afraid to criticize the shallowness of the angels and devils. Like Diome, she was born an only child. He, like her, had few friends. They were misfits and nonconformists striving to be themselves and maintain their morals in a world filled with bitter resentment and rivalry. They were too alike, too similar in many ways. How could Evangelina not love him?

"When you're with the right person, you don't stop to think about how and why they're right for you," Evangelina replied. "Something in your soul, in your intuition tells you they're the one."

"That's a philosophical answer," remarked Merilee. "But could you tell me more details?"

"Be descriptive," Camille added. "We're all hopeless romantics here."

"You sound like Ms. Johansson, my English

teacher." Evangelina giggled. *"Always be descriptive in your essays."*

"She's right, you know." Camille smiled. "All right, now tell us the juicy stuff about Diome. Why do you like him?"

"I'm comfortable around him. He makes me smile. We have many things in common. He never tries to make my decisions for me. With him, it's an equal partnership."

"I hear that many couples like to take on dominant and submissive roles," Merilee commented. "Not that I'm an expert, but how do you feel about that? You said you and Diome are equal partners."

Evangelina frowned. "To be honest, I never liked that saying about roles. A relationship is a relationship. Not a play. There shouldn't be any roles. The two people should be free to be whoever they want as long as they're not breaking any laws."

"Obviously, you don't like the dominant-or-submissive theory," Camille remarked. "Wouldn't you like someone to lead you in life, though?"

Evangelina stared at her. "Would you?"

Camille blushed. "Oh ... Not all the time, I suppose. It'd be like my mother, who's always nagging nonstop."

"That's right. I don't like being told what or what not to do. Honestly, I don't even care about pleasing others. But at the same time, I wouldn't like it if others tried to please me either. That's why I refuse to be dominant or submissive. When I'm friends or more than friends with someone, I don't want to be led like a dog. I expect to get the same respect I give my partner."

It originated from her belief that everyone, angel, human, or devil, was equal. Every life was worth the same, no one nobler or humbler. It was the same in a relationship. Both sides needed and respected each other in equal measure. Because they valued one another and loved them for who they were, they wouldn't attempt to change them.

"What does Diome think?" Merilee mused.

"I can't speak for him, but he and I are very likeminded for sure. It's like I've found a twin flame that mirrors myself. Anyway, I think relationships should be reciprocal. You get as much as you give, and you give as much as you get. Nothing should unsettle the equilibrium. Don't get me wrong, I'm not saying I'll judge Diome just because I gave him a cookie but didn't get one in return. Material things don't matter as much as what's inside— behavior, thoughts, influence, and all that. A relationship is only fair when both sides have the same freedom to be themselves."

"Spoken like a romance expert," Camille complimented her, nodding.

"I don't mean to sound like I'm cleverer. That's just what I believe."

"You shed some new insight on me," Camille replied. "You're very sensible. I think you'd make a great mathematician or philosopher. Most people don't analyze relationships the way you do. They just fall in love and let the tides of romance sweep them off their feet."

"It's a pity people don't think more," remarked Evangelina. "They have no idea how much they missing."

****

Today was tougher compared to the previous few weeks. The teachers were making them work harder, since the midterms were around the corner. Evangelina had three tests in the morning and for the first time, she couldn't wait for the day to be over.

Standing at the school gates, she perused the notes

in her chemistry textbook, cramming the formulas into her mind. It was annoying, as she didn't even understand what she didn't understand. The bizarre letters and numbers might as well be in Spanish. She still didn't know what in the world they meant.

"Never knew you were so studious." A familiar voice rang behind her.

Evangelina turned and smiled. Diome was dressed in a brown blazer, beige trousers, and black sneakers today. Despite his casual attire, he was still the most handsome boy in Horizon High.

"How was your day, Diome?"

"Exhausting. I was thinking of you in class."

That made Evangelina giggle. "Pay attention to the teachers tomorrow. I wouldn't want to be the reason your grades dropped."

"Well, they're not as pretty or interesting as you," Diome assured her.

"You flatter me," replied Evangelina, hugging him. "But that's why I like you," she joked.

"Let's go to the little café in the town square," suggested Diome. "You free?"

"Even if I'm not free, I'd make time for you," Evangelina replied.

"And I would too," replied Diome. "You're my priority."

"For that, Diome, I'll give you all my chemistry notes so that you can copy them. How does that sound?"

Diome perked up. "Sounds wonderful. Maybe you could teach me chemistry."

"How can I teach you when I don't know what in the world the teacher is talking about?"

"You can't be worse than I." Diome chuckled.

"Too busy thinking about me? I've got to make amends for that," replied Evangelina. "All right, I'll do my best to teach you."

"Thank you. I like your clothes today, by the way."

Evangelina had on a fuzzy hot pink sweater, black jeans, and burgundy ankle-length boots. Unlike the fashionistas in Horizon, who were all about designer clothing and jewelry, she was a lot less glamorous than they were. Ironically, she was an aspiring fashion designer who had little interest in dressing up. She preferred admiring tasteful outfits over flaunting them to advertise her wealth. To her, fashion was an art, not a tool to broadcast one's social status.

"I like what you're wearing too," Evangelina replied. "But even if you were dressed in a ridiculous clown outfit with a big red nose, I'd still choose you over any other guy in Horizon.

Diome smiled. "If only you knew how much that means to me."

They entered the café, ordered two lattes, and settled down at one of the tables. Evangelina admired the industrial-style decorations, the bare tubes, wooden tables, and black metal shelves.

"What is your house like?" Diome asked.

"Boring white walls, dark blue sofas and beige carpets. Sky-blue curtains and a white kitchen. It's kind of mundane, to be honest. What about you?"

"You're calling that mundane? My house is full of dark tables, chairs, and shelves. You'd think we lived in a haunted house."

"Not at all," Evangelina replied. "Sounds very quaint and vintage to me. Do you use wood there?"

"Yes, we do. They're charmed so that they won't catch fire in the heat."

A waiter delivered their coffees. Evangelina beamed at the pleasant aroma wafting from the shell-white cups.

"I'm glad we have coffee in the Land of Heavenly Dreams. Is it the same in the Burning Bowels?"

"Oh, yes. We don't grow coffee trees. It's too hot and dry there. We get coffee beans by importing them from the humans."

"Same in the Land of Heavenly Dreams."

"When's your birthday?" Diome asked. "I just realized I never asked."

"It's actually coming up this week. November 15th."

Diome's eyes widened. "Wow. Happy birthday, Evangelina. What would you like as a birthday gift?"

"A date with you. But my family might go out to celebrate."

"We could have dinner together on Friday. How does that sound?"

Evangelina beamed. "Incredible. Thanks for thinking of me."

"You're welcome," replied Diome. "I guess we should start studying now. I don't want to flunk tomorrow's quiz."

Studying with Diome was stress-free and enjoyable. The chemistry formulas didn't appear as difficult as before. Together, they navigated the entire chapter about acids and bases, stopping to consult online teaching videos every now and then. It was already five o'clock when they had a rudimentary grasp of what they were about to be tested on.

"Let's stop here for today," suggested Diome. "I guess this is enough for me to get a passing grade in tomorrow's quiz."

"I'm glad it was helpful," Evangelina replied, rubbing her sore eyes. "We have a test on *The Sorrows of Young Werther* tomorrow in English. Not sweating it, though."

"Oh, is that the book about the guy who died for love?" Diome asked.

"Many books fit that general description, but yes, this is one of them. I was just talking Camille and Merilee this morning about the concept of dying for love. Is it foolish or romantic?"

"It's romantic. To burn yourself like a candle and be there for someone who needs you."

"I think living for someone you love makes more sense." Evangelina finished the rest of her coffee. "People say they would die for their family, best friends, and lovers, but what we need is to people to live for us and give us support. Dying is easy, it takes only one second. But to live for someone is harder. It's a commitment that takes weeks, months, or maybe years."

Evangelina realized the hypocrisy and irony in her words. She thought living for love was harder than dying for love, but if the scenario arose, she would give her life to protect Diome.

"Does it have to be black and white, though?" Diome asked, a thoughtful expression on his face. "Would it be possible to do both? You live for someone and die for them if need be?"

Evangelina laughed. "Nobody could. And anyway, it's not as if something so dramatic would happen to us."

"Hard to say," Diome replied. "But I do prefer a peaceful life without troubles over an exciting one with tons of adventures."

"Me too. I used to wish I was born a human, but come to think of it, don't we have our peaceful days too? Times like now, when all we need to worry about is schoolwork."

"And the existential question about love you just

brought up," teased Diome.

"Yes, and that too. All the chaos in our life only makes those precious moments rarer."

"You know what would make today better?" Diome asked, a playful glint in his eyes.

"What?"

Diome leaned closer to her and captured her lips in an ardent kiss. Evangelina's heart melted, and happiness bloomed in her like the first buds of spring. Something in her told her she would recount this kiss after days, weeks, and months and marvel over the simple yet profound delight it kindled in her bosom.

****

For the next few days, Evangelina's family was aflutter with elation. Turning seventeen was a big milestone for every angel. It marked the beginning of their adulthood, a brand-new chapter of their life. For the entire week, all her parents could talk about was the debutante ball. The invitation—gilded and cream-colored—had arrived at their mailbox on Wednesday, sparking a flurry of excitement in the family.

"You'll meet the angel of your dreams," her mother gushed.

"It's still a month away," Evangelina replied with a shrug. She hoped her mother wouldn't take umbrage at her lack of enthusiasm.

"All the handsome young angels will be dying to dance with you," her father assured her. "Don't be worried, Evangelina. You'll do great."

They must've mistook her apathy for nervousness. They were missing the point, but perhaps that wasn't a bad thing. Evangelina was in no hurry to correct them. As long as they didn't suspect she had a boyfriend already, she was fine with anything.

Diome gave her a little gift the day before her

birthday, much to her pleasant astonishment. It was a silk scarf dyed in a gradient of blue, turquoise, and green.

"Happy birthday to you. Like it?" he had asked her with a twinkle in his eye. He acted like a boy who couldn't be prouder of his report card.

Evangelina had given him a fierce embrace in return. "I love it! Thank you so much. I hope you didn't spend too much on it."

"Oh, just three months of my allowance. It's worth it, though. As long as you like it, I'm glad."

Evangelina remembered the cozy dinner they had had afterwards—nothing extravagant, just some pesto spaghetti and a blueberry milkshake at the Italian diner. However, it was simple in a memorable way. When she reflected on the magical memories she and Diome had woven together, the most ordinary moments stood out to her. Tranquility was a luxury for them, which made the small dates and peaceful days all the more invaluable.

****

Evangelina got up at eight in the morning on Saturday. Her mother had made a reservation at Ambrosia, their family's favorite restaurant. Their relatives would meet them for lunch to celebrate her birthday.

She donned a blue denim shirt and black leggings after washing her face, sat down at her table, and got out her sketches. She wasn't one of those angels who made a big deal out of birthdays. To her, it was just like any other day. If she could have everything her way on her special day, she would invite Diome to join their family gathering. Unfortunately, the chances of that happening were less than zero.

Trying to take her mind off Diome, Evangelina devoted herself to designing and sketching a cocktail dress with a fringe hem. It was a period costume from the

Jazz Age, she realized. Her thoughts wandered back to Diome, whom she supposed was preparing for the exam. Although the imminent test annoyed Evangelina, it was nothing compared to the debutante ball. She would rather take a hundred exams than attend the dance, but complaining about it would do her no good. Like a ventriloquist's puppet, she could only accept her fate.

Abandoning her design, Evangelina rested her head on her chin and gazed at the cloudscape outside. The sky was blue and beautiful, and the creamy clouds were miles below her island. She pondered over freedom. How much control did one have over their life? Freedom wasn't something that could be divided into black and white. Rather, it was a somewhat abstract and relative concept. Whenever freedom existed, so did the opposite—captivity, which came in many forms. Physical imprisonment, mental trauma that refused to relent for years, or the limitation of one's choices, those were all notorious examples.

Evangelina wasn't held hostage in a dark cellar or plagued by a painful memory. Nevertheless, she wasn't free. She wasn't allowed to be herself or even form her own opinion about the rivalry unless she wanted her parents to disown her. Her body was trapped in an invisible cage, her thoughts bound by the shackles of society.

How many angels out there were like her? Evangelina drummed her fingers on her table absentmindedly, staring at the floating islands outside her window. She could see three of them—one rocky and smaller than a classroom, another coated with lichen and with a ring of stones, and the other had a green field and three white bungalows.

"Happy birthday," her father greeted her as she made her way downstairs. It was eleven, and they were ready to leave home.

Her mother wrapped her in a huge hug. "I'm so proud of you, sweetie. Hard to imagine you're seventeen years old today!"

Evangelina smiled. "Hard to imagine that myself."

The restaurant was on Verdana Island, which was a fifteen-minute flight away from home. Evangelina watched the tiny hovering islands pass her as she and her parents soared past them, bathing in the breeze.

"A white ball gown would suit you," Evangelina's mother remarked, smiling. "I can't wait for your dance."

"Why are you so excited about it?" Evangelina asked.

"I had a great time when it was my turn. You'll love it."

Evangelina didn't reply. "How many angels will be there?"

"About a hundred or more, I guess. Your dad and I met at the ball."

Evangelina had heard their love story countless times, but it never failed to fascinate her. "You told me he was the fifth to dance with you."

"I was," her father replied. "The moment I met your mother, I knew she was different from the others. The spotlight shone on her, and the other angels faded into the background. I had eyes only for her."

"Were you an escort?" Evangelina asked. "I thought only female angels were invited to debutante balls "The males only get to be escorts, from what I remember."

"Yes, he was," her mother replied. "Since the ball is a feminine event."

Evangelina frowned. "That doesn't sound fair," she remarked. "I'm sure there are ladies who dislike dancing and gentlemen who are fond of it."

"Those are the exceptions," her mother remarked.

Evangelina did not like the way she glossed over her thoughts and waved away her opinion, but she didn't want to argue with her mother on her birthday. It wasn't that she didn't like dancing, but she knew Diome enjoyed it as much as she did. She couldn't help but feel that her mother was indirectly belittling Diome with her narrow-minded thoughts. One size did not fit all, and it was a pity people dismissed those who defied mainstream conventions.

They arrived at an island, and reached the restaurant, a two-story building with stained glass and surrounded by rosemary bushes and willow trees. Descending on the island, Evangelina saw that their relatives had already arrived. Decked out in vibrant flowing robes of hot-pink, lemon-yellow, and sea-blue, they greeted her and her parents with wide smiles.

"Here comes the birthday girl," cooed Aunt Angela, embracing Evangelina. Her kind eyes crinkled as she beamed at her. "Happy birthday, dear."

"Thank you, Aunt Angela," replied Evangelina.

The other aunts and uncles—Uncle Ulysses, Uncle Melvin, Uncle Anthony, and Aunt Caroline exchanged pleasantries with her parents, and soon, they headed into the restaurant together.

"Happy birthday, Evangelina," gushed Uncle Anthony. "I brought your favorite strawberry cake. This will be a nice party. It's not every day an angel turns seventeen, huh?"

Evangelina beamed. "Thank you. I've always like strawberry cakes since I was a kid. It's never changed."

"So, how's everything going in school?" Uncle Ulysses asked after everyone was done ordering their food.

"It's all right," replied Evangelina. "We have an exam coming soon."

"Are your classmates friendly to you?" Aunt Caroline asked, taking a sip of her lemon water.

"They're nice, yes. I made two friends, and we went to the Halloween dance together."

"Did you have a date?"

Evangelina shook her head. "I went there for the food. And to get a sense of what it's like to be a human high school student."

"I heard that you sent Evangelina to Horizon High on a mission to kill a devil," Uncle Anthony told Evangelina's father. "How did it go?"

"She's trying to gain his trust before killing him," he replied.

Aunt Caroline smirked. "I don't see why you have to bide your opportunity, Evangelina. You could kill him anytime. Sleeping pills, stab him with a knife, push him into a waterfall ... There are so many ways to kill a devil. You could do it anytime. He trusts you now, doesn't he?"

Evangelina sighed. "Yes, but there's the police. I can't stick a knife into his chest in front of a crowd at school, right? They would put me in jail for that." She tried not to sound as sarcastic as she intended to, but her aunt's question was ridiculous.

"Well, you could kill him, flee back to the Land of Heavenly Dreams, and never go to school again. Or if you're worried that'll expose our existence to the humans, you could go on a hiking trip with him and push him off a cliff. He doesn't know what you are yet, I guess?"

Evangelina cringed inwardly at her aunt's casual tone when she elaborated the ways to murder a devil. To her, and to the rest of her family, devils were devils. Lowly, inferior, and hateful.

"Caroline, I think she's doing her best," Uncle Melvin replied. "Remember, devils are crafty creatures. I think it's best if Evangelina treads carefully."

The waiters served them prawn salad and onion soup, and the conversation shifted to how delicious the food tasted. Evangelina was grateful, since she had no desire to quarrel with her family about devils. Nothing condoned their evil actions, but fighting fire with fire was wrong. There were countless innocent devils who had done nothing to deserve their hatred, like poor Diome. Part of her knew she shouldn't let her relatives' obnoxious remarks sway her emotions, but she expected better from her relatives. They were all kind angels who donated large sums of money to charities and spent many weekends volunteering at orphanages for young angels. However, their selflessness and decency vanished whenever they discussed devils.

Evangelina chewed on her lettuce and meditated while the others discussed politics—President Albert Leclair's new education policies.

"Our president's such a piece of work," Aunt Angela snapped. "He wants to edit the history textbooks and include a chapter about the invasions the angels launched on the devils. Is he out of his mind?"

"Must be," Evangelina's father replied. "He's always been a coward. Doesn't want us to battle the devils or provoke them."

Uncle Melvin laid his fork aside. "I'll tell you why. If war breaks out, the angels will be mad at his policies, and he'll lose the next election. It's all political, everything."

At that moment, the sound of glass shattering filled everyone's eardrums.

Evangelina leapt to her feet. "What's going wrong?"

Before anyone could react, several figures in black robes hurtled through the entrance and zoomed at them.

"It's the devils!" Aunt Caroline shrieked. "They've been attacking restaurants, banquet halls, and shopping malls randomly these days!"

And in an instant, the situation erupted into chaos. White and black sparks shot through the air, streaks of light flashing before everyone's eyes. Screaming, the waiters and waitresses grabbed their wings, hurried out of the restaurant, and flew away.

Evangelina could barely breathe. One moment, they were immersed in their discussion of politics, and the next, mayhem ensued. It occurred to her how fragile and vulnerable a brief moment of peace was—it could deteriorate anytime. The question was when and how.

One of the devils charged at Evangelina, and she shoved him away by summoning a shield of light. Thrown off her feet, the devil hit the wall and collapsed, whimpering as a burgundy streak of blood trailed down her cheek.

Meanwhile, her father wrestled a beefy devil, and her mother dueled with another. Aunt Caroline and Uncle Melvin blinded one of them by zapping his eyes, and Uncle Anthony splashed another with a glass of water.

"Our wings!" Uncle Ulysses shouted. "Wear them and run!"

But it was impossible. The devils kept them busy. A moment's distraction could mean death for them.

A black-haired, gray-eyed devil lunged at Evangelina, flooring her. She rolled out of his way as a jet of black light hit the spot where her head had been moments ago. His hands flew to her neck, and she struggled to pry him off.

"Let go of my daughter!" her mother yelled,

flinging herself at him.

"Go away!" he snarled.

Evangelina's mother pushed her out of harm's way, just as the devil hurled a knife at her. As if in slow motion, the blade inched through the air and pierced her mother's throat. Evangelina tried to scream, but no sound came out.

Time stopped.

Blood flowed from the wound like a river. In an instant, relatives were gathered around her.

"Golda, are you all right?"

"Milton, get her to the hospital, quick!"

"Call a chariot ambulance, now!"

Uncle Melvin and Aunt Caroline were still fighting to keep the devils occupied, but everyone else panicked.

"Mom! Mom, can you hear me?" Evangelina flung a streak of light at her attacker to blind him and knelt down beside her mother, not knowing what to do next. Her mother's features were contorted in agony, and she could barely open her eyes. Uncle Anthony had phoned the nearest hospital, and a flying chariot would arrive soon.

The devil who had tried to kill her mother was gloating at the sight of her misery, and Uncle Melvin and Aunt Caroline zapped beams of light to distract him.

Still in a trance-like daze, Evangelina watched her mother stagger to her feet, her quivering fingers curled around the knife.

"Golda, are you ... ?" her father asked.

She flung herself onto the sniggering devil, raised her arm, and drew the blade across his chest, hatred burning in her eyes. Resentment. That was the last emotion her face betrayed before her eyes closed and she collapsed.

"Erik!" the devils hollered, racing over to the injured devil, who was grunting in pain and clutching his wound. One of them shot a black jet of light and floored Uncle Melvin. Carrying their friend, the devils breezed out of the restaurant and flew out of sight.

"Golda, Golda, wake up!" Evangelina's father shook her mother.

Evangelina stared without seeing, her mind unable to process the nightmare unfolding before her eyes. How could it be? She was dreaming. She had to be.

Evangelina crouched down and felt her mother's wrist for a pulse. Nothing.

Her father was administering CPR, pumping her heart and blowing air into her mouth. Within moments, a chariot ambulance descended outside, and the angel paramedics rushed her onto the vehicle.

As the ambulance hurtled through the clouds, Aunt Angela explained what had happened to the angel paramedics, who were pressing a napkin to her mother's throat to staunch the hemorrhaging and performing CPR on her heart. Since there wasn't much room on the chariot, she volunteered to go with them while the other relatives stayed behind. Evangelina couldn't believe what was happening. It was as if she were watching a montage. Their mouths were moving, but none of the words they uttered made sense. Evangelina grasped her mother's hand as if she would perish if she let go. Fear ebbed and flowed in her like tides as she noticed the coldness in her fingers.

Please let her be fine. I'd do anything in exchange for her life.

****

Evangelina's mother was pronounced dead ten minutes after reaching the hospital. That night, Evangelina sat on her bed, staring into space. She was in denial. It had happened all of a sudden, like bandages torn off without a warning. How could it be? Her mother was still with them that morning. She couldn't be dead. And not on Evangelina's birthday, of all days. Her cold body wasn't lying in the funeral parlor, waiting to be loaded into a casket. It was too inconceivable, too flabbergasting.

It was two in the morning, but she couldn't sleep. Her relatives had stayed with her father until midnight. An hour ago, he went out and bought five bottles of beer. When Evangelina tried to stop him from downing all of them, he had lashed out at her. He was obviously drunk. She supposed he was now asleep on the couch downstairs.

Evangelina couldn't blame him for intoxicating himself with alcohol. The grief was too deep. Suddenly, an important chunk of her life had been removed, and there was a hollow ache in her body.

Now that the truth had sunk in, she felt a wave of fury at fate, at the world. It was her birthday. Why? Why had something so devastating befallen her? Part of her stepped back and examined her thoughts. It was bizarre, horrifying even, that her birthday had become her mother's deathday. However, tragedies took place every day. Even on birthdays. Birthdays didn't give people the immunity to avoid catastrophes.

But how could this have happened to her, of all angels? What had Evangelina and her family done to deserve this? Resting her head on her knees, Evangelina let a stream of tears course down her cheek. Her heart was crushed into so many fragments that she could never piece it back together. Curling up in her covers to muffle her sobs, she willed herself to sleep.

Chapter Six
Double Heartbreak
(Diome)

Smiling down at his screenplay, Diome counted the words he had written during the past hour. Computers hadn't been invented in the Burning Bowels, so he could only scribble his play in a notebook. The old-fashioned way, he supposed. Slower, of course, but he liked how tangible it was.

He had just finished an alien invasion scene. Tons of spaceships were zooming toward the Land of Heavenly Dreams and the Burning Bowels, propelling the angels and devils to cooperate. They each sent ten representatives and met in the Burning Bowels for an emergency conference to discuss their tactics and evacuate all the angels and devils. It wasn't the first time the two sides worked in harmony in his play, but in reality, it was impossible. Unlike the play he was writing, nothing would go according to his hopes. Diome was a mere devil among the millions of inhabitants in the Burning Bowels. Too small, too insignificant to wield an earth-shattering influence on the universe. Like a speck of stardust in the galaxy, a shell in the ocean, a tiny rock in a volcano, he hardly held any weight.

Setting his pen aside, he laid his head on his table and fidgeted with his fingers. Today was Evangelina's birthday. What was she doing? Celebrating with her family at the moment, he surmised. Ever since he fell in love with her, he thought about her when he least expected to. A thrill of excitement tingled down Diome's spine as he remembered his birthday was next month. December 22nd. He hadn't had the courage to tell

Evangelina that, but he did want to create a special memory with her on that unique day. Perhaps he could treat her to dinner, or perhaps they could go to an amusement park together. He had never been to one, though he had always been fascinated by the magnificent roller coasters, carousels, and Ferris wheels. Going to the movies with Evangelina sounded amazing too. He had been there once with a human classmate in elementary school, and it was an incredible experience. The atmosphere, the popcorn and soda, and the immense screen made him feel as if he had entered another world. The devils were constructing a movie theater in the Burning Bowels too, but it wouldn't be open to the public until next summer.

What movies would Evangelina be interested in? She didn't appear to be a fan of romantic comedies, but Diome doubted she would love action or horror films. Either way, though, watching a movie with her would be an entertaining and refreshing experience for them both. Whispered conversations, shared drinks and snacks, and one or two fluttering kisses whenever a couple onscreen did the same, those were all a part of the parcel that came with the exhilarating date.

If he turned back the clock and told his past self he would fall head over heels in love with an angel one day, he would've deemed himself a madman. But now, he couldn't stop dreaming about Evangelina. Whenever thoughts of her glided into his mind like pastel streamers at a party, he heated up and smiled. Love made everything around him extra charming. As if he were viewing the world through an iridescent pair of glasses, even the darkest corners had an enigmatic beauty.

"Diome! Come downstairs, quick! It's an emergency!" His mother's voice penetrated the walls and seeped into his room.

Rising to his feet, Diome smoothed the wrinkles on his black robe and made his way downstairs. The moment he entered the living room, he registered the tension in the air. Six devils were gathered in his house, anxiety written on their faces. One of them was wringing her hands, while a few others were pacing back and forth.

"What's wrong, Mom?" Diome asked. He glanced at the couch and froze.

His father was lying on a heap of cushions, a stab wound in his heart. White and burgundy blood splatters were visible on his black robe.

"Who ... what?" Diome stared at the devils, begging for a reply.

"We were in the Land of Heavenly Dreams," one of them answered shakily. "We invaded a restaurant, and one of the angels stabbed your father moments before he killed her."

Invaded a restaurant? Why? What had the angels done to you? Diome thought. But now, his major concern was his father.

"Dad?" he asked, reaching out to hold his hand.

"Diome ... " His father's feeble voice was almost inaudible. "Take care of your mother for me ... "

"No, Erik," Diome's mother was weeping like a terrified child. "Stay with us, please."

Diome stared at them, unable to perceive what was happening. His father, bleeding to death from an invasion. How could it be? Diome had always been a pacifist, for he knew the vicious cycle of attacking and counter-attacking would only result in more deaths, more tragedies, more broken families. Never had he imagined, though, he would be one of them. For his entire life, his father had been an advocate of devil supremacy. He had made it his lifelong mission to eradicate all the angels in the Land of Heavenly Dreams. Of course, Diome had never been a supporter of such a brutal, ruthless ambition. Yet now, his father's beliefs had killed him.

Diome gulped and stared down at his father, filled with turmoil. A tear slid down his cheek, and a lump rose in his throat. "Dad, I love you."

As cruel as he might have been toward angels, he was his father. He had held Diome when he was still a baby. His father had watched him take his first steps and fed him at the dinner table. None of it condoned his racist aggression, but ... It was then that it occurred to him, why the devils had brought his father back home when he needed immediate medical attention. They knew he wouldn't make it, and his family needed to say goodbye. A trip to the hospital would be too late. They wouldn't be in time to bid him farewell.

Diome watched his father exhale one last time. His pulse grew weaker, feebler, trickling to a halt. His heart went silent, and his eyes were closed.

This was how a life ended. Silently but earth-shatteringly, like a shooting star dropping off the horizon. Killed by his selfish desire to eradicate the angels, Diome's father was gone forever.

Diome laced an arm around his mother, who heaved with sobs. Their family would never be the same again. The somber realization pained him to the core, yet there was nothing he could do to reverse the tragedy.

****

A week after his father's death, the others held his funeral. Diome lay in bed that morning, bereft of hope. Evangelina had been absent from school for the past few days, which worried him. The teacher had explained she took a week's leave and didn't mention anything else, so Diome knew nothing terrible had happened to her. He hoped nobody in her family died in the invasion, but he doubted he would have the courage to ask her when she re-appeared at school.

How was he going to face her? Should he even tell her about his father's death? Diome got dressed in his black robe and combed his hair. If his father knew of his relationship with Evangelina, he would be furious. But now, he was in a place he could no longer see or hear him.

Diome's mother hadn't spoken much since the incident. She kept herself locked in her room, her sobs seeping from the crack in the door and pervading the house. Diome wanted to comfort her, but every time he tried to console her, she would start blaming the angels and cursing them. It was ridiculous to fault the angels for fighting back when the devils were the ones who provoked them in the beginning. Yet nobody around Diome appeared to have an iota of common sense. Blinded by hated for their enemies and indignation for their cohort, they vowed to kill every single angel that escaped the restaurant. The furious angels launched an assault on the Burning Bowels later that day, but the devils chased them away after managing to hold the fort for an hour. That, if anything, aggravated the tension on both sides. Diome was used to it, though. A perfect, peaceful day could erupt into chaos. He had known that since he was a little devil, and nothing had changed after all those years.

Nodding at his mother when he reached the dining room, Diome sat down. He turned to the right end of the table where his father used to sit all the time. Once again, the loss hit him like a hurricane. The grilled toast on his plate had suddenly lost its appeal. He knew his father wasn't immortal, and that there would come a day when he would die, but he wasn't expecting it to be so soon, so abrupt. Their house was too big for him and his mother. Every room and every corner reminded them of the innumerable memories the three of them had created together. No, they weren't a perfect family, but at least they were a happy one.

After breakfast, Diome and his mother flew to Orange Seas, the "cemetery" where the funeral would be held. It was a beach where many devils held funerals. After the event, they would push the casket into the lava ocean and let it become one with the Burning Bowels.

They passed a bridge, a forest of unburnable trees, and a community of red bungalows. The lava ocean seemed dimmer than usual today, Diome noticed. Or perhaps melancholy had tinted his vision, making everything depressed and miserable.

When they reached the site, dozens of relatives were already present. They exchanged hugs and condolences. Diome found himself embraced by his many aunts and uncles. A lot of them were crying and wiping tears from their cheeks, but Diome went numb. He hadn't cried as much as he thought he would due to his conflicting emotions. He was heartbroken his father was gone, but at the same time, he hated him for launching an attack on the innocent angels. His malice had killed him, and much as Diome hated to admit it, his death was a comeuppance.

Part of him felt aghast such a thought had entered his mind. He was his father, not just any random devil. How could Diome be so heartless to his family? It felt like betrayal. But was judging the matter from an objective perspective wrong? If his father hadn't invaded the Land of Heavenly Dreams, he would still be with them. There was nobody to blame but himself and his accomplices.

The latecomers trickled in, and everyone gathered around the casket and paid their respects one by one. In the Burning Bowels, there were no hosts at funerals, only mourners who commemorated the deceased together.

"Rest in peace, Dad," Diome murmured when it was his turn to approach the coffin. The other relatives were a safe distance away from him and out of earshot. "Wherever you are, I wish you repose and reprieve. If there's something I regret not telling you, it's that I love Evangelina. I know you'd be angry if you found out about my relationship with her, but she's the one for me. I never liked the rivalry between the two clans, and neither did Evangelina. Often, I dream of the day you let go of your anger toward the angels and give me and Evangelina your blessing. Dad, I don't expect you to forgive me for being with her, but I hope if you're watching over me and Mom somewhere out there, you'll understand why I chose her one day."

Diome had a million wishes. He wished he could marry Evangelina—not elope with her as if they were having an affair, but having a grand wedding with hundreds of attendees. He never was one to favor extravagance, yet despite that, he'd be proud of the prospect of marrying Evangelina. He wanted to show the world how much they loved each other, how they disdained the hostility between the two clans, and how their love knew no barriers or confines. However, the idea was absurd. Nobody would accept them together unless they fled to the human world, disguised themselves as humans, and hid their powers. Reality was that brutal to them.

As Diome watched the casket glide toward the lava ocean and sink into the fiery waves, rocking side-to-side like an infant in a cradle, he hoped with all his heart not only his father but all of the angels and devils would come to their senses and make peace with each other. Only by maintaining peace could future tragedies be prevented.

****

With the guilt and sadness reigning in him, Diome could barely focus on his academics. School was boring without Evangelina. Many times, he gazed at the cerulean sky outside the window, dreaming of playing hooky. He wanted to fly to the Land of Heavenly Dreams and seek Evangelina. Of course, he didn't have the audacity to do so, but he ached for her company.

As he twirled his pen in his hands during math class, he contemplated the possibility Evangelina was furious at him. Could that be it? Might that be the reason for her absence? She didn't want to see him, and therefore, she took a week off to avoid him. What if that was the truth?

But then again, Evangelina didn't seem like that kind of person. She was kind, forgiving, and clever, and she was well aware of the fact Diome hated the animosity between the two clans as much as she did. He couldn't imagine her sulking in her room and cursing him under her breath. No, she was far above that.

He felt angry at himself for entertaining such notions, for having irrational fears that were unconfirmed. However, it wasn't as if he had anything to lessen his anxiety. He had no friends at school, and at home, his mother retreated into her shell and spoke little. She never was one to show her emotions, so it was predictable she would prefer healing alone in solitude after an unfortunate event.

Diome sighed and studied the barcode on his notebook, hearing without listening as Mrs. Rainer droned on with her algebra nonsense, numbers and symbols filling the air and aggravating him. The last thing he cared about was what x was. Math hadn't been his worst subject, but he was struggling with eleventh grade math more than any other subject. Even physics and chemistry weren't half as annoying.

If Evangelina emerged all of a sudden, what was he supposed to tell her? The idea both excited and terrified Diome. He assumed he should apologize for the devils who spoiled her special day. Somehow, it felt right. She deserved an apology. If the devils weren't willing to take responsibility for their wicked ways, he would apologize on their behalf. Even so, he wasn't going to admit his father was one of them.

When Diome entered the art classroom the next period, he found a huge surprise waiting for him. Evangelina. She was in her usual seat, scrawling on a piece of paper. His heart rate accelerated at the sight of her. A torrent of vertigo overcame him. What should he say to her? How should he greet her?

Diome made his way over to her. The thirty-foot distance between them practically stretched on for miles. It was as if he were walking from a side of a football field to the other.

"Long time no see, Evangelina." Diome sat on the stool beside her.

Evangelina glanced up at him and smiled. Her eyes were fatigued. "Good to see you too. I missed you."

Good. She wasn't mad at him. Diome wanted to ask her if she was all right, but the glaring insensitivity in that foolish question was comical. Her drooped head and sagged shoulders were more than enough to suggest her sadness.

"What's wrong?" Diome asked instead. "I'm really sorry about the invasion."

Tears pooled in Evangelina's eyes. "The restaurant my family was at got attacked by the devils, and my mom died during the fight."

It took Diome ten seconds to realize what she was saying. "Oh, Evangelina ... " He didn't know what to say.

No wonder she was grief-stricken. Losing her mother was devastating, but worse than that, she died on her daughter's birthday.

"A devil with black hair and gray eyes killed her. She stabbed him moments before she died, and the devils hurried away."

Could it be his father? Diome fell silent. The world was spinning. No. No, it couldn't be. The thought was unbearable. His father killed Evangelina's mother, and she had stabbed him back in self-defense? Things like that occurred in dramas, not real life.

"What happened on that day? Why did they target your mother?" Diome heard himself ask.

"The devil was trying to kill me at first, but my mom dueled him. She stepped in front of me at the last moment when he flung a knife at me. I heard her killer died later that day after the devils helped him home. The angels who invaded the Burning Bowels said so."

"What was his name, the devil who tried to kill you?" Diome asked, although he wasn't certain if he wanted to hear the answer.

"The others called him Erik."

Diome could barely breathe. His father. That was his father. He couldn't believe it. His father had tried to murder Evangelina but killed her mother instead. What were the chances of such a dreadful coincidence befalling him and the girl he loved? He and Evangelina had lost a parent on the same day, and more than that, they were each other's killers.

"I'm sorry," murmured Diome. "Evangelina, I'm so sorry that happened. I wish I could do something to make it up to you."

Evangelina shook her head. "Don't be sorry, Diome. I knew it wouldn't be easy for us the moment we became a couple, but we shouldn't let their rivalry tear us apart. We're not letting them win, the angels and devils who want us to antagonize each other."

Evangelina was comforting him when her mother had fallen into battle with the devils. Shame filled Diome to the brim. He didn't deserve her. She was too pure, too innocent, too selfless and generous. He had expected their relationship to be challenged and threatened again and again, but he hadn't thought she would lose her mother during a devil invasion. Evangelina's refusal to push the blame on him made it all the more unbearable. What if she found out he was the son of her mother's killer? Would she abandon him? Would she leave Horizon High and never return? Possibilities churned in Diome's mind, each one plaguing him more than the previous. Because of his father, Evangelina's family was shattered. Even if it had nothing to do with Diome, he felt responsible for her mother's death. If he had stopped his father from leaving the house, if he had known his plan to ambush the angels in the Land of Heavenly Dreams on that day, he could have prevented the incident. It was his fault.

After the last bell struck, Diome left school alone, unable to face Evangelina. Self-hatred welled up in him like a tsunami as he ambled along the road, aimless. The sky was as gray as his mood. He wondered if it would rain soon. Perhaps the icy shower could wash away his depression and the memories he was dying to forget.

Diome spotted a park ahead of him, and he walked over to the swing set and sat down, exhausted. Why did misfortune favor him and Evangelina so much? His father's face glided to the forefront of his memory. For a moment, he felt a wave of fury at him and realized it was possible for him to hate his own father. He had tried to kill Evangelina, the angel he loved. How could he? Evangelina had done nothing wrong. She had a heart of gold. Anyone who knew her would be infuriated at the attempted murder. Diome was relieved she hadn't been harmed in the end, but her mother didn't deserve death. And even though Evangelina had survived the ordeal, she would be scarred forever.

A soft hand landed on Diome's shoulder, and he startled. The corner of his eye caught a glimpse of platinum-blonde hair.

"Hey," began Evangelina. "Are you angry at me? You didn't wait for me after school."

She sat down on the swing beside him. Diome averted her gaze and ignored the lump in his throat.

"I'm not angry at you," he assured her. "I'm ... "

"Guilty? Diome, you know I don't blame you the least. To fault you for what happened would be insanely stupid. I took the last few days off because I needed time to cope with ... with what happened. Not because I'm upset at you."

Diome closed his eyes and balled his hands into fists. "It was my father, Evangelina. He was the devil who tried to hurt you but ended up stabbing your mother and getting killed by her."

He half-expected Evangelina to start screaming or slapping him. As calm and serene as she was, this was the most horrific, the most appalling news one could receive. She could vent her anger in any way she wanted. He was ready.

"No," Evangelina squeaked. "It can't be true. There must be a mistake. How did you know?"

"You told me his name. Erik. And you described his appearance. He ... he died moments after the devils escorted him back home."

Every syllable pained Diome like never before. He saw the shock in Evangelina's face, the hurt in the downturned corners of her lips, and the deep agony in her tearful eyes that echoed his own. At that moment, a deep disgust for himself brimmed in every fiber of his being. He was supposed to comfort her and provide her solace, but he couldn't pull even himself together.

"I'm sorry." He wiped his eyes, on the brink of a meltdown. "If I'd done something to stop him ... "

Evangelina buried her face in her arms. "Diome ... How did this happen to us?"

His name came out muffled, but her grief and disappointment were raw and real. Diome stared at the ground, developing a sudden interest in the rubber tiles padded around the swing set. He ached to reach out to console Evangelina, but he had no business doing so when his father was the reason for her heartbreak. In fact, he would never be able to face her for as long as he lived. He owed her, and he couldn't pay her back. No matter how much love they had, it wouldn't be enough to fill the hole her mother's death had left in her. Perhaps it was a mistake, their romance. It was destined to fail from the start.

"Evangelina, I hate to say this, but ... " Diome took a deep breath. "I can't be around you anymore."

Her head jerked up. "What do you mean?"

A raindrop landed on Diome's nose. "You don't want me to be around you, do you?"

"What are you talking about?" Evangelina asked.

"I never thought things would become the way they are today, and Evangelina, I'm sorry everything went wrong."

"Diome, I lost my mother already. Don't make me lose you too," Evangelina implored, her voice cracking.

Her words, if possible, only increased his guilt. He couldn't stay with her and look her in the eyes. Not after her life had been ravaged by his father.

"I can't cope with the guilt," admitted Diome.

"I forgave you," Evangelina assured him. "This is

nothing, Diome. I don't see why we must end our relationship."

But she was oblivious of the haunting regret in him, the tides of insecurity and his hatred for his identity. She was the goddess of perfection. Instead of punching him and screaming her anger for his malicious clan, she pretended as if nothing had occurred, as if the son of her mother's killer wasn't standing in front of her at this moment.

"What if this happens again?" Diome asked. "What if my mother or your father finds out we've been dating and they kill one of us? Evangelina, I don't want to hurt you."

"You're hurting me by leaving me," she wailed.

Diome felt a familiar stab into his chest. He turned away from her so she wouldn't see his tears.

Silence lingered between them. A drizzle of rain showered them, the raindrops blurring into long, thin, gray lines before Diome.

"Won't you reconsider?" Evangelina asked. "We've only got each other left."

"What if one of us dies? What if more of our family members die?"

"We knew from the start our clans hate each other. Neither of us wanted all the battles to happen, but they did. Why should we let them affect us?"

"You don't understand," murmured Diome.

"Then let me," Evangelina replied.

It wasn't an insult, but the truth. Since the devils were the more aggressive ones, it was natural he felt extra insecure. Evangelina didn't understand the guilt he felt whenever the devils returned from a battle they initiated, smiling at the mention of how many angels they eliminated. It was sick, perverse, and twisted. He couldn't bear the thought of being a devil, just like those crazed killers. Surrounded by perpetrators, he felt as if their sins were contagious, and he was corrupted and contaminated by the evil aura that permeated the Burning Bowels.

"I'm sorry about your mother, Evangelina." He had uttered those words to her countless times today, but they would never be enough. "I wish I could do something to help, but I can't stand the guilt anymore."

"What are you sorry for?" Evangelina asked. "I told you I didn't—"

"It's not about you or me, it's about us." A tear rolled down Diome's cheek, mingling with the rainwater. "Now that I lost my father and you your mother, I'm scared what the devils and angels will do next. What if our families start targeting each other?"

"I don't care!" cried Evangelina, hands on hips. "And I thought we agreed we wouldn't let their rivalry affect us. What happened to our promise?"

The last question crushed Diome. Every word needled into his heart. He felt like a coward for leaving her alone, but at the same time, his family had done enough damage to hers. He would never forgive himself if they harmed her.

Diome stood up and made his way to Evangelina. "Take care," he murmured. He fought the temptation to wrap his arms around her in an embrace of farewell but thought the better of it.

"Don't go!" Evangelina cried. "Diome, come back!"

But he couldn't. He would rather die than face her and confront the overwhelming shame and hatred for himself. Instead, he sauntered out of the park and down the street.

"Diome!"

Another tear coursed down Diome's cheek as he heard Evangelina's shout. He didn't bother to wipe it away, since the rain was intensifying at an incredible speed. It pounded on the streets and roared in his ears.

The blinding neon signs and the golden street lights bloomed like glowing flowers before his eyes. Diome walked on like a machine, fighting the wave of memories rising in his mind. He thought of the first day he met Evangelina, remembered the conversation they had had at Cassie's Flower Shop, recounted the splendid night of the Halloween dance. They had been perfect recollections worth their weight in diamonds.

Was leaving Evangelina the right decision? Nobody could tell him the answer. All Diome knew was that he wanted to protect Evangelina. If their families somehow found out they were in love, they would destroy them. The happy ending they craved would end up in ashes. There was no correct choice, no best answer.

But Evangelina apparently disagreed. Diome could understand why. Their romance had just started budding. She wanted to give herself false hope and believe they could stay together, a naïve dream that love could conquer all. Real life wasn't that simple, though. As far as Diome knew, the sneaky devils and angels would go to any lengths to eliminate them. He wouldn't be shocked if he and Evangelina were being followed.

Halting at a red light, Diome watched the cars, buses, and motorcycles whoosh by, bathed in the colorful glow issuing from the shops and stores. The rain was still pouring, and his clothes were soaked. The heat in the Burning Bowels ought to dry him up in a few seconds, but he didn't want to go home now.

Already he missed Evangelina. Standing alone, he watched the people come and go on the streets, bags of groceries in their hands. He wondered if any of them shared his troubles and smiled at the absurd thought. None of them were devils or angels.

Night was encroaching upon the sky, dyeing it inky black. The pedestrians on the streets and the bright, flashing lights made Diome feel even more isolated. He blinked, and the streets became a bokeh of mingled hues. It was beautiful in an odd, bizarre way. At this moment, he was willing to focus on anything to take his mind off Evangelina. It was cruel, leaving her in the park like that, but it was for the best for both of them.

The signal greened, showing a little man jogging on the dark screen. As Diome sauntered to the crosswalk, he spied a giant shadow emerging to his left. A car running a red light. Something crashed into him before he could move. The last thing he remembered was hitting the ground before his world faded into darkness.

HERMIONE LEE

Chapter Seven

Next Move
(Evangelina)

"Diome!" Evangelina shouted.

Where was he? What was he about to do? She dreaded to contemplate his next step. Never had she seen him in such a state of distress. For five minutes she had been hurrying down the street despite the violent torrents of rain that whipped her face. Where could he be?

Evangelina knew he was distressed, anguished, and appalled at the turn of events, at the fact their parents had killed each other. However, she couldn't let him go. She had already lost her mother. She would lose her last shred of her will to live if Diome left. No, never in an eternity would Evangelina break up with him. She couldn't.

The streetlights were aglow, golden light permeating the townscape of Horizon. Evangelina had never seen the town at night, but she wasn't in the mood for admiring the buttery yellow hues. Instead, she turned left and right, ahead and behind her, trying to find Diome's figure.

Diome couldn't leave her like that. It wasn't his fault the devils had barged into her birthday party and killed her mother, and it wasn't Evangelina's fault her mother stabbed his father in self-defense. Why should they break up because of the adults' rivalry? She and Diome were only two victims, two innocent lovers impeded by the angels and devils' bitter resentment for each other. Neither of them were to blame. It wasn't fair their relationship had to end just because a series of misfortunes and tragedies which they had no power over took place. The more fate was determined to keep them apart, the more it strengthened Evangelina's will to stay with Diome.

A idea flashed in her mind like one of the many neon signs that lined the streets. The possibility made her halt, a bout of anxiety washing over her. What if Diome hated her? What if he was furious at her mother for murdering his father, and that was the true reason he refused to continue their relationship? Evangelina felt as if she had been hammered by a bolt of lightning. Was that why he insisted on leaving her, because she was the daughter of his father's killer?

Tears formed in Evangelina's eyes, blurring the lights and hues in her vision and turning them into a field of bokeh circles. She blinked, and when they flowed down her cheeks, wiped them away forcefully with the back of her hand.

A moment's hesitation. Should she continue? Should she seek Diome, or should she leave him alone? What if this horrible incident formed an iceberg between them, and no amount of love could melt it?

She stood under a street lamp, gazing at the street with defocused eyes. A group of figures were gathered around something on the road, snippets of conversations wafting toward her. Talking in high, frantic voices, they were anxious. The blinding beams of a car's incandescent headlights could be seen behind the crowd, slivers of light slicing through the shadows.

Evangelina approached them and spotted an unconscious figure sprawled on the ground. Her heart almost stopped.

It was Diome.

A streak of burgundy blood was coursing down his right temple, and a small puddle of it had pooled on the asphalt. Evangelina's heart thumped against her chest, drumming in her ears. Time froze. She couldn't move her feet. It was as if they were glued to the ground by an invisible force. The sights around her blurred.

"W-what happened?" Evangelina asked a bystander. Her mind had drawn a blank. It was refusing to make sense of the sight before her.

"A boy got hit by a car," he replied. "We've called the police and the ambulance."

The truth hit Evangelina like a violent hurricane. "Excuse me," she mumbled, fighting through the crowd. Crouching down beside Diome, she grabbed his hand for a pulse. Relief flooded through her when she realized he was still alive. She held his hand for support, not knowing what else to do.

"Miss, are you his family?" a woman asked her.

Evangelina glanced up. "Yes," she replied without hesitation. "Did you know what—? How—?" She couldn't phrase her question properly, couldn't even string two words together. Every word she knew evaded her mind, and in it, chaos roared like a waterfall.

"He was trying to cross the street, and a car collided with him," a third bystander explained. "Help is coming soon, don't worry."

Within moments, the wail of a siren announced the arrival of the police and an ambulance with a glaring red light on top in tow. As still as a statue, Evangelina watched the paramedics lift Diome onto a stretcher and place him in a gurney on the vehicle. She had no idea what to do, how to help. Her mind was still spinning, and her heart was still thundering in her ears.

"Miss? Are you coming aboard?" one of the paramedics asked.

"I-I suppose so," Evangelina mumbled. Her voice didn't sound like her own, and when she walked up into the ambulance, she wore a stranger's skin. As if she were an actress in a movie, nothing felt real. Overcome with shock, she sat down beside the gurney, gazing at Diome's closed eyes. One of the paramedics dabbed at the cut with a wet cloth, while another draped a blanket over him.

Evangelina watched the street lights and shops whoosh by her in the window as the ambulance sped through the night. The shock had robbed her of her ability of speech.

"Is he in any danger?" she asked the paramedics when an ounce of common sense had returned to her mind.

"He'll be fine, dear," one of them replied.

Evangelina bit her lip. A concussion didn't sound any less serious than a hemorrhage or a broken bone.

"You are his ... sister?" the paramedic, a young man with red hair and freckles, asked her. "Could you inform his family?"

Evangelina hesitated for a moment. The abruptness of such a request made an alarm sound in her mind, jerking her back to her senses. She acknowledged the seriousness of the situation and realized there was no way she could let Diome's mother know what had occurred. The exposure of their magical clans was at stake. There was only one way out—she had to fabricate a story.

"I'm his friend, but I don't have his mother's number," Evangelina answered.

The paramedic nodded. His eyes softened, registering sympathy.

"He's got dark blood," one of the paramedics remarked, making Evangelina's heart jolt. "I've never seen blood like this. Almost burgundy."

But at that moment, the ambulance pulled over at a hospital and stopped. The paramedics pushed the gurney outside, and fortunately, nobody made any remarks about the anomaly of his blood. Evangelina followed them into the building, narrowing her eyes when the sharp sting of the white lights stabbed them like knives. They entered the emergency room. Evangelina braced herself for the worst scenario possible. She didn't want to be pessimistic, but it was hard, maintaining a positive outlook when surrounded by groaning patients and their anxious families. She dug her fingernails into her palms so that she would have something else to focus on rather than Diome's terrifying situation.

"Hold on for a second, miss," a male nurse told her. "Dr. Ross will be coming soon."

Evangelina nodded. "Thank you."

She stared at Diome's unconscious form and reached out to grasp his hand. He was so still, so pale, but the steady pulse in his wrist assured her he was all right.

Not realizing how exhausted she was until now, Evangelina leaned her head beside his on the soft pillow. She hadn't recovered from the shock of almost losing Diome. What if the car accident had been worse? What if he died on the spot? Evangelina had deemed herself the most unfortunate angel in the Land of Heavenly Dreams when she fell in love with Diome, only to realize their families were rivals. However, she couldn't be more grateful that he was still alive. Had the car been bigger, had Diome been slower, had any unexpected factors complicated the situation, he might not have survived. If the hand of fate had trembled, if the conditions were any different than what had been, it could have yielded a different outcome. Diome could be breathing his last right now. But because fortune took pity on them, they were granted a sliver of hope.

The doctor, a kind old lady in her fifties, came, and so did two nurses. They told Evangelina they would perform some tests and x-rays on him later—for they had other patients to tend to. The various tests would take about thirty minutes. If Diome behaved normally and showed no signs of a concussion or internal bleeding, he could leave Horizon Hospital tomorrow. Evangelina thanked her again and again, and decided to stay with him until he came to. She wanted to be with him when he woke up, wanted him to know he meant the world to her. Anyway, her father wouldn't notice her absence, since he was consumed by alcohol and grief.

As Evangelina was lost in her thoughts, Diome's hand twitched, and he stirred. His eyes fluttered open. Apprehensive yet relieved in equal measure, Evangelina leaned close to him.

"You're awake," she cried. "Are you all right?"

Diome gazed up at her. "What happened?" he murmured.

"You got into a car accident," she replied. "How are you feeling?"

"A little dizzy, but other than that, I'm good."

"The doctor told me you have to stay for a night. I don't know how yet, but I'll try not to get your mom involved in this."

Diome nodded. "Thank you."

Evangelina forced a smile. She wanted to ask him if they stood a chance of getting back together but feared now wasn't the best time to have such a conversation.

"Evangelina," began Diome. "I'm sorry if I upset you."

Evangelina averted his eyes so he wouldn't see the pain tearing her apart inside. "If I ask you something, will you be honest?"

He tightened his fingers around hers. "I promise I will."

Evangelina took a deep breath and balled her other hand into a fist. She buried her fingernails into her skin so that something would pain her more than Diome's reply. "Do you hate me because my mother killed your father? Is that why you want us to break up?"

A pause.

Diome's eyes widened. "No. No, of course not. Evangelina, why would you think that way?"

"Why would you want to be with the daughter of your father's killer?"

"Then why would you want me? The devils from our clan destroyed your party and took your mother's life. I would never have the audacity to beg for or even accept your forgiveness."

Evangelina pressed her lips into a thin line. "I ... I told you already. It's not your fault. You had no control over what happened."

"Neither did you." Diome squeezed her hand. "I thought we made a pact to not talk about the rivalry anymore. Evangelina, if you forgive me for what the devils did to—"

"I already do. Look, Diome, I lost my mother last week. I don't want to lose you too. We both lost a parent. And if there's anyone who knows the guilt and frustration in me, it's you. My dad, he's been getting drunk every day to numb the pain of losing my mom. The only person in the world who knows what I'm going through now is you. I need you, Diome. When you told me that we should break up, did you mean it?"

Diome shook his head. "I didn't. Evangelina, I was just worried you wouldn't want to stay with me."

"I'd never leave you." Evangelina sat down beside him on the gurney and squeezed his hand. "So, we're back to normal, aren't we?"

Diome wrapped his arms around her frame. "Of course. I wish the tragedy hadn't happened, but I'm glad you're still willing to love me for who I am."

"Always," murmured Evangelina. "Always together."

She pressed her lips to Diome's, who held her closer to his chest. The warmth of his velvety lips assured her everything was back to normal, that they would overcome any barriers in the future, as they did this time.

****

The next day, Diome was discharged, having sustained only a mild concussion and a few cuts. It happened to be a Saturday. Since Diome refused to press charges and the driver's insurance would cover his medical bills, the matter was resolved. He told Evangelina the next day that his mother didn't notice he was gone. When he returned home, she didn't even utter a word to him. Evangelina sympathized with his sorrow, but she too dealt with the grief of losing her mother. Diome's father was "cremated," his casket burned in the lava ocean. But on the contrary, Evangelina's father insisted on having a proper burial for her mother in the Heavenly Cemetery.

Every night when she was in bed, she thought of her mother. What happened to a person's memories when they were dead? Did they take them to the afterlife, assuming there was one? Or did they dissolve into nothingness and become a form of irretrievable history? Her mother hadn't been a perfect parent, but she was a decent one. When Evangelina was a baby, she had cradled her, sung her lullabies, and kissed her tiny infant limbs. Although Evangelina's mother hadn't always respected her opinions, she loved her more than any mother loved their children.

There was one thing weighing on Evangelina's heart—her mother's wish. She made her promise she would murder Diome. However, that was something Evangelina would rather die than do. Diome was her soulmate, her significant other. She loved him with all her heart. Killing him would be like stabbing a sharpened blade into her own heart. Diome was her one and only, her sun and moon, her every waking thought.

Yet what would her mother say if she knew Evangelina had been concealing such an enormous secret from her family? She had sacrificed her life to ensure Evangelina's safety. Like the day her mother gave birth to her baby angel, she had again on that fateful day, seventeen years later, breathed her last in exchange for her child's life.

I'm sorry, Mom. I can't kill Diome. I love him too much to hurt him.

It was Diome who saw the beauty in her character and imbued colors and delight in her life. With him, they could climb the highest mountain, swim the deepest ocean, and turn ashes into gold. She could always lean on him when in need, for he was willing to support her at all times. In their relationship, nobody was better or worse, higher or lower, dominant or submissive. They were each other's twin flames and mirror images, equal. He couldn't fill the hole her mother's absence had carved in her heart, but he could heal the traumatic memories she had had that day. Diome was her only hope for reprieve, her only ticket to a future of bliss. Evangelina hoped if her mother was truly watching over her, she would one day understand why she had such unwavering faith in her romance with Diome.

****

Two days later, Evangelina and her father left their house, heading to the funeral. Their thirteen aunts and uncles would be present as well. Evangelina had donned a somber black robe for the occasion, her flowing tresses piled in a bun and secured with a silver hairpin.

She and her father soared through the clouds in

silence. He had stopped drinking yesterday and was endeavoring to adhere to his goal of quitting forever. As a strong, stoic man, he rarely showed his emotions in front of his daughter. Evangelina wished he would confide in her more. A death in a family, however tragic, was also an opportunity for bonding.

The puffy clouds today reflected her gray mood. Evangelina felt reminded of her disastrous birthday, for that was the last time she and her family had gone out together. But this time, her mother was missing. And never would she return.

As she gazed at the floating islands that passed them, she thought of Diome and his wish to come visit her in the Land of Heavenly Dreams. It was common for ordinary couples to visit each other's homes, but for them, it was impossible. Why? Everything originated from the meaningless animosity between the two clans. If they hadn't been so determined to maim and kill each other, her mother would still be alive, and Diome ... He could walk with her in the sunlight, literally and figuratively. But because the angels and devils pursued instant gratification and preferred revenge over peace, because the presidents on both sides were too weak, selfish, and cowardly, because their forbidden love was destined to be challenged, impeded, and threatened again and again, the situation evolved into what it became today. She and Diome were both left with shattered hearts. Their families would grieve forever, while their hatred for each other mounted like a tsunami.

Evangelina and her father landed on an island bigger than the others. With manicured lawns, snow-white lilies, and rows upon rows of headstones, it was the sacred, revered cemetery where all fallen angels were laid to rest.

Most of her relatives had arrived—she could

make out Uncle Ulysses, Uncle Melvin, Uncle Anthony, Aunt Caroline, Aunt Angela, and her cousin, Julia, who was two years her junior, and she had barely spoken to. Everyone was garbed in identical black robes and wearing the same solemn, mirthless expression like masks.

"Milton," began Aunt Caroline, making her way to him. "I'm sorry for your loss."

The others greeted them with a nod, and some embraced Evangelina. She noticed a golden casket on the grass beside them, and tears pooled her eyes as she thought of her mother's body, devoid of warmth and life, stiller than a statue. Her voice, her soft touch, and her lovely sea-blue eyes were gone with her.

As heartbroken as she was, Evangelina sensed the hypocrisy and irony in her extremist relatives. They were all mourning for her mother's death, but what about Diome's father? None of them cared when devils fell in battle. No, they delighted in their demise. To them, devils were nothing but specks of dirt which they felt the responsibility to eliminate from the world. By invading the Burning Bowels, they were heroes and guardians protecting their kind and avenging their fellow angels. However, that was far from the truth. The devils also had families and friends. They had beating hearts, blood pumping in their veins, and a desire for love. It was pretentious, how the angels—and quite a number of devils, she was certain—to grieve for their kind only. Had life dealt a different hand and the angels were born as devils, they would be the ones in the Burning Bowels.

The funeral began after the stragglers trickled in, and the family had all arrived. Everyone took turns delivering a eulogy. When it was Evangelina's turn, she approached the casket and knelt down before it. She took a deep breath, preparing herself for the last words she was about to say to her mother.

"Rest in peace, Mom," Evangelina whispered, a hand on the casket and the other on her heart, as if she could somehow link them together and impress upon her mother the profound sorrow and utter loss echoing in her. "I know you always loved me. You were a selfless mother, so selfless you gave your life to protect me during your final moments. That's you, prioritizing me and putting me in the center of your world forever. Mom, I can't repay you for what you did. Nobody can. But I can take care of myself well and live each day to its fullest.

"I won't make every decision the way you would want me to, but I promise I'll treasure the time I have and make my life the best it can be. Life is too short to be a conformist, isn't it? I've taken pride in being myself and obeying my morals, and I will continue. Although you're not here with me anymore, I'll take the baton of responsibility and live a beautiful life. In my next lifetime, Mom, I would like to be your daughter again. Thank you for everything you've done for me. I love you."

One of the uncles conjured a bouquet of pink lilies, handed it to her, and she laid it on her mother's casket. Evangelina wished she could summon flowers, but she wasn't powerful enough to. With a touch of her hand, the casket sank into the ground, buried itself, and the grass above it closed the rift.

Mom, please forgive me for dating Diome. I need him as much as he needs me.

****

"Evangelina, I'd like to talk to you for a while."

They had reached home after an emotionally exhausting morning. Evangelina's father wiped his eyes and sat down on the fluffy azure couch in their living room. It was his first attempt to initiate a conversation after her mother's passing. Knowing how much he needed her support, Evangelina took a seat beside him.

"Yes, Dad?"

"Your mother mentioned to me a day before your birthday that ... " he quavered before clearing his throat. "Your coming-out ball is next month. December first. She hoped you could find love in the debutante ball like she did. I didn't think much of her words, but now that I come to think of it, it's one of her last wishes."

Evangelina nodded, placing a hand on her father's. "I'll go, Dad."

Attending the ball didn't mean she had to exchange vows with an angel she called her lifelong partner. No, her heart still belonged to Diome, and nothing could erase her affection for him. However, she knew how eager and ecstatic her mother had been about the ball, how much she longed to see her daughter blossoming into a grown-up beauty and presented to the eligible young angels. Evangelina would attend it, but only for her mother's sake and to honor her memory.

Evangelina's father beamed tearily. "I hope you find an angel to take care of you for the rest of your life, Evangelina. Never had I thought she ... your mother would be gone so soon. You need a new family, someone who will love you, protect you, and support you the same way I did your mother. She would be so proud of you."

"I miss her," Evangelina admitted. The house suddenly felt too large, too empty without her. Although they'd quarreled a lot about Diome, they rarely argued or disagreed with each other before that. Growing up, she had been nurtured in a loving environment. Her parents seldom fought, and they pampered her like a little angel princess. They could be controlling and overprotective at times, but Evangelina knew that was because she meant a great deal to both of them. Unlike Diome's family, in which he was deprived of love, her family was the definition of harmony.

However, now that her mother was gone, and the funeral had ended, it was time to move on—not by forgetting her and erasing the tragedy from her memory, but to carry on with her life while keeping her mother in her memory. Evangelina had witnessed her mother's death, witnessed life leaving a body like a petal parting from a wilted rose. That, if anything, made her realize how fragile and vulnerable life could be and strengthened her will to be herself, abide by her conscience, and heed her mind. She would rather pursue love and let the light in her soul guide her heart than devote her time and energy to pleasing others and complying with societal expectations in her case, antagonizing devils, and widening the canyon between the two sides.

"I love you, Evangelina," her father murmured.

Evangelina wrapped her arms around him, hoping that in the future, he would understand why she had so vehemently disobeyed them when they ordered her to assassinate Diome. It was all for the greater good, for the bigger picture. *One day,* she told herself, *one day, he will know.* Yet part of her questioned whether she was convincing herself so because she had enough faith in him, or was it because she was so desperate that she needed something—anything—to cling onto and provide her an illusion of hope and security?

Chapter Eight
Life and Death
(Diome)

Diome stared at his history textbook, unable to cram a word into his mind. They had a quiz on the Holocaust tomorrow, but he couldn't digest any of the facts in his textbook. Not only because he was too anxious about Evangelina and whether she was safe, but also due to the fact he didn't have the heart to read about all the unspeakable horrors the poor Jews were forced to endure. It hit home too much. After losing his father, he couldn't bring himself to go through the details of how Hitler had tortured the Jews. Concentration and labor camps, gas chambers, medical experiments, all sorts of inhumane treatments printed in black and white.

Diome couldn't believe it. The Holocaust took up only a chapter in his textbook, but it was a tragic genocide that had affected millions of humans. The scars it left in the human world were unremovable. Countless people had lost their loved ones, only because of some foolish eugenics nonsense. The Holocaust represented an entire era of terror and uncertainty, not only for Europe but also the entire world, for nobody knew whether Hitler would target their race or ethnicity next. And yet everything was written and summarized in his history textbook, real and raw yet unfeeling. The simple words and short sentences carried so much weight it was unbelievable. The book covered all those significant yet tragic historical events—not only the Holocaust but also the countless battles in history—the Siege of Orléans, the Revolutionary War, the Battle of Waterloo, the Civil War, World War I, World War II, the Cold War, and innumerable major and minor conflicts throughout the course of history. The way the textbook described the events as if they were merely the plot of a novel somehow bothered him. Something about it just wasn't right. Each name of a war weighed on his mind like a heavy stone as he thought of how similar the humans were to the devils and angels. Hurting people who, like them, lived and breathed and bled. Somehow their lives didn't matter, their pain went unseen, and their screams were unheard.

Flipping a page and forcing himself to continue, his eyes glazed over when the picture of a concentration camp caught his eye. The dull faces, the empty pits of their hopeless eyes, the somber black and white, the evidence of the massive destruction, a glaring blot on humanity ... It was almost too much to bear. History was overwhelming. The scale, the events, the frustration and indignation it brought.

Every human life extinguished by the Nazis marked the end of a lifetime. How many memories, how many dreams, how many possibilities and prospects has been reduced to ashes because of Hitler's hateful supremacist beliefs? With the termination of every life, the lost dreams, faded memories, silenced hopes, dead futures, extinguished possibilities, and smothered potential each person had possessed were gone forever, crushed into the dust to history, where they would melt into oblivion. Hitler had vowed to annihilate the entire Jewish race only because they were people who were different from him, people who were non-Aryans. Racial hygiene, ethnic cleansing, eugenics, and genocide, those were similar to the tribal rivalry between the angels and devils. The perpetrators believed they were doing the world a favor by eliminating the spares, as if they weren't human lives and were pesky insects instead. Had fate dealt a different hand, the supremacists who disdained other races would have been the ones to suffer for being foreign.

What good did eradicating diversity do? Would the world be a better place if everyone was the exact same? Similarly, what good would eliminating all the angels or devils do to them? Families would be torn apart, hearts would be shredded, and the genocide would leave an irreversible mark on their history. And the guilt and shame would be passed on to their future generations, a price nobody wanted to pay.

"Diome," his mother called.

Diome left the room and headed downstairs. "Yes, Mom?"

"I'd like to talk with you." Her face was cold, devoid of emotion.

Diome nodded, still standing awkwardly by the tufted couch she was seated on.

"Sit," she ordered, and he obeyed. "I'd like to talk to you about your father."

Diome didn't reply. After perusing the depressing depiction of the Holocaust, he couldn't get involved in a discussion about his father, which would no doubt lead to a diatribe against those "vermin that deserved to be exterminated."

Tears collected in her eyes and glossed her gaze. "Diome, the angels killed him."

No, thought Diome. The rivalry between the angels and devils killed him. If the devils hadn't invaded the Land of Heavenly Dreams, none of that would have happened.

"Now that you're older, you should participate in battles and help the devils too."

Diome knew losing his father was a huge hit for her, but none of her views made sense. He wanted to embrace his mother, but his hands refused to obey him every time he thought of her twisted, wicked beliefs.

"Promise me, Diome," his mother continued. She wiped away the tears in her gray eyes with her thumbs, yet Diome remained motionless. "We must take revenge on the angels. Kill any angel you happen to come across. They sometimes come to the Burning Bowels in flocks. Slaughter them if you see them, shove them into the lava ocean if necessary. I want to see every angel burn, every feather on their wings torn and crumpled."

"What good will it do?" Diome murmured. "This vicious cycle of killing, it's never going to end. Two wrongs never make a right. The endless revenge will only breed more revenge. More blood will be shed, and more lives will be lost. How is this going to benefit us?" *Or the angels?* he wanted to add, but hadn't had the courage to.

His mother gave him a stern look. "Another angel down. That's the benefit."

Diome shook his head. "That's not a benefit. That's a crime. Murder."

Annoyed, his mother exhaled loudly. "Murder doesn't count when the victim isn't a devil. The angels are sanctimonious, hateful animals who think of themselves as pure, harmless creatures. They must die, all of them."

"And then?" Diome challenged her. Perhaps it was due to the infuriating and distressing historical events that had met his eyes earlier, but for some reason, he felt an inexplicable urge to argue against her. She was wrong, more wrong than ever.

"And then what?" his mother snapped.

"Yes, and then what? What benefits will we get if the entire clan of angels die?"

Of course, Diome never cared about obtaining any benefits. But in an attempt to convince his mother, he had to speak her language. To her, the angels' rights mattered not. She only cared about the devils and their needs.

"If all the angels die, if we're the only magical creatures that exist, if our grandchildren's grandchildren learn of our great achievement of annihilating all the angels, think about how proud they would be. We proved ourselves to be the more powerful clan with our actions."

"They wouldn't be proud," Diome contradicted her. "They'd be ashamed. The disrespect for life is baffling."

"For goodness' sake, what's gotten into you?" His mother's voice was now sharper than a blade. Her words pierced into his ears as her stabbing glare prodded him like needles. Diome detected hurt in her gaze, but he wasn't about to bow down or concede.

"Nothing's gotten into me. But can't I have my own opinion?" he asked.

"If you're siding with the angels, you might as well leave this place," she declared. "I will not house a traitor to our kind, and I refuse to live with a devil disloyal to his own clan."

"I never sided with them. I'm not saying they're innocent either, but I'll never join any battles or murder any angels that don't pose an immediate threat to my life."

"How can you say that? Their very existence poses a threat to us, to devilkind!" Never had his mother been so appalled. Disgust gleamed viciously in her eyes.

"I just wish the devils would stop—"

"Don't you say that to me! How dare you have your lips dripping with those traitorous words? I just lost a husband to those vile creatures above us!"

"You didn't just lose a husband," Diome argued. "I lost a father, too. Instead of seeking comfort or offering it, you're obsessed with revenge—"

A stream of black sparks escaped his mother's palm and zoomed at him, leaving a streak of red on his forearm.

"You are a disgrace to our kind!" his mother yelled, angry tears streaming down her face as her complexion crimsoned with anger. "Get out of my sight and go back to your room!"

Diome marched away, his head held high. When he closed the door, though, all he felt was a deep sense of melancholy instead of satisfaction at defying his mother's absurd beliefs. How someone could easily claim a life without hesitation was beyond him. Although Diome knew it was wiser to keep silent in front of his mother while she was lecturing him on how all the angels deserved to perish, he couldn't stand her speech without interrupting her. The reason behind it was a heartbreaking one—he believed in his mother. She had been a decent one, and she had held him when he was a baby, despite being rather strict on him at times. Devils like her ought to know better. However, she, like every other devil he knew, was obsessed with being the better clan. He was disappointed in her, and yet at the same time, he didn't want to give up faith and trick himself into believing she was hopeless and there was no way to convince her otherwise.

Diome sat down at his table and closed the history textbook. He had read too much, more than he desired to know. When he closed his eyes, he imagined the faces of the tortured, the wounded, the killed, Evangelina, and countless innocent angels among them, abused because they were themselves, killed because they were not born devils.

He contemplated the topic of life and death. Death. It was one of the easiest words to pronounce, but behind it there dwelled an incredible amount of heaviness. It was the very epitome of destruction, something that affected countless people and made them never the same again. People—devils, humans, and angels alike—couldn't be revived after dying. They would never get another chance to open their eyes, to breathe the air, to live another day. Life wasn't like taking a test, which you could always try again if you failed. When life ended like a candle burning down to its demise, that was it. Dead was dead. Nobody got a second chance.

It was appalling how many devils (and angels) glorified death, celebrated the demise of the opposing clan, even. More appalling than that was the fact his own parents were two of those lunatics who delighted in the death of the angels. What difference was there between them and Hitler, Stalin, Lenin, and all the tyrants in history? Deriving pleasure from another's suffering just because they couldn't feel the pain they had inflicted on their victims?

Comparing his own parents to those hostile leaders responsible for millions of deaths sickened Diome. However, the perversity was unbearable. Diome was grateful for his parents for offering him a home, but that did not mean he agreed and tolerated their irrational, unreasonable, outrageous beliefs in mass-murdering angels. It took a great deal of courage to stand up to one's adversaries, but even more when confronting their loved ones and calling them out on the impropriety of their deeds or thoughts. But truth be told, Diome never craved to be a hero. By rebelling against his mother, he wasn't fulfilling his dream of becoming a righteous voice of reason and justice. On the other hand, he was simply articulating his beliefs, and making his small, feeble, yet undeniable voice known in a world where devils like him were isolated and muted, their opinions unheard and their thoughts dismissed.

Chapter Nine

Another Event Gone Awry
(Evangelina)

"What do you think, Evangelina?" Merilee asked, winking at her.

Evangelina blinked. "What were you talking about?"

Camille frowned, worry creeping into her expression. "You've been acting a bit weird these days. What's wrong?"

Evangelina shook her head and forced a smile. "Nothing. Just tired."

She noticed the change in herself. After her mother's death, Evangelina became less talkative and outgoing, and the smiles that frequented her face had lessened. Sadder and worldlier, she spoke less and kept her silence most times. She wanted to confide in Camille and Merilee, but she couldn't mention her mother's death. Even if they didn't ask for the details, she didn't want to dwell on it.

Apart from that, something else—a serious, frustrating matter—was weighing on her heart too. The debutante ball. It was all her father could speak of. Evangelina knew she had to attend it to please him and fulfill her mother's wish, but she had no intention of making any new acquaintances. Her heart already belonged to Diome. Dancing with any other angel felt like a betrayal to him.

Rumors were flying among the angels already. Her neighbors told her she would be the most dazzling angel at the ball, the top choice for all the eligible bachelors. Evangelina only nodded in politeness but registered no signs of joy. When they asked her, in a concerned demeanor, why she was so gloomy and depressed, she told them it was because of her mother's passing. She hated using the tragedy as a shield to avoid further questions, but at the same time, she would do anything as long as it meant they would leave her alone.

On most days, Evangelina didn't want to work on anything. She lost interest in the library books she had borrowed from school—even soaring among the clouds no longer brought her joy. It could only numb her sadness for a while, and once the thrill and the euphoria was over, she was left alone with frustration, self-hatred, and helplessness again.

Was this depression? Evangelina stared at the hallway ahead of her, drifting among the chittering crowd.

"See you around, Evangelina," called Camille, waving to her as they reached the stairs.

Evangelina smiled and nodded at them before turning right at the end of the corridor and entering her classroom. Diome hadn't arrived. She sat down in her usual seat and rested her head in her arms.

Should she tell Diome about the ball? Would he be upset? But she had no choice. Not attending the ball meant she already had a love interest The angels would gossip, and she would be plagued nonstop. She would have to be insane to admit to them about her relationship with Diome, so that wasn't an available option either.

Evangelina feared if she confessed everything to Diome, he would be furious at the prospect of her dancing with other angels, and in that case, she couldn't blame him. She would never want a devil to share Diome. He was hers as much as she was his. However, did she have a choice?

The debate with herself made a headache bloom.

As she rubbed her temples, a wave of anguish flooded her. Why did she have to conform to the societal expectations and attend the ball when she had already met the love of her life? But then again, did she have the courage to refuse her father and tell him she wouldn't go? No, she didn't. Because she was too timid, too much of a coward to confront him and reveal her romance with Diome. However, it was for the best. Unraveling the truth would do her no good. They would be forced to break up, and her father would no doubt punish her for "fraternizing with the enemy."

Did being prudent mean the same as being weak? Or did it vary? The jury was out. Evangelina supposed it depended on what the circumstances were. So many factors could come into play. If a person avoided taking action and rationalized their behavior by using "prudence" as a shield to avoid responsibility, that had to count as weakness. But if she was being prudent to obtain what she wanted and take the bigger picture into consideration—being with Diome with her father's intervention, that was a whole different story.

"Hi," Diome, who walked into the classroom at that moment, greeted her.

Evangelina nodded at him. "Good morning, Diome."

Her heart was racing, and she felt lightheaded all of a sudden. She glanced down at her math textbook, staring at the algebra exercises even though she could barely make sense of them.

"What's wrong?" Diome asked. "You look very disturbed."

"Nothing," Evangelina replied absentmindedly. "I-I'm studying."

Diome chuckled. "You're not a very good liar, are you? Your math book is upside down."

"Oh gosh, is it?" Mortified, Evangelina turned the book right side up again. How foolish was she?

"Well, that proves you do have something on your mind." Diome's voice softened. "Is it your father? Did he give you a hard time?"

Evangelina bit her lip. "Let's talk this over at recess."

Diome nodded. "Of course."

Evangelina couldn't focus on anything in first period. Her heart was suspended in her chest, and she was restless. What would Diome say, and how would he react to her mentioning the ball? Anxiety grew in her like a parasite, consuming her mind and tugging her heartstrings.

When recess came, she exhaled, relieved, and mustered her courage to tell Diome the truth.

"All right, so what happened?" Diome asked the moment they exited the classroom.

Evangelina took a deep breath. "Well, the angels have a tradition that all seventeen-year-olds must attend a coming-out ball. A formal debutante dance."

Diome nodded, donning a perplexed expression. "I see."

Evangelina lowered her head. "I have to go. Diome, I don't want to, but I can't tell my dad about us. He'd force us apart."

"Well, then go to the ball to please him," replied Diome.

"And you're fine with that?" Evangelina asked, bracing herself for a harsh answer.

"You're upset about what I might think?" Diome asked, comprehension dawning on his face.

Evangelina pursed her lips. "I thought dancing with other angels at a socialite ball like this would be a betrayal to you."

Diome's eyes widened. "A betrayal to me? Evangelina, you're kidding, aren't you? Why would I think that way?"

"Well, you know what debutante balls are like, right? They expect you to find a romantic partner at those dances."

Worry loomed over Diome's face, and his forehead creased in a frown. "But you won't, will you?"

Evangelina shook her head. "I'm going just to please my father because my mom cared about the dance a lot when she was still with us. There's no way I'm going to find another romantic partner."

The tension left Diome's face, and he relaxed. "Good. Have fun, then."

Evangelina stared at him. "Have fun? Diome, do you know how much I hate having to go to this ball?"

Diome's eyes registered pity. "I wish I could help, but I can't. Maybe you could go there just to enjoy the food and somehow manage to have fun."

"If only you could come and be my dance partner," Evangelina sighed.

Diome smiled. "I wish. We could recreate the lovely memory of the Halloween dance."

Evangelina's eyes widened. "Yes, yes! That's a terrific idea. We need to do that someday!"

"That's fabulous. I'd love to see you in the black gown you wore last time. What will you wear to the debutante ball?"

"I haven't been thinking about it at all," Evangelina admitted. "The mere thought of going to that silly dance makes me stressed and depressed. Don't you devils have debutante balls?"

Diome shook his head. "That's not a thing in the Burning Bowels. I'd give anything to dance with you again, though."

Evangelina smiled and leaned closer to him. "We can imagine we're dancing anytime. Let's go to Horizon Park this afternoon and go on a date."

"Why not?" Diome asked. "There's nothing a date and an afternoon snack can't fix."

Evangelina blinked. "Snack?"

"It's on me," returned Diome. "There's a coffee shop beside Horizon Park. Have you noticed before? It's called Sweet Nothings."

"Oh, I never noticed. That sounds like a nice place for a date. Let's see if it's as sweet as its name after school."

Diome laughed. "As you wish, sweet angel."

"Is that a pet name for me?" Evangelina asked, amused.

"If you like it." Diome kissed her on the cheek.

Evangelina hugged him. "Yes, I do."

He ruffled her hair. "You're the best. I can't wait for our little gathering this afternoon."

****

Evangelina had never appreciated how beautiful afternoons were until today. The dazzling sunlight, the gusts of cool breeze, and the cerulean sky seemed to delight in her excitement. Another date with Diome. He deserved a small reward for surviving the car accident.

A rustic cabin with a black roof, Sweet Nothings was an adorable café. The tiles were dotted with tiny flowers, and the walls were painted in jungle colors—green, brown, and a dash of yellow. The little poufs were shaped like toadstools, and the tables were large tree stumps with annual rings emanating like ripples.

"How cute!" Evangelina exclaimed. "It's called Sweet Nothings, but everything's very sweet in here."

"For sure. Take a seat and let's order." Diome chose a window seat and sat down. "What would you like?"

"Anything. Let me see. Some pesto risotto and a glass of sparkling apple soda."

"Sounds like a good idea," remarked Diome. "I'll have the supreme pizza."

They placed their order and returned to their seats.

"I don't want to sound offensive, but is your dad still asking you to kill me?" Diome asked.

Evangelina shook her head. "No, luckily. He's forgotten why I came to Horizon High in the first place."

"Enemies-to-lovers. Quite an incredible story. We're acting more mature than the adult angels and devils around us. If our tale goes down in history, would the angels and devils from future generations see us as the Romeo and Juliet of this era?"

"I hope we have a much happier ending," Evangelina remarked. "I'd rather have a mundane but happy romance than an epic but tragic one."

"Me too," added Diome. "I'd rather be a poet than a poem. To portray others but not be portrayed. As a wannabe playwright, I can tell you how much more interesting creating dramatic situations is than being depicted in a play. A creator has power, but a character is destined to be submissive."

"I wouldn't want to be submissive and voiceless when my future is at stake," replied Evangelina. "You're too right. It's way better to create than to be created."

A waiter brought them their meal, and they ate in silence. Evangelina loved hers. The spices brought out the intriguing flavor of the curry, teasing her taste buds. The apple soda added a tang of sweetness to her mouth, icy thrills dancing along her tongue.

"You said you wanted to be a fashion designer before. That's a form of creation. Have you done any designs?" Diome asked.

"Oh, I've drawn a couple of sketches, but I've never really made any clothes." Evangelina giggled.

"You could make a dress for the debutante ball," Diome suggested.

Evangelina rolled her eyes. "Why do you keep mentioning the ball?"

"I kind of envy you, I guess," admitted Diome.

"You envy me?" Evangelina asked, appalled. "What? Why? This ball is insane. You don't know how annoying the rules are! It's technically the epitome of high society and fine etiquette and all that nonsense. I'd give anything not to go."

"Do you need an escort? Like the debutante balls we read about in history class?"

"It's optional in our debutante balls," answered Evangelina with a shrug. "But we do have to wear ridiculous white ball gowns and gloves and act all prissy and ladylike."

Diome smirked. "I bet you're no fan of that idea."

"You don't say," Evangelina replied, shaking her head. "But I don't mind the etiquette stuff as much as being required to dance with the other guests. It's that part that bothers me. Say, why would you envy me?"

"The last ball—the Halloween dance, I mean, was a great memory. The lights, the music, the atmosphere. I wish I could go with you this time."

"Great, come," said Evangelina. "It's on Splendor Island. Dress up as an angel and blend into the guests. As long as you don't reveal your dark magic and your burgundy blood, nobody else will notice."

"Are you telling me to sneak into the ball like Romeo?" Diome asked with a mischievous smile on his face.

"Why not? Let's face it, the odds of spilling your blood or attacking angels with your magic at a dance is pretty minimal."

"You're kidding, aren't you? I can't go. The price is too big to pay."

Evangelina contemplated her insane proposal and had to reluctantly admit it was too preposterous. "You're right, Diome. We've made it to this day. Our relationship is almost a month old, and truth be told, I'm shocked it managed to survive for nearly thirty days. Nobody has found out about us yet, and we should keep it that way."

"I'm proud to be in love with you, Evangelina," Diome said. "If only I could declare it in front of a crowd."

"When we get married, yes," Evangelina replied, smiling at that thought. "Right now, we can only dream about it. But maybe if we both move into the human world when we grow older, we can have a secret wedding."

"Elope," Diome suggested.

"Like two carefree young lovers," Evangelina replied with a dreamy sigh. "Finally, there's something I can look forward to in this life."

"We'll stay together forever," Diome promised her. "Maybe we're not great activists who will change history and melt the iceberg of hatred between the angels and devils, but we're two non-conformists who promise to love each other until the end of time. We may not be great or influential enough to go down in history as the heroes who brought peace to the two clans, but at this point, I couldn't care less about the rivalry between the angels and devils. I just want to have a future with you, Evangelina."

And it was then that Evangelina realized that nothing mattered as long as she and Diome could have the happily-ever-after they deserved. The sky could collapse, the mountains could sink, the valleys could rise, and the world could fall apart at the seams, but all she cared about, all that concerned her was whether she and Diome could marry each other and be the blessed prince and princess in the fairytales.

****

"You're attending the annual debutante ball?" Allison, the seamstress of Sparkling Fashionhouse, a boutique that sold formal outfits, buzzed around Evangelina like a bee.

"Yes," replied Evangelina, trying her best to hide her reluctance.

Her friend Carol was already flitting between the racks of white gowns like an elated butterfly.

"We have a wide collection of debutante dresses. Strictly white and floor-length. It's also necessary to wear white gloves and stockings."

Evangelina was already rolling her eyes in her mind. A dance was supposed to be enjoyable, not formal and smothering. The dress code idea sounded very meaningless and laughable.

Sitting on a pink ottoman, Evangelina gazed at the shop, studying the interior decorations. With fuzzy white rugs, pink silk curtains, and rows upon rows of white dresses, it was the biggest couture boutique in the Land of Heavenly Dreams.

"Evangelina!" Carol squealed, stepping out of the dressing room in a white mermaid gown adorned with silver sequins at the hem. "How do I look?"

"Lovely," replied Evangelina.

"Go pick one and try it on," gushed Carol. "What do you like?"

"Nothing too fancy." Evangelina shrugged.

She sauntered over to the racks and glossed over the boring and identical dresses.

Carol glided over to her. "What's wrong? You

don't seem excited about the ball."

Evangelina sighed. "Well, it's just that I already have someone I like. A-a human classmate. He doesn't know what I am yet, though."

She hated lying to anyone, her friends in particular, but she could never reveal what Diome was.

"Ah, I see. Does he like you, then?" asked Carol, donning an amused smile.

Evangelina set her lips in a thin line. "We're in a relationship."

Carol nodded. "Oh, that's why you're not excited about the ball. Everything makes sense now."

"I don't want to dance with the other angels. It'd be a betrayal."

Carol pondered for a while. " I know how you feel. I'm not particularly interested in finding a partner."

Evangelina glanced up at her. "Really? Then why do you look so enthusiastic about the ball?"

Carol smiled. "Well, I figured that whether I like it or not, my parents will make me go, regardless. So, why don't I try to enjoy the whole process and have fun? Come on, Evangelina. Lighten up! It's not every day you get to wear a fancy white gown and dance with other handsome young angels. They'll all be dying to have a dance with you."

Evangelina smiled glumly. "Maybe, but Diome is the one for me."

Carol laughed. "What's this lucky guy like? You're so in love with him. Tall and handsome and charming?"

Evangelina thought for a while. Diome and she were about the same height. While he was indeed handsome, he wasn't popular. His attractiveness was unconventional. He didn't smile much, and he was shyer than he was masculine. Unlike the heartthrob of Horizon

High, Andrew Scott, who was outgoing and humorous, Diome rarely hung out with anyone and had an insecure streak. But with him, Evangelina felt at ease. Comfortable enough to be herself. And that, she believed, was what mattered the most in relationships.

"Why does he have to be tall to be handsome and charming?" Evangelina asked. "To me, he's perfect."

Unlike most of the other devils, Diome refused to antagonize the angels. He had a kind heart and shared her values, and to her, that was more than enough.

Carol tilted her head. "Well, you're right. Since he loves you so much, he would want you to enjoy yourself at the debutante ball. Instead of grumbling, why don't you take the opportunity to dress up and have fun? At least I'll be there. Plus, there will be food at the venue, right?" She added with a playful wink.

Evangelina smiled. "You're right. And seeing what all those angels are like might make me appreciate Diome even more. I'm sure nobody can compare to him, and I have full confidence they'll prove me right."

Carol laughed and gave her a high-five. "That's the spirit! Now, off you go to pick a dress! If you have fun at the ball, you and your human boyfriend could recreate it and have a little dance of your own!"

Evangelina grinned. "You do know how to cheer me up, Carol. Thank you."

"No problem."

Evangelina sauntered from one room to another, browsed the racks of dresses. Some were slim and sleek, while others were wide and puffy. Some were beaded, some were embroidered, some had fluffy tiers of ruffles, and some were embellished with intricate lace appliqués. Evangelina had hoped to choose a plain gown, but all the others were equally appealing. In the end, she selected three dresses and brought them to the dressing room—a hexagonal space with mirrored walls.

Carol was humming to herself when Evangelina exited the dressing room in a satin gown with an empire waist and a form-fitting skirt.

"Hmm." Carol tapped her chin. "Very neat and simple. You like it?"

Evangelina twirled before the mirror. "Well, not much. The design is too bland. Not something I like."

Carol giggled. "A minute ago, you weren't the least interested in picking an outfit."

"You talked some sense into me. Since the ball's inevitable, why don't I make an attempt to enjoy it? Anyway, it won't have a significant impact on my life. It's just a random event. I'm going to try on the others."

The second dress Evangelina tried on was a puffy ball gown with a frothy skirt adorned with white floral lace. It was heavier than she had expected, but it made her feel beautiful. With long, lacy sleeves that reached her wrists, it transformed her into a princess. She twirled in front of the mirror, watching the tulle skirt flare around her like a blooming peony.

Carol gazed at it. "I think it's prettier than the last. What about you?"

Evangelina admired the voluminous skirt and the swirling pattern of pearls. The hem caressed the floor in scallops of lace, edged with gold. Without a hoop underneath, the shape was supported by three layers of fluffy net fabric.

"I agree it's more extravagant than the previous one." Evangelina smiled at her reflection. "I still have another to try on, though."

She donned the third dress, an A-line gown with sheer balloon sleeves dotted with tiny rosettes. With white sequins on the skirt and a bow on the waist, it had a smooth, elegant, and tasteful design, but Evangelina felt it lacked something. In the end, she chose the second gown, which stood out the most among the three.

"You're going to look stunning!" exclaimed Carol as they headed over to the accessories section and perused their options.

"Not as much as you," replied Evangelina with a smile. "Doesn't look like we have many options here. I'll go with the pearl earrings and crescent moon necklace."

Carol picked a pair of silver-studded earrings and a necklace of crystals. "This ought to suit me. Glad to see you're getting into the mood of the ball."

"I'm still not in the mood to go, but you made me decide to enjoy it instead," Evangelina answered.

"You could tell your dad the angels there are too shallow for you, and maybe he'll support your relationship with your human boyfriend," suggested Carol.

Evangelina lapsed into a spell of silence, a tide of sadness washing over her. If only Diome were a human. But he wasn't, and her father would never in an eternity accept him.

****

A week passed, and then came the night of the debutante ball. Evangelina braided her hair into a partial updo and pinned a few white roses around the bun to secure it. Her white satin pumps clicked on the stairs as she made her way downstairs, taking extra care to not trip over her skirt.

Her father watched her glide down the stairs, tears of pride glistening in his eyes. In a white tuxedo with a matching shirt and bow-tie, he too was in his proper attire for the ball.

"You're beautiful, Evangelina. Your mom would be so proud."

Evangelina smiled. "I want her to be."

That was the main reason she had consented to attending the ball. Her mother would have loved to see her all dressed up for a special occasion.

Her father disappeared into his study and returned with a white box, a pink satin bow nestled atop it. "A gift from me and your mother."

Curious, Evangelina accepted the present and unraveled the silky ribbon. In the velvet box was a bracelet of pearls with her initials *EL* engraved on one of them.

Her father's eyes glossed with tears. He swallowed and forced a smile. "This was your mother's. She wanted you to wear it to the ball."

Evangelina picked the bracelet up and slid it onto her wrist, surprised that it fit like a glove.

"She wore it to her debutante ball. Last month before your birthday, she wanted to pass it on to you, so she had a jeweler engrave your initials on one of the pearls. We were going to present it to you before the ball as a last-minute surprise. Do you like it?"

Evangelina examined the soft sheen of the milky pearls on the bracelet. So sleek, so smooth. She thought of her mother, of how delighted she would be if she were here.

"I love it, Dad," she told her father, beaming at him and blinking her tears away. "Thank you so much."

She embraced her father, his warmth enveloping her figure. She felt a nagging urge to reveal everything to him—at that moment, he was a loving father who would never judge her for the decisions she made, who cared about nothing but only her happiness. However, she knew too well the touching moment would dissipate immediately if the truth escaped her lips now.

Dad, I have something to tell you, but I'm worried you'll be upset.

Not at all, dear. I'm your dad. No matter what decision you make, I'll always support you.

I ... I'm in love with Diome Lenoir.

Is that true? Does he love you?

More than anyone ever has. He and I are kindred spirits who are blessed to have each other.

I'm worried the other angels will view you as an outcast if they know you're associated with him. But if you truly believe he's the right one, I'll stand behind you.

If only such a conversation could take place in reality ... A blade of sorrow stabbed into Evangelina's heart at that thought. Fortunately, the doorbell rang before she could dwell on it.

"Your friend Carol's here." Her father wiped away his tears. "I suppose it's about time to go."

Evangelina and her father made their way to the front door and spotted an excited Carol and her parents outside.

"Evangelina! You look stunning!" Carol squealed.

"Thank you. You're gorgeous tonight as well," returned Evangelina.

Carol looked like a goddess, her hair piled in a bouquet of curls and littered with tiny, glittering stars.

"Good evening, Milton," chirped Carol's mother, Mildred, who was clad in a sapphire-blue velvet gown and a white furry shawl. "Evangelina looks gorgeous. All the angels would kill to be her partner."

Evangelina's father laughed. "Carol's blossomed into a young little beauty as well. You must be so proud of her."

Carol's father, Jack, checked his watch. "The event starts in fifteen minutes. We should leave now. Splendor Island as usual, everyone."

The five of them donned their wings and took off, sailing through the navy-blue sky. There were barely any clouds tonight, only a few wisps of mist trailing below them like stray threads. The full moon was glowing above them, painting the serene cloudscape silver. It was a whimsical sight, five angels soaring in the nocturnal sky and bathing in the alabaster moonshine and starlight.

The clouds grew in number as they neared Splendor Island. A regal white building with ornate pillars and carved windows loomed into sight, bright candlelight seeping from the windows.

"Wow," murmured Carol. "I can't believe this is it. The venue."

Evangelina beheld the grand edifice, studying the intricate swirls engraved on the doors. A little garden with a fountain and heart-shaped hedges was nestled in front of the entrance. Evangelina smiled at the rose bush, recalling the rose she had given Diome on the day of the Halloween dance. It had been a little over a month, but to her, the magical night seemed as if it were only yesterday.

"Let's go in," suggested Carol. "Maybe we can meet the other debutantes and talk with them."

They removed their wings in the foyer and hung them on the numbered hooks on the walls. An immense pair of golden doors swung open as they approached them, leading to the ballroom.

The interior was far more resplendent than Evangelina had assumed. Sparkling chandeliers dangled below a vaulted ceiling, dripping crystals and streaks of rainbows all around the vast room. Glossy beige marble floors reflected the angels upside down. A flight of stairs led from the entrance to the dance floor, a snow-white carpet cascading all the way down like a pristine river.

"Guests, please be seated downstairs," an usher was telling the parents of the debutantes.

Evangelina spotted a cluster of young angels—

about sixty of them—gathered by the balustrade of the balcony that overlooked the dance floor. Like her and Carol, they were appareled in white gowns and gloves.

"Hello." Carol struck up a conversation with a girl who wore her red hair in a braided crown. "What's your name?"

Evangelina stood a little apart from the angels, observing them. She wasn't keen to approach them, for many of the debutantes were shooting envious and hostile looks in her direction. Some whispered to their friends, pointing fingers at her, while others frowned and donned sour expressions, as if they had swallowed lemons.

"That angel thinks she's better than us, doesn't she?" one of them muttered.

"Well, she is," another replied. "Look at her hair and her dress. She's perfect."

Evangelina bowed her head and made her way to a window. At that moment, she felt a strong desire to smash the window with her magic, escape the venue, and fly away. However, she knew she had to stay. Not for the precious memories, for she had no expectations for the ball, but to honor her mother's memory.

At seven, the host, Auntie Josephine gave a brief speech about how it was her honor to host the annual debutante ball and how it was a delight to watch the charming young angels blossom into lovely young adults. She announced the debutantes' names, and Evangelina watched each of the angels make their way down the stairs, curtsey to the guests, and take their places at the dinner table.

The host moved past the Cs and Ds. Evangelina knew it would be her turn soon.

"Emily Leclair," she announced.

After Emily had made her entrance, Evangelina readied herself for her turn.

"Evangelina Leclair."

A thunderous storm of applause greeted Evangelina as she descended the steps, her hands folded before her skirt. She dipped in a low curtsy when reaching the dance floor, smiling to acknowledge her father when he waved at her among the crowd.

The dinner table, long and rectangular, had placards with each debutante's name written on them. Evangelina found her seat and sat down, not forgetting to applaud the next angel who was presented onstage.

When all of the angels were introduced, the dinner party began. A great many of them had brought male escorts—some even had two—which meant the debutantes who didn't have an escort would still be guaranteed a partner.

Eggplant salad, smoked salmon, beef stew, roast chicken, shepherd's pie, baked potatoes, stuffed peppers with cream cheese, and creamy chowder soup were served. Evangelina's mouth watered as the alluring aromas permeated the air. The salad was flavorful and savory, and the beef was tender and chewy. For a moment, Evangelina no longer regretted coming to the ball. This was one of the most delicious meals she had ever had.

After dessert—vanilla cake, chocolate caramel pudding, and strawberry and grape punch—was served, it was time for the debutantes to pair up with the escorts. As expected, Evangelina spotted five boys making their way toward her.

"May I have the first dance with you?" one of them, an angel with honey-blond hair, brown eyes, and a handsome face asked.

The others gazed at her with expectant looks, hoping she would reject.

Not wanting to hurt his feelings, Evangelina

nodded and took his outstretched hand. "It would be my honor," she replied with a curtsy.

Disappointment etched on the other angels' faces, they set off to find another partner, their shoulders sagging and their heads drooping.

Evangelina and her partner flitted onto the dance floor, waiting for the music to begin. She took her time to appreciate the gilded mirrors in the ballroom, which doubled the vast space. Stars gazed at the jovial dancers through the tall, arched windows, twinkling in the inky sky.

An orchestra of angels played a lively, colorful waltz to the piano, violins, and cello. Evangelina's partner placed a hand on her waist and held her hand with the other. The two of them drifted into motion, spinning, dipping, and bobbing to the beat of the dulcet melody.

"So, what's your name?" the boy asked. "I'm Daniel, and I'm nineteen. I'm one of the escorts."

"I'm Evangelina. Seventeen years old. I study at Horizon High."

"Horizon High?" Daniel lifted an arm to twirl her. "Why?"

"I wanted to learn more from the humans," Evangelina lied. She wasn't about to tell him about her task of eliminating Diome, for she had never known an angel who didn't detest his kind.

"You want to be an inventor? Is that why you study in a human school? Good for you. I look forward to the day they introduce electricity to the Land of Heavenly Dreams," remarked Daniel, to which Evangelina responded with a polite smile.

"Indeed, who wouldn't welcome technology?"

Daniel spun her around and caught her by the waist.

"I hear the devils have been learning from the

humans too. Nasty creatures, aren't they, the devils? Always attacking us."

Evangelina's heart sank. Daniel was also a firm supporter of the rivalry between the angels and devils. She had so desperately hoped she would meet someone like her, an angel who believed the resentment between the two tribes was pointless, but she was a maverick among the shallow angels.

"Don't you think the angels should stop launching attacks on the Burning Bowels, then?" she asked, a bold endeavor to challenge his beliefs. "If we stopped provoking the devils—"

"They're barbarians, Evangelina. We need to teach those savages a lesson and dominate them. Perhaps one day, the Burning Bowels will be ours."

"What about the devils, then?" Evangelina had the courage to ask.

Daniel raised his eyebrows. "They must all die, of course. Not a male or female or baby devil should be left alive. We can't lose to them. They've initiated so many battles and wars in the course of history, and they should pay for the consequences of their actions. We can't let them win, right?"

"Right," Evangelina lied.

She thought of the Native Americans in her history textbook, and how they became victims of colonialism, their homes stolen and their tribespeople killed. To the explorers, Christopher Columbus was a hero, but to the indigenous Americans, he was the cause of their endless nightmares. Why would anyone with a conscience ruin a perfect land and a group of people who protected, respected, and loved their home? It was hard to believe the handsome angel standing in front of her—and many others, probably—were advocates of eradicating the entire devil race.

The melody ended with a long, slow note. Evangelina was relieved. She thanked Daniel before hurrying off to the refreshments section, planning to busy herself with the punch and raspberry cakes so that she could ignore any other incoming invites.

"Evangelina," her father called, rushing to her. "I just met my old friend Steven, whose daughter is also one of the debutantes. We're going for a drink at the bar on Moonbeams Island, all right?"

"What's the bar called?" Evangelina asked.

"Tropical Bar. I won't be home before midnight. Hope you won't mind if I don't stay here at the ball, but it's been three years since I last saw Steven, and we have a lot to catch up on."

Evangelina smiled, and his apologetic expression relaxed. "No problem. See you, Dad. Enjoy yourselves."

He embraced her before departing with his friend. Evangelina added three ice cubes into a crystal goblet, filled it with the punch, and took a sip. It was sourer than she had expected. Had any lemons been added to the concoction?

"Miss, may I have the next dance?" asked another angel. This one was an older boy with curly brown hair.

Behind him stood a queue of ten angels, all waiting for her to turn the first one down. There were many debutantes on the dance floor who had yet found a partner, but most of the angels were more interested in Evangelina than anyone else.

Evangelina's lips parted, her mind whirring to word a courteous rejection. "Sorry, I—"

A deafening sound of an explosion blasted through the ballroom. Evangelina whirled around as the floor-length window shattered, and a torrent of what she could've sworn were black bats barged into the ballroom.

"The devils!" one of the angels shrieked. "They're

going to kill us all!"

Another invasion? Now? Evangelina couldn't believe it. One moment, the angels were still searching for partners, and the next, screams, shouts, and cries of terror were reverberating in the room. The angels scrambled to find their wings and fly away, but there were dozens of devils. Black sparks zapped from their fingers, striking a few angels. Many of them were carrying spears, bows, and arrows, and were shooting at any angels they saw.

Evangelina ran for cover, bolting toward the curtains. In her mind was a tangled mess of thoughts. She tripped over a series of small steps amid the commotion, and pain assailed her senses. A jet of black sparks struck her hand, and she winced in agony.

A devil with messy brown hair was hovering above her, smirking at her predicament. He descended to the ground and seized a handful of Evangelina's hair.

"What do you want?" Evangelina squeaked.

The devil slapped her across the face. "Shut up!"

He pressed her against a wall, but Evangelina kicked him in the thighs with the heel of her shoe and hurried away. She saw Carol and her family escape through the shattered window and felt a rush of relief, but still, there were hundreds of angels who were still trapped in the ballroom. Specks of blood rained down from the battling pairs, and black and white sparks filled the air, sizzling like firecrackers. Specks of blood dotted the marble floor, some injured angels and devils sprawled on the surface. Many were moaning for help, but the others remained as still as fallen statues.

My wings. Evangelina berated herself for not remembering to collect them the moment the devils invaded, but she had been so overcome with shock then that she had forgotten the most obvious way to escape.

Seizing her skirts, she darted past the groups of fighters on the dance floor and zoomed up the stairs.

"You angels launched an attack on us this afternoon, and we told you we'd make you pay the price!" one of the devils snarled at a bleeding angel whose wings were torn. "How does it feel, you all?"

So the angels had provoked them this time? Amid all the panic and flurry, Evangelina felt a wave of fury boiling in her. Nothing condoned the devils' invasion, but didn't the angels deserve it? They had brought this disastrous attack on themselves.

Evangelina sprinted to the foyer, donned her wings, and flew to the entrance. Just then, a hand seized a tuft of her hair and jerked her backward. She uttered a cry of pain, but was unable to resist the force yanking her in the opposite direction.

A devil with flaming red hair was grinning down, her face alight with victorious glee. She had a dagger attached to her belt.

"Let me go!" Evangelina yelled, summoning all her strength to break free from the devil's iron grip.

"Never!" she snarled, dragging Evangelina to the balustrade of the balcony.

Three other devils raced to the entrance and slammed the doors shut.

"Let us out!" one of the debutantes screamed, tears streaming down her face.

The devils advanced on her, black sparks emitting from their fingers and zapping at the poor angel. They floored her, and Evangelina uttered a cry as one of the devils impaled her neck with a knife.

"One more down," the angel's killer announced, as if he were checking off tasks on his to-do list instead of destroying a life.

"Pity." Another devil gazed down at her dress.

The white bloodstains were invisible on the immaculate gown, but nevertheless, Evangelina could see them. "She's a pretty one. But it doesn't make her any less innocent than the others."

Just then, Evangelina's captor flung her to the floor. The marble tiles collided with her head, and pain arrowed through Evangelina's body. A stream of black sparks zoomed at her, and ignoring her headache, Evangelina retaliated by deflecting the dark magic. A film of mist blossomed from her hands and formed a shield, separating the devil from her.

With an angry bellow, the devil crushed the shield with a wave her of her hand. She punched Evangelina in the stomach and shoved her against the wall. Pulsing waves of pain flooded Evangelina's body. She sank to the floor, waiting for the ballroom to stop spinning. A feeble white spark escaped her fingers, but it was nothing compared to the hailstorm of black sparks that pricked her skin like needles.

"Know why I haven't killed you?" the devil snarled in her ear. "To kill you off immediately would be too merciful. I'll torture you until you beg for death."

Evangelina wanted to scream at herself. She shouldn't have been so weak, so feeble, so useless. But the invasion had caught her off guard, and she was still in a state of shock. She used to wonder why the angels weren't quick enough to save their family members from the brink of death during devil attacks, but now, it was evident why. When an invasion or anything appalling took place, nobody had the time to slow down and contemplate their next step. Frozen by the abruptness of the catastrophe, they were too flustered to react, too panicked to confront the problem.

More and more black sparks assailed Evangelina. Numb from the pain, she felt the blinding lights of the ballroom blur and mingle into a golden haze. A wave of vertigo took over as the ambient sounds faded by degrees. Within moments, Evangelina's surroundings plunged into darkness, into oblivion, into nothingness.

Chapter Ten

With All His Heart
(Diome)

Diome gazed at his reflection in the mirror in his room. A black tuxedo, a white bow-tie, and polished leather shoes. He would look the same as all the other attendees, right?

Tonight was Evangelina's debutante ball. "Reluctant" was a drastic understatement to describe how she felt about the dance. Evangelina regarded it as a burden, an inevitable responsibility to shoulder. But to him, it sounded amazing. Having rarely attended any formal events in his life, he found fancy occasions interesting and mysterious. How did people act? Did they use flamboyant language and make flowery gestures? Was it like being in a movie?

High society. It was a concept he had only studied in school. The Regency Era, the Victorian Era, and the Edwardian Era. Nowadays, nobody—human or devil—held any debutante balls, or at least, nobody that he knew of. To get a glimpse of what it was like would be amazing. As long as he didn't reveal his dark magic and leathery wings, nobody would know what he was.

Studying his reflection, Diome acknowledged the seriousness of his absurd plan all of a sudden. It was insanity. What in the world was he doing? Imitating Romeo and sneaking into Evangelina's debutante ball was amusing to imagine, but now that he was actualizing his plan, it felt surreal and insane. His stomach fluttered with anxiety, and sweat beaded on his forehead.

What was he to say when reaching the venue? *Splendor Island.* Evangelina had mentioned the name of the island during one of their chats. But could he locate the island without any assistance from the angels?

Diome sat on his bed, pondering over the details. He couldn't be discovered by the angels. Was this too bold an endeavor? How was he going to get past the angels on the floating islands without being spotted? It wasn't as if he would lose in a fight. However, he had no intention of harming any angels.

What if he was fortunate enough to make it all the way to Splendor Island without running into any angels, though? He could tell whoever hosted the ball he was Evangelina's escort, and due to some family affairs, he was late to the dance. A smile crept onto his lips as he thought of how excited Evangelina would be to see him. They could dance the night away, and it would be like the Halloween dance, only this time in a different venue— much brighter and more lavish. Like a duke and a duchess in old times, he and Evangelina would have the time of their lives. He wondered what she was wearing and how she had styled her hair. But even if she wore a ragged shirt or a hideous dress to the ball, nothing could detract from her breathtaking beauty. The flawless features, the heart of strength and innocence, and the riveting charm she possessed would never fail to mesmerize him. She was perfect. Both on the inside and the outside.

A knock sounded on the door to Diome's room, and he opened it.

His mother crossed her arms, a frown creasing her forehead. "Where are you going, all dressed up like that?"

"Oh, there's a-a school dance," Diome lied. "Didn't I tell you last week?" He did his best to feign astonishment.

His mother shook her head. "I don't think you've

mentioned it. Or maybe something's gone wrong with my memory. Oh, never mind."

Diome felt an urge to clap himself on the back. For his convincing act, he deserved a Best Actor award for fabricating a story and improvising in a matter of moments.

"Did you know there was an invasion in the East District this afternoon?" his mother asked. "Three devils died."

The Burning Bowels was split into four districts—the North District, the South District, the East District, and the West District. Diome and his family lived in the North District.

"Why didn't we see the angels?" Diome asked. "They should have passed us before reaching the East District."

His mother sighed. "It was three in the afternoon. All the devils must have been napping then. Very cunning, aren't they, those nasty angels?" A devious smile lifted the corners of her lips. "Now, all hell is breaking loose in their Land of Heavenly Dreams. They can rename it the Land of Heavenly Nightmares after tonight's big event."

Diome froze, and his mind blanked. "W-what do you mean, Mom?"

She smirked. "The devils decided we should give them immediate payback for what happened earlier. Thirty minutes ago, five dozen devils who volunteered to avenge the victims of this afternoon's invasion set off for the Land of Heavenly Dreams. One of the spies reported there would be a debutante ball on Splendor Island, one of their many floating islands in the sky. Good opportunity for a genocide, huh? I wonder how many causalities there's been."

The world stood still at that moment. *Splendor*

Island. The ball. Evangelina. An invasion. Random words and fragmented phrases stirred in Diome's mind like leaves disturbed by a gust of wind, but he was unable to make sense of them or even form a complete sentence. His senses sharpened and heightened, he became suddenly aware of every little movement around him, every second that ticked by, every breath that entered and exited his nose. The air felt dense, almost too thick for him to inhale. Numbing terror gushed through his veins as he tried to figure out his next step.

He had to remain unfazed, had to don a serene, if somewhat joyful demeanor. "Oh, good," he heard himself say in an enthusiastic voice that sounded unlike him. It sounded bizarre, as if the lips that moved weren't his, as if the vocal cords that vibrated belonged to a stranger, as if he were a guest in his body.

His mother nodded. "After we teach those angels a lesson and someday eradicate their disgusting existence, we can claim the Land of Heavenly Dreams as ours."

"That sounds wonderful," choked Diome. "I want to help the devils. Can I?"

His mother regarded him with astonishment. "You want to join the battle?"

Diome nodded. It was his only chance of rescuing Evangelina, his only hope of protecting his beloved angel. Now, her life was at stake, and whether she could survive the invasion depended on him, on whether he could arrive in time and whisk her away from the danger.

"Off you go, then, son. The devils will be glad to have some reinforcements."

Without another word, Diome donned his wings and hurtled downstairs, almost hitting his head on the ceiling. Time was precious, and there wasn't a moment to waste.

Soaring out of his house, Diome flapped his

wings and glided across the lava ocean. Questions swirled in his mind. How many angels and devils had fallen in battle? How intense was the fight? Was Evangelina safe? Was her father all right? Although her father was an evil supremacist, Diome didn't bear any ill will toward him. He was Evangelina's family.

A stream of cold air greeted his as he left the cave. It was December first, Diome remembered just then. Winter was approaching. There was a chill in the air that hadn't existed before. However, nothing mattered to Diome, nothing but the fact Evangelina was in great peril.

Was Evangelina terrified? Was she wounded? Always strong and independent and never fearful, she would fight them and no doubt defend herself well, of that Diome was certain. However, it did little to combat his anxiety.

Flapping his wings and craning his neck, Diome ascended into the skies for the first time in his life. He had had many dreams about flying in the sky since he was a child, but never had he imagined the first time he navigated the sky would be at nighttime. The puffs of clouds were warm and wet, cloaking him in soft, airy blankets of moisture as he glided by them. He had never been in such close proximity with the pearly moon, the queen of the stage above the clouds. The winking stars, the full moon, and the ocean of clouds made an ethereal sight, but Diome wasn't in the mood for admiring the picturesque scenery around him. Evangelina's life was his primary concern.

As Diome rose higher into the clouds, a series of floating islands sank below him. It was a whimsical sight to behold. Some of them were tiny, no bigger than a boulder and too small for him to land on, while others were larger. Many even had trees, rose bushes, and flower fields growing on them. There were enormous islands with lakes, small hills, and waterfalls too, he discovered. It was incredible, how the wonders in the Land of Heavenly Dreams never ceased.

Diome searched for the devils who had gone before him. He flew past a rocky island, another with an apple tree and a pond, and another with a hedge maze, sleuthing for any clues as to where Splendor Island was.

"Devil!"

The next moment, a stream of arrows came sailing at Diome. He flapped his wings in a mad attempt to escape and zoomed away. Several blinding white sparks told him the angels were on his heels. Swerving past four islands, doing a backflip in the air, and dashing past a dense cloud, he managed to get rid of them without resorting to violence. He was in the Land of Heavenly Dreams to save Evangelina, not to eliminate any angels or provoke them. In a way, he was on their side by being neutral.

A sting on Diome's arm made him gasp in terror. He spotted a trio of angels—triplets—crouched on a floating island, shooting white sparks at him. They hadn't ruined his jacket, but the force of the sparks still hurt him. Small bruises began to bloom on his skin.

"You're not welcome here, monster," spat one of the angels.

"Go back to your Burning Bowels," another growled at him, crossing her arms.

Diome ignored them and flew in the opposite direction. He could have moved faster if he hadn't had a tuxedo on and was garbed in his usual black robe, but now, he couldn't care less.

A white spark landed on Diome's shoulder, and he uttered a cry of pain. It was as though a tiny bullet had struck him. He turned and fired a stream of black sparks at his attackers, careful to target their arms and legs instead of their heads, which would be fatal. He couldn't tell them he was neutral and meant no harm, for it was impossible they would believe him.

Diving out of the angels' way and gaining height and speed, he hurtled away, mounting the clouds as he went. In the distance, he spotted a group of devils garbed in black robes. Diome's heart leapt—could it be? Had he reached Splendor Island? There was a tall white building on the island they were circling. Shafts of golden light issued from the immense windows, and Diome saw a ballroom with a shattered floor-length window. Shards of broken glass mingled with puddles and pools of blood, telling a tale of death and destruction. The mangled bodies of seven angels and a devil could be seen sprawled on the marble tiles, their wings crumpled and their eyes closed.

For a moment, Diome hesitated, appalled by the sight before his eyes. What if Evangelina was one of the dead? Many of the fallen angels were young, some still in their debutante dresses. Had they ever imagined the jubilant celebration would take a grim turn and claim their lives? What was supposed to be the most important day of their life marked the end of it instead.

Summoning his courage, Diome forced himself to proceed. He neared the shattered window and flew into the ballroom, searching for any signs of Evangelina among the turmoil. Many angels and devils were still battling in the air, shooting sparks and zapping beams of light at each other.

Could she have escaped on her own? Diome contemplated the possibility just when a redheaded devil seized his attention.

Lenora Lenoir. A dagger was clutched in her hands, blood dripping from the silver blade that gleamed like the fangs of a brutal beast.

Lying on the floor beside her was an angel in white, unconscious.

Evangelina.

Lenora smirked down at her like a victorious predator hovering over its prey.

"Pretty little angel," Lenora drawled. "You'll have less than ten seconds to live."

She raised her dagger, aiming it at Evangelina's throat.

No. Not Evangelina. Before Diome realized what he had done, he flung himself at Lenora and crashed into her, knocking her down. The dagger she had been holding sliced into her abdomen. Lenora's eyes widened, almost bulged as the truth dawned on her.

Diome could hear nothing but his own pounding heart, could sense nothing but the palpable tension solidifying the air. He killed Lenora. There was no way she could survive after sustaining the fatal wound.

All around him, there was dead silence. The devils had called a truce and were staring at him.

"Did he ... save that unconscious angel?" someone whispered, flabbergasted.

"Killed a devil to ... to rescue one of our enemies," another murmured, shaking her head.

Blood was gushing from Lenora's neck like a fountain. In her hazel eyes, a mixture of shock, consternation, and resentment glared at Diome. Horrorstruck, he could only gaze at her, unable to move a muscle. Panic and terror had numbed his senses and deprived him of all his vocabulary. Like a strangled beast, she made an odd, shrill noise and lunged at Evangelina. Diome flung himself over Evangelina's comatose form, shielding her from harm, and shoved Lenora away.

"For her?" Lenora hissed. "You ... you would die

... for her?"

Having recovered from his initial shock, Diome crossed his arms. "What did she do to you? Why target her?"

"I ... didn't t-t-target ... " Lenora's eyes widened, and hatred flashed across them. "You love her? Is that why ... why you came? To ... to save her?"

Now no less than ten devils were staring at them, agape at the fact there was a traitor among them. Acknowledging the seriousness of the situation, Diome knew he had no more time to spare. Since he was exposed, he might as well rescue Evangelina and escape before everyone started attacking him. Ignoring Lenora's hissing, he crouched down, scooped Evangelina into his arms, and flapped his wings to leave.

"What are you waiting for?" one of the devils demanded. "Kill that traitor!"

A storm of black sparks sailed at Diome, and he dodged them. Three devils blocked his way as he was approached the window, snarling at him. Diome zapped them with black beams of light, and one of them plummeted to the ground.

"Kill him! That's Diome Lenoir!" a devil cried.

Cries, screams, and shouts filled the air. Diome had to circle the ballroom to avoid the devils' sparks and spells. He winced every time a spark hit him. It was pain beyond pain. The only way to fight back, to end this disaster was to summon darkness, but he couldn't focus on his magic now. Powerful magic like that required an incredible amount of concentration.

"Traitor! Trash! A piece of filth!"

"You killed one of us just to protect an angel?"

"How long have you been with her?"

"How many secrets of our clan have you spilled?"

"You're a disgrace to the devils! Burn in the

bowels, you wicked monster!"

The catcalls and insults didn't faze Diome, not even the least. He had been ready for this since the moment he fell in love with Evangelina. She was still in his arms, and he was grateful that she was much lighter than he had expected. After zooming out of the ballroom, he could descend on the nearest island and check on her.

Diome passed the balcony where he had found Evangelina and spotted Lenora lying on the floor, her eyes closed. She was dead. He knew it from the deathly pallor in her skin, from the awkward angle her arms and legs were bent in. Diome had never wished anyone— even any of the devils—ill. He never liked their revolting supremacist beliefs, but at the same time, he pitied them for their ignorance and shallowness. However, he couldn't pity Lenora. She had attempted to murder Evangelina, tried to destroy the purpose of his life. Had Diome been a second too late, he would have lost Evangelina forever. He loved her with all his heart. If she died, he would be irrevocably destroyed. His heart would be crushed, and he would be sentenced to a horrible life of guilt and depression.

"Bastard! You killed Lenora for that scum!"

A devil flung herself at Diome, who blocked her with a wave of his hand. She hurled a knife at him, and he lowered himself, avoiding it by inches. He had to end the battle before any more of the devils or angels lost their lives. It was up to him to terminate it—by conjuring darkness, none of them would be able to see their allies or foes, and that would be enough to dispel them. They were all too indignant, too furious, and none of them were keen to end the fight.

One of the devils guarding the broken window flew at Diome, who dived out of the way and zoomed at the window, kicking the others away in the process.

Black vapor blossomed from his fingers and formed a shield, blocking the fallen devils. Diome pictured a curtain of velvety darkness descending on the ballroom, visualized the bright candles and glistening chandeliers devoured by a void of blackness.

But Evangelina—

I'll check on her later. Focus. Just focus now.

Waging a war against his fear, panic, and uncertainty, Diome imagined darkness—deep, profound darkness—descending on the world and enveloping everything in black. His life depended on it, and so did Evangelina's.

At that moment, he felt a wave of power escape him, unleashed by his fingers. Diome opened his eyes and saw a puff of black smoke blanketing the ballroom, drowning all the candles and engulfing everything in utter darkness.

Relief flowed through him like a river. He was safe. Taking advantage of this opportunity, Diome turned and flapped his wings, becoming one with the night. Now that he had survived the battle and managed to rescue Evangelina, Diome felt a surge of confidence gushing through him. He had done it. He had slapped the devils in the face by being himself and exposing his love for Evangelina. The act of rebellion brought him an inexplicable torrent of satisfaction. There was no need to scream reason at them, no need to accuse them of lusting for bloodshed. No, all he had to do was to show them how proud he was to defy tradition, how adamant he was to rescue Evangelina. Love made him fearless, unstoppable, if only to remain with his beloved for a moment longer.

Diome glanced down at Evangelina, still unconscious in his arms. He thought of everything that had transpired, everything that had built up to this moment. Minutes ago, he had almost lost Evangelina. He felt Evangelina's wrist for a pulse. She was alive. The notion coursed through his mind like warm honey, calming and imbuing hope in him.

"Stop!"

Diome spotted an angel on a floating island above him. A silver arrow whirred past him, and he retaliated with a stream of black sparks.

"He killed one of us, and he's stealing her body!" another one cried. "Go get him!"

Torrents of black and white sparks and streaks of light zapped at each other, lighting the night. Diome was alone, all alone. There were no devils around, but even if there were, they would never help him. He had exposed himself as a traitor, and everyone would soon learn of his betrayal. An exceptionally strong spark struck his cheek, and he grimaced. Diome did not wish to fight back, but now, he had to attack the angels in self-defense.

Where could he fly to? All the floating islands around him were either blanketed with moss or had rocky surfaces. Could he make it all the way to the human world, or could he find a secluded island to hide on? Diome swerved around five islands, dived through a funnel of clouds, and came across an immense island with an endless forest. Under the moonlight, it looked dark, ominous, and foreboding. Yet it was the safest place in the Land of Heavenly Dreams. The muted hues of green beckoned to him, inviting him to take refuge in the darkness.

He flew into the forest, seeking the sanctuary of the shadows, and laid Evangelina on the velvety grass. The angels hadn't seen him heading into the forest, of that he was certain. A fortune among a misfortune. Nursing his sore arms, he wiped the sweat from his forehead with the back of his hand. He sat down and leaned against a tree, trying to banish all the horrifying memories tonight. Any moment, and he could be caught. Any moment, he could die. However, he survived. As close a call as it was, he made it.

Beside him, Evangelina stirred, and her eyes opened. "Diome?" she murmured.

Diome helped her into a sitting position and lifted her into his arms. "Yes, Evangelina. It's me. You're safe now."

"Where are we? And how did you know that ... ?"

"We're in a forest on one of the floating islands. I found you unconscious in the ballroom and brought you here."

Evangelina shivered. "It was horrible. One second, everyone was dancing, and the next, the devils came. They flew in like bats, and they destroyed everything."

"It's over," murmured Diome. "Nothing can hurt us now."

Evangelina nodded fearfully. "How ... how did you find me?" She gazed at Diome, tracing his outfit. "And why are you dressed like this?"

Diome wanted to smile, but the thought of all the angels and devils who died in the invasion made him utter a sigh instead. "I wanted to sneak into your debutante ball and give you a surprise, but my mother told me the devils were launching an attack on Splendor Island, where there was an ongoing dance. I told her I was going to help the devils, and I flew to the Land of Heavenly Dreams at top speed."

"How did you know where Splendor Island was?"

"A couple of angels attacked me. When I was flying away from them, I spotted some devils gathered around an island with a ballroom in a white building. I flew in and carried you out, and after escaping from a few angels who thought I killed you, I came across this island and decided to use it as a hideout."

Evangelina frowned, confused. "Before I blacked out, I remember a redheaded devil who tried to kill me. What happened to her?"

Diome hesitated for a moment. "She tried to stab you, but I saved you at the last moment. She ended up slitting her throat by accident. I didn't mean to kill her, but when I tried to knock her out, she dropped the dagger, and it cut into her stomach."

Evangelina's eyes widened. "Did the devils see you saving me?"

Diome nodded, and Evangelina's hand flew to her chest.

"But ... but you just exposed yourself! They'll kill you for that!"

" There's no way I'm going back to the Burning Bowels. They'll execute me the first chance they've got."

Evangelina gazed at him with a mixture of awe and astonishment. "But where will you go?"

Diome shrugged. "Somewhere. I'll live on the streets if I must."

"Why did you come for me?" Evangelina asked.

Diome studied her face, acknowledging how beautiful her features were under the silver moonlight. "I couldn't let you die in there. Actually, I'll tell you a secret. I know the devil who tried to kill you. Lenora, that's her name. She ... " He winced, preparing himself to utter the truth. "She ... she liked me."

Evangelina frowned. "Really? I never saw her before. How could she have known we're in a relationship?"

"You think she tried to kill you out of jealousy? I thought it was just a coincidence."

Evangelina bit her lip. "But what if she spied on

us before? What if she knew, and that's why she targeted me?"

"Did she target you?" Diome asked, his concern for the issue mounting.

Evangelina contemplated his question for a while. "No, I guess. The devils were killing any angels in their way. When they dueled each other, they didn't leave the angels alone until one of them was dead ... " She trembled and faltered. "Maybe it was nothing but a coincidence Lenora tried to kill me."

"It's all over," Diome murmured, stroking her back. "No matter what Lenora knew, it won't bother us from now on."

"I'm sorry, Diome," Evangelina cried. "You risked your life to save me tonight. I never wanted—or thought—I would ever need someone to rescue me, but ... " She shrugged.

"It's all right," Diome replied. "Even the strongest fighters have times when they need help."

That made Evangelina smile. "You're hurt," she noticed, her expression melting into concern.

Diome dabbed at the cut on his cheek. "One of the angels zapped me when I was fleeing from the ballroom."

"Hold on for a moment." Evangelina stood up and made her way to a bush squatting by a tree across from them. Stooping down, she plucked three pink flowers from it and returned.

"What are those?" Diome asked as she picked up a stone and pounded it on the petals. Pink liquid oozed from the flowers.

"The Blossom of Angelica, the angels' spirit flower," replied Evangelina. "Also known as the healing flower. Its pink liquid can heal minor cuts and gashes."

She dabbed some of the liquid on the gash on Diome's cheek. He winced, a throbbing sensation making his features contort.

"It's all right," cooed Evangelina. "You'll be good as new in a minute."

A warm tingle replaced the pain, and Diome's gash mend mended itself. He placed his hand on his cheek tentatively. Not a scar was left on his face.

"Thank you," he told her. "You're literally my healing angel."

Evangelina beamed. "Anything for you. We look like a lost bride and groom wandering in a dark forest, don't we?"

Diome glanced down at his black tuxedo and her white gown. "That's an accurate observation. Where are we going, my bride?"

"On a date, maybe," Evangelina replied.

"I should send you home," Diome volunteered. "Just in case the devils attack you."

Evangelina shook her head. "I don't want to go home, though. I want to stay with you here forever."

Diome smiled. "We barely made it out alive. For that, we definitely deserve a reward."

Evangelina gazed at him, confused. "A reward for us?"

Diome leaned closer to her, and their lips met each other's in an instant. A spectrum of vibrant colors came alive before Diome's eyes. The night was no longer black and white, but alight with a thousand hues. Evangelina's lips were as soft as feathers. They reminded him of rainbows, honey, sunshine, sugar, and everything sweet and pleasant. How could he have known what euphoria meant before this beautiful moment? Lost in a world of pure bliss, all he could think of was Evangelina, her tender skin and graceful figure. He was beyond fortunate to have and hold her for the rest of eternity.

After what seemed like an hour, the two of them

leaned back for air. Diome saw his delight reflected on her face, and he reached out to hold her hand. "That's our reward. How do you like it?"

Evangelina leaned her head on his shoulder. "I love it, Diome. But not as much as I love you."

Before Diome met her, he would never have had the courage to fly to the Land of Heavenly Dreams, much less fly into a battlefield to save her. But Evangelina's love had changed him, dispelling his fear and anxiety and replacing them with the will to keep their relationship burning, to guard their love at all costs. By rescuing Evangelina, he was paying her back for the bravery and strength she'd imbued in him. Because of her, his life had a purpose. Because of her, every day was a new adventure—thrilling, exciting, and full of surprises. Now that he came to think of it, love wasn't only about hugs, kisses, and sweet nothings. Rather, it was complex. It was about sacrifice, about devotion, about supporting each other during the toughest of times.

Evangelina was an angel he trusted with all his heart. In many romance novels he read, the protagonists were always up to something fun, a picnic, a candlelight dinner, or a ride to the countryside. However, his relationship with Evangelina was much rockier, paved with one challenge after another. Nothing was easy for them, for their love was forbidden, a romance destined to be tested again and again. Yet against all odds, they braved through everything and were still willing to accept each other for who they were. To Diome, that was the most charming, the most magical, the most touching part of it.

Most couples wanted to look their best in front of their partner by either donning makeup, spraying cologne, or making witty remarks. But with Evangelina, Diome was at ease with being himself, while she was also comfortable in his presence. This was raw, real romance, boiled down to the core. They loved each other for their uniqueness, quirkiness, and their mutual rebellion against their clans. Their hearts beat in sync, and their futures were intertwined with one another's. Diome knew in the deepest depths of his heart that they were soulmates, bound together by destiny. She was his beacon, his hope, his everything.

"Should we leave now?" Diome asked after another few minutes. "I don't know the time. When is your dad expecting you to be home?"

Evangelina shrugged. "He might be out drinking until midnight."

"I'll send you home." Diome squeezed her hand. "I insist."

Evangelina responded with a warm smile that melted his soul. This time, she made no objection.

Chapter Eleven

Soaring Through the Skies
(Evangelina)

Out of the forest and toward the rim of the island, Evangelina and Diome went. In the night, the stars, clouds, and shadows had become one. In perfect harmony, they gemmed, painted, and adorned the night with their splendor.

"Is it safe out there?" Diome asked.

Evangelina scanned the place for enemies. "I think so. There's nobody in sight."

Diome heaved. "Good. I don't want to get murdered by anyone, angel or devil. Right now the two sides hate me equally."

Evangelina still couldn't believe he had rushed into the ball and rescued her moments before Lenora could kill her. She was so close, less than an inch away from death. And yet, it was her best friend, the love of her life who had swept her away at that critical moment of imminent danger. Always, she had thought of herself as someone invincible, infallible, but now, she realized even for the most invulnerable of angels, there were times they had to be rescued, times when they were in mortal peril. She could not complete everything alone and be the hero every time, and neither could anyone else, angel or human or devil. As reluctant as the most pompous person in the world was to admit, there weren't many things one could achieve independently, for nobody had much control over their fate.

The greatest generals in history couldn't win a battle without a powerful army; the most sagacious president wouldn't be who they were without all the previous leaders; the wisest scholar wouldn't have had a vault of knowledge without the findings and philosophies of those before them. Everything relied on everything else, and everyone more or less relied on everyone else. Nobody could truly be independent, a lone, detached island that had nothing to do with the others. In one way or another, everyone was connected to each other in an unending circle.

"Are you well enough to fly?" Diome asked worriedly.

Evangelina still felt unsteady and shivered from her collapse. "Give me a moment." She spotted a giant rock by the nearest tree and sat on it.

"I'll wait for you." Diome joined her. "Are you okay?"

Evangelina nodded. "I am. Just still a bit unsettled is all. The way everything erupted into chaos all of a sudden the same way it did on my birthday ... It just brings back so many awful memories."

Diome put his arm around her, pulling her closer. "It's over," he murmured to comfort her.

Evangelina analyzed her emotions. She never was one to cry when terrified, but was it terror bubbling in her now? Anxiety, more like. A dread for the unknown. She had no desire to contemplate to future, to ponder over how the enmity between the angels and devils could worsen—before the ball, she had thought their mutual hatred of other had hit rock bottom, but things always had a way of contradicting her assumptions. It wasn't only anxiety she felt now. The sickening sensation in her stomach was a blend of fear, uncertainty, and trepidation.

"When will these attacks stop?" Evangelina cried.

Diome hung his head. "If I were braver, I would be an activist. I'd fly around the Burning Bowels and advocate peace."

"Don't," Evangelina pleaded. "The presidents can't stop this. How can we be so foolish to assume we can? I used to think we could be the ones to change history, but now, that's no longer my wish. I just want a peaceful life with you. Nothing else."

"Me too," Diome replied. "It's every angel and devil for themselves. As much as we want the rivalry to end, it's not up to us. At this point I dare not take anything for granted. Every peaceful day can be our last."

"Our last ... "

Evangelina stood up and glided to the end of the island. Epic and sublime as always, the stars glittered above her, streaks of dreamy clouds streaking the endless, and a canopy of inky black. An enormous, luminous pearl high in the sky, the moon observed them, shining, smiling. The profusion of undulating clouds churning below sparked an inexplicable surge of excitement in her, despite the unpleasant event earlier. If fate was determined to kill them, why not let it go, if only for a night's wild, carefree fun?

She turned to face Diome, all of her fatigue and apprehension evaporated in an instant. Her breathing quickened, and a surge of boldness flooded through her veins.

"Do you want to surf the skies?" Evangelina asked.

She had not an inkling why such an insane notion had struck her mind, but all she knew was that life was too fleeting to leave any regrets. Tomorrow, the day after tomorrow, she might cease to exist. One more time, she wanted to soar through the clouds and drink in the beauty of the Land of Heavenly Dreams, and more than anything, she craved Diome's company.

"When did you become so adventurous?" Diome asked, half-amused, half-baffled.

"Just now. I want to take you on a trip through the clouds. We can visit and stop by some of the empty islands."

"No, we can't! Aren't you scared the other angels will spot us? Aren't you worried we'll get killed?"

Evangelina stared at him. "I'd rather die living than live dying. We can go to a remote part of the Land of Heavenly Dreams. Might be a little far, but there's a nice little restaurant. My parents and I used to go there for celebrations."

"Are they open in the night?" Diome asked.

"Oh, only in the night. It'll be an incredible experience."

"Who are you, and what did you do to the terrified Evangelina?" Diome asked with a laugh of wonder.

"Come on, just for once, let's leave everything behind and create a wonderful recollection worth remembering together."

She extended a hand to Diome in an invitation, the same way she had done on the magical night of the Halloween dance.

Diome edged closer to her, but did not take her hand. "And if we die?" he whispered, as though fearing inauspiciousness could be transmitted through words.

Evangelina hesitation for a fraction of a second. "Then," she declared. "We'll fall together."

Diome lapsed into a spell of pensive silence for a while. When Evangelina thought he was going to refuse her offer, he replied with a smile. "Why not?"

Hand-in-hand, they walked to the edge of the island, her gown and his robe fluttering in the breeze that caressed the clouds and ruffled the grass.

"Ready?" Evangelina asked breathlessly.

"Ready," murmured Diome.

The two of them plunged down and dove into the clouds.

"There," Evangelina told him, pointing right. "That direction."

They flew past large puffs and slender tendrils of gossamer clouds, past a constellation of tiny green islands, past a giant one with a waterfall plummeting down a hill and forming a lake that glistened under the moonlight. Unlike the flamboyant, blinding beams of sunlight, the moon had a soft power of its own. The pearly, alabaster glow it emanated doused everything in a filter of soft white light, making the world a dreamy wonderland of white and silver. It was an ethereal, breathtaking sight worth more than a thousand words, as if a painting had come alive before their eyes. Even though she had cruised through the clouds alone before many times, Evangelina still could not believe how charming, how mesmerizing the cloudscapes were. There were no words for this, no words for something so grand yet mysterious, so magnificent yet priceless, so celestial yet whimsical.

"Do you like it here?" Evangelina asked Diome, riveted by the nocturnal scenery.

"It's divine," he whispered. "Am I dreaming? Tell me I'm not. This—it's the setting of a fairy tale. It's otherworldly."

Evangelina laughed. "You're not dreaming, Diome. Welcome to the Land of Heavenly Dreams."

With their hair whipping in the light, airy breeze and the pleats of their gown and robe flowing behind them like the tail of a kite, they immersed, they relished, they indulged themselves in beauty and magic all around them. Somehow, soaring through the sky instilled euphoria, ecstasy, and excitement in Evangelina. Spreading her wings and feeling the wind feather against her skin was relaxing. It had a cathartic impact on her. All the burdens and concerns that plagued her dissolved, and her mind, no longer bound by the shackles of past events, was uncaged. Joy, sheer, uncontaminated joy seeped into her heart and circulated in her veins.

This was freedom, pure and perfect; this was freedom, a calming breath of fresh air when she longed for it the most; this was freedom, in a realm where nobody would judge her and Diome for being themselves. This was utmost freedom, utmost bliss.

"If I remember clearly, the restaurant's down there," mused Evangelina.

"How come you remember it so well?" Diome asked. "There are no roads here, and the clouds change every day, don't they? How do you keep track of where everything is?"

"Angels are born with a good sense of direction in the sky," she replied. "Our instincts tell us where to go."

They lowered themselves and descended on an island with verdant slopes framing a rocky grotto. Diome removed his wings, shrunk them, and stuffed them into the pocket of his robe.

"There's a restaurant here? Where?"

"Over there, behind the patch of trees."

Evangelina led him through the shadows, past the tall, ghostly poplar trees, and to a clearing with several sets of chairs and tables sporting curly legs and ornate carvings. Every table had a blazing candle and a simple centerpiece of pink and red flowers Evangelina failed to recognize. Flurries of jasmine fragrance wafted from the candles, teasing her nose.

"It's an outdoor restaurant?" Diome asked.

"Yes. So the angels can watch the stars as they eat. Let's go and place our order."

Diome hesitated for a moment. "Won't they

recognize me?"

"It's hard to tell whether you're an angel or devil without looking at your wings, blood, or magic." Evangelina mused. "Come to think of it, those are the only differences we have. Apart from our blood color, wings, and brands of magic, we're pretty much the same."

She and Diome entered the restaurant, ordered some whipped cream and waffles, pesto spaghetti, and a glass of iced grape tea. Then, after claiming their order and paying, their retraced their steps and went back outside.

Dining under the starry universe was a marvelous experience. It was like having a candlelight dinner under a velvet canopy dotted with tiny diamonds. Evangelina and Diome shared the plate of spaghetti, forking the noodles on the same plate.

"I love the food here," gushed Diome. "It's delicious."

Evangelina smiled. "I'm glad. This is the most unique restaurant in the Land of Heavenly Dreams."

"What's it called?" Diome asked, shoving another forkful of spaghetti into his mouth.

"Starry Soirée."

"A romantic name that suits the atmosphere," replied Diome. He shook his head. "I can't believe the devils launch attacks on the Land of Heavenly Dreams, a world so charming and lovely. Have they destroyed any islands before?"

"Plenty." Evangelina sighed. "If they could lay down their weapons and take a moment—just a moment—to appreciate the beauty here, perhaps they would stop."

Diome nodded. "It's sublime. Honestly. I hope one day the angels and devils can visit each other without worrying about getting killed. Maybe someday, we can have parties in the clouds and celebrate eternal peace. That would be nice."

Evangelina took a sip of the grape tea. "Definitely. They could sit and frolic on the floating islands, and the little angels and devils could play hide-and-seek among the clouds." She sighing, realizing such innocent dreams were nothing but empty illusions. Reality was much crueler. While the little angels and devils hadn't been poisoned by hatred, none of them could make a difference. The resentment the angels and devils had for each other had been rooted deeply in their hearts like a century-old tree. Even the presidents' calls for peace could not dispel the bitter loathing both sides had for each other.

Was it due to insecurity? Perhaps the angels and devils detested each other because somehow, belittling the other clan brought them a notch higher on the totem pole of competition—there was no competition, of course, but to the supremacists, nothing mattered more to them than overpowering their enemies. Life was all about conquering and not cooperating with whoever they deemed their rivals.

But now, Evangelina abandoned the annoying thoughts and focused her mind on the present. Here she was, enjoying dinner on a floating island with Diome, something she never dared to dream of. At this moment, on this night, they were two regular teenagers who longed for a minute of tranquility, two innocent souls who craved peace. They were together, boldly, proudly, audaciously together. Defying gravity, defying their families, defying societal norms and conformity.

"Looks like we're the only ones sitting here," Diome noticed. "The other angels are gone. I wonder how late it is now."

"Oh, don't worry about the time," Evangelina replied. "My dad won't be home until after midnight. He's drinking with his friends now."

"Must be difficult for him to cope with ... You know, your mom's death."

Evangelina nodded. "Yes, but he and I still talk normally. It's just that he doesn't really show his emotions. He's not big on expressing himself and all that touchy-feely stuff. What about your mom?"

"Mom ..." Diome sighed and shook his head. "She still thinks it's the angels' fault Dad died. It's crazy. I should comfort her, but I can't bring myself to do that. I can't be comfortable when she's nagging about how angels are ... Sorry, I shouldn't talk bad about the angels in front of you."

"Never say sorry to me." Evangelina took his hand. "I understand. We didn't choose who we were born as. We can only decide who we want to be."

"And I want to be yours," Diome vowed.

They leaned closer, and their lips brushed against each other's with an unsettling amount of tenderness that melted her core. He was the one—he was her one and only. When her lips were devoured by his, all Evangelina could think about was the warm, glowing sensation radiating in her. She could see her future glittering before her eyes—a world of rainbows, light, and magic. A utopia of the purest bliss imaginable.

At the same time, they drew back for air and smiled at each other, delighting in their presence.

"Should we explore the skies a little more before ending this surreal night?" Diome asked after finishing the last of his iced tea.

"Oh, yes. Of course," Evangelina replied, stuffing the last bite of waffles into her mouth. "Follow me."

They sauntered to the edge of the island and with

a flap of their wings, flew into the night once again.

"So where should we go?" Evangelina asked.

"Why do we have to go anywhere?" Diome replied. "The skyscape here is sublime. Let's just cruise in the clouds and sail through the skies."

"Good plan."

Evangelina watched the shiny stars, gauzy clouds, and phantom shadows rise and dip around them as they soared, glided, and flew through cloud after cloud. Moist droplets of water clung onto her skin as she threaded her way past them.

Before them was a tunnel of funnel-shaped clouds, all in various shades of black and navy blue. The colors of midnight. Evangelina wove her way into the tunnel, clutching Diome's hand. They swayed right, leaned left, dipped down, and rose up as they traversed through the winding labyrinth of clouds.

"Who would have thought there would be a maze of clouds way up high in the sky?" Diome marveled at the soaring walls of clouds.

"Right? The Land of Heavenly Dreams is filled with wonders."

"Have you tried dancing in the clouds before?" Diome asked.

Evangelina shook her head. "Never."

"That's because you never had a partner, I guess. Want to do it with me?"

Evangelina nodded, more than a little perplexed. "How?"

Diome reached out for her hands, and she took them. With a dip and a swirl, he dragged her downward and spun her around.

"Interesting," Evangelina giggled. "So this is dancing in clouds."

"Indeed," replied Diome, a sparkle his eye.

He lifted a hand to twirl her around, and she did the same with him. Soon, they were inventing their own moves—flipping cartwheels, turning somersaults, and performing backflips among the clouds.

"This is amazing," Diome said. "I can't believe how incredible it is above the clouds."

"We're lucky it's midnight," Evangelina replied. "Almost none of the angels leave their homes during the nighttime. Even better, nobody can see your wings through the darkness."

Diome did a somersault and flew higher. "I see an island above us. Want to check it out?"

"Anything special about it?" Evangelina asked.

"It's very small. Barely big enough to fit three angels."

"Oh, there are tons of tiny islands. The Land of Heavenly Dreams consists of about ten thousand islands, big and small."

The two of them landed on the tiny island and sat down. It was rocky and uneven, clad with nothing more than a thin layer of green moss. However, Diome seemed to love it.

"Staring down at the ocean of clouds and floating islands in the moonlight, it's so therapeutic, isn't it?" he asked.

"It's peaceful beyond words," replied Evangelina, lying down on her back and gazing up at the endless universe of stars. The thin blades of grass on either side of her framed the vast galaxy, swaying in the cool breeze.

"What if the stars were sentient?" Diome asked out of the blue. "What if the reason they're up in the sky forever is because they swore an oath to love each other forever?"

"That would be a good idea for a play," Evangelina replied. "You could explore some deep themes in it. For example, what is love? Is it as powerful or as fragile as we think?"

"As powerful or as fragile?" Diome asked, tilting his head to look at her.

"Yes. There's a saying that goes, 'Love makes the world go round.' In some ways, it's true. Love gives us courage to fight for our loved ones. It instills a bout of bravery in us, a determination to be strong for our partner. But at the same time, is it that unbreakable? Might it collapse at the slightest bit of scrutiny? It sounds so perfect, so rosy and divine, but what if it's just an existential illusion? As powerful love is, it can't make lovers immortal."

"But does it have to?" Diome asked. "Love itself is immortal. When you love someone until they die and until it's your turn to join them on the other side, doesn't that count as immortal love?"

"Of course, but with all the literature glorifying love and romance, you'd think there would be more to it. But the truth is, love isn't a shield that makes one invincible. Think about poor Romeo and his Juliet. They had an undying love, but wasn't it their love that killed them in the end?"

"What do you mean? Their family rivalry killed them, not their love. Juliet wouldn't have drunk the potion if she hadn't wanted to escape the wedding with Count Paris, and Romeo wouldn't have committed suicide in the Capulet's burial chamber."

"Yes, but it was all for love. Right? I didn't expect the play to be a tragedy. Thought it would be like some cheesy fairy tale, in which they 'lived happily ever after'. But no, the play has way more depth than that."

"Are you saying you prefer tragedies over comedies?" Diome asked.

Evangelina contemplated the question. "There's a

poignant beauty in tragedies. Those are stories you'll remember because they touched or even broke your heart. Take another book, *The Sorrows of Young Werther,* for example. The ending was far from satisfying. But maybe that's why people will remember it. Maybe that's why it holds significance in some people's hearts."

"Just like what you said when we first met. 'Flaws can highlight the rawness and reality of things and bring out their beauty instead.'"

Evangelina nodded. "Yes, just like that. Tragedies are like scars in your memory. They won't let you forget them. Happy endings are more likely to be glossed over and forgotten because there's no element of pity and imperfection in them. Everything went well, so life goes on. But bitter endings will claw their way into your heart and make you remember the sadness you felt for the characters."

"Back to what you said about love," continued Diome. "You said it could be fragile, and it doesn't make people stronger."

"No—yes, well, it depends. Love is neutral."

As life-changing as it was, love could make one lose their sense of direction. It had destroyed Werther's will to live and pushed him into the abyss of heartbreak and sorrow. But at the same time, how many people delighted in the glow of it, the warmth it brought, the charm it held? Evangelina herself, for one, saw all the beauty and brightness. As divine as it was, though, everything had a dark side to it, and love was no exception. If Diome was gone, if he fell in battle, what would become of her? Like Alice in *Alice's Adventures in Wonderland*, she had fallen into a pit that led her to a beautiful wonderland before she could think of escaping, and now, she could never leave it. Her life was bound to Diome's in so many ways that she couldn't imagine losing him.

"I'm not demeaning the concept of love, because being neutral isn't a bad thing. It's like fire. Without it, you can't cook food, heat water, or light candles. But at the same time, fire can be dangerous. It can burn down buildings, and choke people with smoke. In fact, many things in the world are neutral. It depends on how everyone thinks and sees them."

"How is love neutral? It's supposed to be the most powerful emotion in the world."

"It can either breathe meaning into your life or ruin it with extreme, unhealthy obsession. Despite its bright side, hardly anyone mentions the disadvantages. But then, as powerful as it sounds, it can't stop death or save lives."

"Maybe not," Diome replied. "But it can make a life worth living. And isn't that what matters the most? We can't choose how long we want to live, but we can determine how full we want our lives to be."

Evangelina nodded, acknowledging the profound depth in his words. "Wise words, Diome. I'll always be proud to have you in my life."

"And I you," he answered. "You changed my life, Evangelina. I'm proud to have showed the devils I'm not one of their kind and how I'm against killing angels."

"But where will you go now?" Evangelina asked. "The devils might murder you if you go back to the Burning Bowels."

"I'm not going back there. Treason is a crime punishable by death. No one would be foolish enough to commit suicide."

"But you can't stay in the Land of Heavenly Dreams," Evangelina lamented. The realization that tonight, like everything beautiful, would come to an end made a tide of melancholy wash over her.

"Isn't it obvious? I'll have to stay in the human world. It's the only place safe for me."

Evangelina stared at him. "But where will you live?"

Diome smiled. "Nowhere. I'll wander on the streets, lonely as a cloud. Live like a nomad on the run."

"I ... But—"

"That's the only way I can survive. What difference will it make if I stay in the Land of Heavenly Dreams or return to the Burning Bowels? The angels and devils will kill me, sooner or later. I'm a criminal everywhere. Gosh, I wouldn't be surprised if they joined forces on a hunt and targeted me together. Perhaps their hatred for me will make the two sides unite at last."

Evangelina sighed. "I'm sorry, Diome. I never wanted this to happen. If you hadn't come and saved me—"

"Nobody wanted anything to happen. But I don't regret flying in to save you. Had I been a minute later, Lenora would've killed you."

"Yes, but it's so unfair. You saved me at the risk of losing your home and the devils' trust."

"Some sacrifices are worth it," Diome asserted. "I know you don't like to be escorted, but could I fly you home? I want to take a good look at the cloudscape, since I might never come back here again."

Evangelina nodded. "Of course."

They sat up, donned their wings, and took off.

"It's a beautiful night," Diome remarked. "Magical and surreal. If only it can last forever."

"Nothing beautiful lasts forever," Evangelina replied. "Roses wilt. Clouds dissolve into water. Snow melts. Angels, humans, and devils die. But memories exist as long as someone remembers them, right? You and I will always treasure tonight and keep it in our hearts, right?"

The alabaster moonshine, the undulating ocean of clouds, the glittering universe, and the love flowing between them, those would always remain etched in Evangelina's permanent memory.

Diome nodded. "We can't freeze time, but we can always hold onto the good memories."

Too soon it was that they reached the floating island Evangelina's house was located on. They made their descent, and Evangelina sighed with relief when she saw that the lights were still out—her father hadn't returned yet.

"Stay here for a bit," she told Diome. "I'll get something for you."

Unlocking the door with her magic, she rushed upstairs to her room, grabbed a bag, some sweaters and trousers, and hurried back outside.

"This is a magical bag that can fit in everything. I put three sweaters and trousers of mine in it, so you'll have spare clothes to change into. We're the same height and everything, so I think they'll fit you fine."

Diome gave her a hug. "Thank you, Evangelina."

Evangelina shook her head. "I did nothing."

"You did everything," Diome corrected her. "So how do I get back to Horizon Park? I'll wash up there and see if I can find a place to sleep there."

"Just past those clouds, and fly all the way downward. Be careful, Diome. I don't think there are any angels awake now, but it's best to be careful."

"I will. Good night."

They kissed each other goodbye, and Evangelina watched his black figure soar across the rippling clouds, dip low, and leave her view.

Veiled by the vapory clouds, the serene moon remained perched in the sky, surrounded by thousands of stars. Evangelina retraced her steps into her house, her mind still replaying the whimsical memories they had woven together. Worth their weight in gold, they were recollections she would treasure for an eternity. In her mind, heart, and soul, tonight would last forevermore.

HERMIONE LEE

Chapter Twelve

Sacrifices
(Diome)

A light fog misted Horizon Park, whispering chills in the air. Glittering dewdrops clung onto the tufts of grass, some plummeting to the ground while others trailed down the length of the grass like snails. Diome summoned a black fireball and dried himself after making sure no humans were nearby. When he made sure nobody was looking in his direction, he built a small black bonfire on the ground on the pile of sticks and twigs he had gathered.

He was on the run, but he didn't mind being homeless. Anywhere was better than being in the Burning Bowels. He loved the Land of Heavenly Dreams, but could not stay there and risk being discovered by the vengeful angels. They would all murder him in no time. Here, in the shadows in the woods by Horizon Park, he was safe. Uncomfortable and bedraggled, but at least he had a chance of surviving. The tree roots, twigs, and dry leaves were his companions, and the lush canopy of verdant leaves and thick branches were his roof. After sleeping on the mattress of leaves for a long while, he had gotten used to his new identity as a runaway devil.

It had been two weeks since Evangelina's disastrous debutante ball. For many nights, he slept in Horizon Park, washed up in the river in the early morning when the birds were chirping, and headed to school afterward. Evangelina had given him two sweaters, three pairs of jeans, and a bar of soap, and those were the only things he was living on. Diome had never considered himself strong, but now that he had no other choice, he could only grow. His only two options were one, returning to the Burning Bowels and getting executed by the devils after a possible public shaming, and two, staying in the human world and praying the devils wouldn't capture him. Neither sounded appealing. He only wanted a peaceful life with Evangelina, but an invisible force conspired against him.

Nevertheless, Diome wasn't defeated. The harder he fought to maintain his relationship with Evangelina, the more he loved her. Like the immaculate moon that accompanied and watched over him like a guardian every night, she was his beacon, his light, his everything. He would climb every mountain, cross every ocean, and travel to the ends of the world if she told him to do so. It was his love for Evangelina that kept him striving, that gave him hope, that kindled faith in him on his darkest nights. He had promised to remain with her no matter what. A little coldness and fatigue was nothing compared to the dazzling future they would have together.

On many sleepless nights, Diome remembered how powerless he had felt when realizing he loved Evangelina. Love had seemed useless to him then. Rather than an invincible diamond, it couldn't break through any barriers or shatter the age-long rivalry between the angels and devils. But now, he realized how wrong he had been. Unlike a bomb, love couldn't destroy the angels and devils' hatred for each other, but it gave them—him and Evangelina—hope. As long as there was hope, as long as hope was still alive, everything would still be possible. Hope gave them the audacity to dream, to believe, to make a wish. Like a booster shot, it mounted their will to march toward a better, brighter future. The knowledge that Evangelina would forever stay with him and never abandon her commitment instilled an unprecedented strength in him that he never imagined existed. Alone, he couldn't have braved the disasters that threatened to thwart their romance, but now that they were together, they were unstoppable. With hope for the best, support for each other, and eagerness for their future, he and Evangelina could conquer every obstacle in their way and make the impossible a reality.

****

After a morning bath, Diome donned his clothes and washed his dirty ones. He stuffed his sweater, pants, and undergarments into the magical bag Evangelina had given him, got out his books, and set off for school. He missed the hot showers, the food, and his bed. However, if living in the park for one more day meant he could stay alive and keep Evangelina safe one more day, he would do it in a heartbeat. Therefore, he had no complaints. Everything he did, every choice he made was for the best.

"Diome," Evangelina called.

He glanced over his shoulder and smiled, his face lighting up in an instant. "Evangelina, it's you."

Every day, he looked forward to seeing her. The brief few hours at school were enough to fuel him with courage to face the long, endless nights.

He and Evangelina entered the cafeteria, and she purchased two muffins and sandwiches.

"One each for you." She handed him a muffin and a sandwich. "You must be starving."

"Thank you," replied Diome.

Evangelina studied him, guilt evident in her gaze. "I'm so sorry you made so many sacrifices just for me. You shouldn't—"

"For you? For us, you mean. Evangelina, I want a future with you. I'm not a billionaire or a celebrity. I'm not rich or famous or successful in any way. But I will catch you whenever you fall, and I want to stand with you forever and ever. I want to grow old with you, see your hair gray, and I want to see our children age. We've got so many unfinished dreams, so many possibilities together. This—being on the run, it's nothing compared to protecting our love."

Evangelina sighed and rested her chin on her palm. "I wish I could do something to help. Yesterday and the day before that, I navigated all the floating islands by my house—ten of them, actually. But none of them are safe enough."

Diome shook his head. "You know there's no way I can live in the Land of Heavenly Dreams."

"If you lived closer to me, I could bring you food and necessities," Evangelina insisted, though her confidence was dwindling like a candle burning down to its core.

Diome grasped her hand. "Don't feel guilty. Perhaps I can sneak back into the Burning Bowels one day and find a cave to hide there."

"But when? When will all this end? You can't come to the Land of Heavenly Dreams, and you can't go home either. This is all my fault, and—"

"That's not true," Diome insisted.

"It's a fact. If I hadn't been at the ball, you wouldn't have to save me."

Diome rubbed his eyes, exhausted. "But it's the devils who initiated the fight. Like they always did."

"Don't blame yourself, Diome. It's got nothing to do with you. I wouldn't be here if you hadn't come for me in time and stopped Lenora. That was very noble of you."

"I knew it would expose myself—the devils would know I was on your side, but it looked like an accident, right? She tried to stab you, so I waved her hand away, and the knife fell and cut her in the stomach. I didn't want to kill her either, but that was an act of self-defense."

Evangelina nodded. "I know you meant well, Diome. It's the most gallant thing you've ever done. But it's so unfair that you have to suffer because you did something so noble. The devils won't ever accept you because you exposed yourself to protect me. It's all my—"

Diome held up a hand to interrupt her. "It's nobody's fault. None of us asked for it. Neither of us wanted all these tragedies to happen. From the start. We didn't deserve this, the rivalry, the battles, the trauma of losing family members. But just because we didn't deserve them doesn't mean they won't happen. If there's anything I've learned during the past few weeks, it's that life isn't and never has been fair. Come to think of it, it's destined to be unfair from the start. Nobody gets to choose their parents, their family, and the house they grow up in. You have the extremist devils jabbering about how ruthless and sanctimonious angels are, and on the other hand, you have moderate and pacifists devils whose only wish in the world is for the rivalry between the two sides to end. But the truth is, nothing works in their favors—either way. For the extremists, the angels won't be eradicated from the world, and for the moderates and pacifists, the war will never end. Let's face it, none of us have as much control over our lives as we want. Accidents happen out of the blue, and so do surprises. Nobody knows whether tomorrow will be better or worse than today. Nothing is predictable."

Evangelina finished the last of her muffin. "That's true. And who's to tell? I wish I could do something to help you, though. It's not any of our fault things evolved into what it is now, but even if I didn't feel a sliver of responsibility, I don't want to see you alone and homeless every night. I wish you could live in a hotel or something, but I can't ask my father for money. If he knew what I'd do with it—"

"Evangelina, it's all right," Diome comforted her. "Please, you don't have to do anything more for me. Just stay with me until the end."

Anxiety flitted across Evangelina's face like a bird. "The end?"

"Until all this drama ends ... assuming it ever will. We just have to have faith, I guess."

"Easier said than done," Evangelina replied. "It's hard to have faith when everything is so bleak."

Diome kissed her on the cheek. "We never know what will happen tomorrow, do we? And no matter what happens, we'll run at it and not run from it. In that case, if we're going to face every tomorrow with courage, why don't we remain optimistic instead?"

The old Diome would never have said that. But like a metamorphosis, the time he spent with Evangelina had wrapped his insecure self in a chrysalis and transformed him into a butterfly. Now he was no longer the devil he had been, the devil who feared to pursue his dreams. Evangelina had filled up the void in him and shown him he had the capacity to be stronger than he ever knew. They were two sparks of light navigating a labyrinth of tunnels in a cave of darkness, two fireflies who needed each other's glow to see through the blackness unfolding before them. Only by staying with and helping each other could they brave the turmoil resisting their efforts to conquer the obstacles in their way.

****

The six periods of class—homeroom, English, geography, physics, math, and P.E. passed in no time, and soon, school ended.

"I'll treat you to some afternoon tea," Evangelina

proposed when they met each other outside the school building.

"Sounds fantastic," replied Diome. "One day, I'd like to go to Horizon Beach again."

"To recreate our first date?" Evangelina asked. "I'm in."

They arrived at a vintage coffee shop with a patio in front of it. Evangelina ordered a peach milkshake, and Diome got some chocolate waffles with whipped cream.

"One day." Diome took a bite of his snack. "I'll invite you to afternoon tea. I can find work somewhere and make money. Anyway, I can't return to the Burning Bowels. I might as well settle down here."

Evangelina abandoned her interest in her peach milkshake. "What will they do if they capture you?"

"Execute me, perhaps. I don't know the penalty, though. None of the devils have been accused of treason for fraternizing with the angels before. I might be the first in history."

It was something to be proud of, something worthy of a badge. Diome was the only devil he knew of who dared to rebel against the majority, who had the audacity to question their beliefs. However, he didn't have the courage to fly back into the Burning Bowels and accept the consequences of his actions. He couldn't die. He had to live on for himself, for Evangelina, for the prospect of them having a blissful future together.

"You're a hero," gushed Evangelina, her eyes shining with respect. "I mean it, Diome. Weren't you scared that night?"

"I was scared," Diome admitted. "But bravery isn't being unafraid. It's overcoming fear when you are afraid.

"Spoken like a true philosopher," replied Evangelina, nodding in fervent agreement.

"Who am I, then? Socrates, Aristotle, or Plato?" quipped Diome, making her giggle.

"You're the fourth philosopher." Evangelina humored him.

"Oh, I wonder why you're the only one who knows my name as a great philosopher," Diome joked.

"You went against the grain and didn't fit the societal expectations," Evangelina replied.

"But so did those three, right? They didn't care what people thought of them. Instead, they stuck to their beliefs and promoted their philosophies."

Evangelina suddenly donned a solemn expression. "They're kind of like us, you know. Pioneers. Outcasts. Misfits. They couldn't stand the conformists and went out of their way to question things others took for granted. We never thought it was right to take a life, angel or devil, while everyone else around us pretends it's as normal as eating breakfast."

"We're way above the sheep-like fools who believe in destroying innocent lives," Diome agreed. "But come to think of it, they're kind of pitiful. They've been fed propaganda by their families, brainwashed to hate each other, and probably scolded when trying to challenge their parents' beliefs."

"Do you think there are any angels and devils like us out there?" Evangelina asked.

Diome pondered her question for a while. "There must be. We're not the only ones."

"How so?" Evangelina asked. "And how can you know for sure?"

"Well, it's nice to assume we're not the only ones fighting for our beliefs, right?"

Evangelina smiled. "Confirmation bias. But I like your theory. Either way is possible—either we're the only misfits or we're not. Since we have no way of finding out the truth, why don't we just believe whatever comforts us the most?"

"Speaking words of wisdom," began Diome. "I'm glad we think alike."

"Of course. That's why we're more than friends," Evangelina replied.

When the sun made its descent, Diome walked Evangelina to Horizon Park and watched her take off, ascending into the twilight skies, a charming palette of purple and pink. He yearned, more than anything, to join her above the clouds. The Land of Heavenly Dreams was an ethereal realm of utmost beauty. Now that Diome had seen all the floating islands, satiny lawns, and vibrant blossoms in the divine, celestial nation way up high, he longed for the possibility to stay with her in the clouds forever.

Perhaps, he thought as he wandered the streets, past the assortment of shops and the rainbow of signs, there would come a day when the angels and devils could negotiate together at a table and talk peace. Maybe someday they could visit each other freely, court each other, get married, and have baby demi-angels and demi-devils together. They could go to the same schools, frolic in the Land of Heavenly Dreams in summer, and evade the frigid winter in the Burning Bowels. One day, when mutual peace was no longer a luxury for them, they could all co-exist in pure harmony and be a huge family together.

Footsteps. Coming from behind him. Diome paused. The pounding feet stopped. He glanced over his shoulder and spied two strong men standing behind him.

"That's the one," the taller man snapped. "Take him."

Before Diome could process what was happening, someone punched his head. A tide of darkness swept away his consciousness.

When his sluggish mind encountered reality, his body was draped over a hard rock. The red air around him made him realize, with a pang of horror, that he was back in the Burning Bowels.

Diome struggled to sit up, and he spotted a crowd of devils—there must have been at least a hundred of them—around him. The two thugs who had knocked him out were standing beside him, tall, blazing torches clutched in their hands.

"He just came around," the shorter one cut in. "Can we tie him to the stake, sir?"

"Stop asking questions and do it," snapped the taller devil.

No, thought Diome. The sudden realization of his dire situation rattled him, and he fought back against the pair of arms that grappled with him. Struggling to kick away the devil, he got to his feet.

"I can't," whimpered the short devil. "He's too strong."

"Useless thing," the tall devil spat. He breezed over to Diome and punched him in the stomach.

Pain reverberating in his body, Diome crouched down, his face squishing with anguish. He had no other choice but to comply with the devil. A rope bound his right hand to a sturdy plank, and another wound itself around his left arm. The devil knelt down and tied his feet to the stake, while Diome, who had surrendered to his predicament, closed his eyes.

"Look here, devils," the tall devil told the crowd of bystanders. "This thing, he's a traitor to our kind, a backstabber who murdered a fellow devil to save an angel, a lowly piece of filth."

A roar of outrage erupted from the crowd, their faces tinted vermillion by the furious glow of the lava ocean below. Among the constellation of angry faces, Diome could see his mother weeping in the back of the crowd. When her gaze met his, her expression contorted into one of wrath.

"Kill him!"

"That we will," the tall devil declared. "But not so soon. He deserves a punishment worse than death."

Diome saw his mother making her way to the front of the crowd. "Jackson," she addressed the tall devil. "May I speak to the crowd?"

Jackson nodded. "You may."

Diome's mother turned to face the indignant devils. "Devils of the Burning Bowels." She knelt before them. Her black, hip-length curls flapped in the sizzling heat. "I apologize to all of you for the evil deeds my son has committed. I too mourn and grieve the death of the innocent, heroic devil who fell in battle, Lenora Lenoir. Jackson and Robert ventured into the human world to bring my son back, and for that, I am grateful. To ensure justice can be done, I give them permission to punish my son in any way they so desire."

"Mom," quavered Diome.

His mother stood up, faced him, and slapped him across the face. "You are no son of mine!" she growled. "I will not bear the shame of being associated with a traitor to our kind!"

With livid red eyes, she stormed back into the crowd without a second glance at Diome.

"Thank you, ma'am, for your support and for not obstructing in justice," Jackson continued. "Indeed, every culprit deserves a punishment befitting their crime. And as for you, little traitor ... "

Jackson dumped a bucket of water on Diome's head, and a chill spread through his body. He shivered, his ears grazed by the jeers and cheers thundering from the crowd, an uproar of approval. Something long and black like a snake flew toward him, a whip of thorns. It struck his legs again and again, inflicting agony beyond agony. Diome bit his lips, determined not to let a cry of pain escape his lips. Bound to the stake, he remained indifferent and tight-lipped, as if his body was burning with the agony of a thousand flames.

Blood. It trickled down his legs, hot and fierce. The metallic tang made him sick. His stomach churned, and bile rose to his throat. He coughed, but nothing came out. His legs were a patchwork of gashes that told a story of unspeakable horror. Tortured flesh, skin cut and sliced without mercy.

Something was tearing at Diome, shredding him apart. Had he imagined it? He wished it would stop. Fire was sizzling, scorching, searing in him. His blood was turning into something hotter than lava. It boiled in him, burning his veins and spreading through him like a wildfire. A thousand scalding knives were pressing at his skin, white-hot pain devouring him the same way a ravenous beast devoured its prey. Unable to bear the torture anymore, Diome screamed, cried, kicked, flailed, implored to nobody in particular. He thought of Evangelina, the sweet angel who had been the purpose of his life. In his final moments, she was the only person he missed. If he had never met her, the situation would never have erupted into the chaotic mess that was the present. However, if he could die for her, if his dying meant the devils' hatred for the angels—or at least for Evangelina and her family—would lessen, he would embrace death, greet it like a friend. He felt not an iota of remorse for his actions, and no, he didn't lament everything he had sacrificed for her, for their beautiful romance. His only regret was that if he couldn't survive the torture, if he lost his final battle and died at the hands of the insane devils who were fueled with rage and vengeance, he would never again get to see Evangelina's angelic face or hear her sweet, smooth voice.

Diome imagined the innumerable adventures they could have had, the countless possibilities that awaited them in the future. If he died, he would never get to propose to her or see the joy glistening in her eyes. He mourned the numerous delightful memories that would dissolve with his existence the second he breathed his last. Their wedding, the sight of her in a pristine white gown gliding down an aisle like a swan, the memorable moment when they found out she was pregnant with a baby, the baby's first cries, first words, and first steps ...

No, Diome had to hold on, had to cling onto dear life, if only to be the guardian of the countless recollections he would create with his beloved Evangelina. Now numb to the constant flow of pain flooding every inch of his body, a bizarre cloud of oblivion fogged his mind as his head drooped. He drifted, drifted, drifted, until he was no more.

Diome's mind flitted in and out of consciousness during what felt like the next hour. The excruciating torrents of pain hadn't ceased their ruthless attacks. The agony came in bouts no longer a steady stream of pain. He lost his sense of time, and soon, he couldn't feel his limbs anymore.

The crowd was still cheering and egging Jackson on, but Diome no longer cared. Blood, sweat, and tears became one on his face and cheeks. They pressed their torches to his bloody legs, and he screamed until his throat grew hoarse. His clothes were soaked, and his wings were torn. He knew they would mend themselves in a matter of days, for devil wings could heal themselves when damaged, but he would never live to see them mended. He thought of the saying his fifth grade English teacher had mentioned in class: *If you plummet into a valley, the only way you can go is up.*

Diome wondered where the dead went when disembarking from the mortal plane. That was his last thought before oblivion closed around his mind again.

****

A haze of red and orange bloomed before Diome's eyes as he came to. He was still alive. That was the first notion that entered his mind.

Alive. That meant he had hope, didn't he? As feeble as it was, like a flickering candle in the wind, one couldn't deny its existence.

Diome sat up, navigating his surroundings. A cell with metal bars. That was where he was locked.

Was there an exit? A window, perhaps? He gazed around and spotted, to his surprise, a window high above him, right below the ceiling. Whoever locked him here hadn't removed his wings, a careless move. Now, a beacon of hope had been lit in his dull, hopeless heart.

Diome was still in pain, in great agony. His skin was red and raw, and blood streaked down his legs in rivers of burgundy. However, the physical agony was nothing compared to his will to live. Ignoring the pain that clawed at his flesh, he moved his wings, felt his feet depart from the ground, and neared the window.

Since it was locked from outside, Diome needed a hammer or a tool hard enough to shatter the glass. He shot a stream of black sparks at the glass, but it remained intact. Then, he fired a zap of black light at the window, but his attempts ended in vain.

What tools could he use? His cell was empty, with only the bars, the bricked walls, and the small window on top. And as for him, he had nothing with him that could do enough damage to the window, except ...

Diome's gaze landed on his boots. Might they

prove to be useful? He would make a massive racket, that was for sure. But for freedom, for the chance to meet Evangelina again, he was willing to try.

Removing one of his boots, he moved away from the window. Summoning all the strength he possessed, he smashed it at the little square of glass. Nothing. Diome tried again, although every muscle in him was burning in pain. Still nothing. He edged closer to the window and scrutinized it. Was it strengthened by magic?

Then, he spotted it–a small crack zigzagging on the glassy surface. It was thin and tiny, so small it could have been invisible. However, the sight of it imbued an unnamable flood of energy in him. Fueled by determination, he smashed his boot into the window another three times, and with a crack, it shattered.

"Who's there?" someone cut in.

Diome didn't look over his shoulder. Squeezing through the window, he pushed himself out, relieved his was slim enough to fit through the hole.

"It's the traitor, Diome Lenoir!" another exclaimed. "Grab him!"

With a flap of his leathery wings, Diome took off, soaring through the air and crossing the lava ocean. He ignored the pain coursing through him, through his wings. Heat burned and blazed in him, and a searing sensation tore through his senses. Yet now, he couldn't be more grateful for the pain. Every ounce of it reminded him he was alive and that he had survived the torture. Currents of air flooded his nose and issued from it in streams.

Diome breathed, savoring the clean air. He was a free devil now. Behind him, he could hear the furious shouts of the guards in the jail, but he was far from them. A few skillful maneuvers around three buildings, and he could no longer hear the flapping of their wings.

He would return to the human world and seek help at the hospital. It was the only place he could be safe, away from the devils who wanted to see him broken, to hear his screams, to see him beaten and broken. Although he could understand their fury, he didn't regret protecting Evangelina. He hadn't stabbed Lenora. No, she had brought that on herself. All Diome had done was shield Evangelina from a fatal blow.

As he reached the cave that connected the Burning Bowels to the human world, he found his stamina sapping, his strength dissolving. Perhaps it was from fatigue, or perhaps the adrenaline pumping through him had faded now that he was out of danger. Diome's wings beat in a wild attempt to rise to freedom, to escape the shackles this infernal dungeon of flames and darkness.

It was a tough ascent, for he waged a war against not only his intense fatigue but also his wounds. Still, he couldn't surrender. The guards would come across him if he didn't take action now. Since he was captured in the human world, they might figure out his destination. He couldn't let them imprison him again. If they caught him and executed him, all his dreams would turn to dust. Worse, he would never see Evangelina's charming face again. There would be no proposal, no wedding, no newborn babies, no family memories.

And it was that very notion—the need, the want, the longing for his Evangelina that boosted his spirits, that made him forget his exhaustion and resurrected his ambition.

Driven by a madness, a primeval, instinctive desire to survive, Diome shot up, hurtling through the darkness. Warm air whooshed in his ears, and even though his injuries had slowed him down, his determination was enough to overpower the limits of his feeble condition.

Miracles happened, he told himself. After being tormented and humiliated in public, he was in great pain, but his heart was still beating, and his pulse was still vibrating in his wrists. The old Diome, a coward, a loser, a timid devil, could never have braved the trauma and scars. But now, he was born anew.

Diome rose, he rose, and he rose from the pit of darkness, an unstoppable rocket on a sacred mission. He felt superhuman for some reason. His steely will had taken full control over his mind. No longer in captivity, he knew the only person he could rely on, the only guardian he could trust right now was himself. He turned left at the end and exited the tunnel that connected his world to the humans'.

Outside, fresh, sweet oxygen greeted his lungs. The glittering sky, gemmed with billions of bright, sparkling stars, appeared to delight in his success. Diome flew over the cliff and landed in a smooth touchdown.

It was over. The torture was over. Finally. At long last. Diome removed his wings, shrunk them, and hid them in the pocket of his dirty trousers. Then, he took refuge behind a lush shrub large enough to shield his figure from the cave. He lay down on the grass, his limbs consumed by relaxation despite the nagging stabs of pain. The sight of the silver stars in the sublime universe misted his eyes as he recounted his treacherous journey and the power the shame and torture had ignited in his heart. He was a general who had won the most crucial war, a warrior who had overcome his biggest enemy—himself.

Closing his eyes, he inhaled a lungful of air. Before this moment, he had never contemplated how divine it felt to be free.

HERMIONE LEE

Chapter Thirteen
Because of Love
(Evangelina)

Evangelina donned a black asymmetrical sweater, a white pleated skirt that reached her knees, and a pair of dark brown boots. Today was a Friday, and soon their exams would be coming up. It would be wise to go to school early today, she had thought, but the cold weather made inertia mount in her.

No matter what, though, she had to get up at seven o'clock and go to school. Donning her wings and bidding goodbye to her father, who was still asleep in his room, she left the house and made her descent. He knew about the devils' invasion during the ball, but Evangelina left out all the details about Diome. It was fortunate their little date afterward went undiscovered due to the perfect timing that her father had returned home later than she. When she told him her handsome rescuer was a devil, though, he refused to believe her. None of the angels at the venue were conscious enough to remember Diome and how he had saved her, so his noble, chivalrous gesture became a secret between him and Evangelina.

The clouds lay flat and low today, a thin sea of white below her. Different from the swirling waves of fluffy clouds on most days, they weren't as flamboyant. The sun was shining, its incandescent and iridescent rays streaming down on Evangelina, engulfing her in a canopy of golden light. Yet despite the gentle warmth emanating from above, the air was cold and frigid. Typical for a mundane December day.

Evangelina loved mornings. That was the time of a day she could never be depressed. Every morning, the world, awake from its deep slumber, came alive again. Everything glowed with the jovial enthusiasm of a new life, a flawless beginning.

When she arrived at Horizon Park, her emergence went fortunately unnoticed by the senior citizens, who had taken a sudden interest in a baby in a passing stroller. She removed her wings, shrunk them, and stuffed them into her school bag at top speed. Then, she hurried away before anyone else could see her.

The security guard, Ms. Jenson, stopped her at the gates.

"Yes?" Evangelina asked.

"A letter for you from Horizon Hospital." Ms. Jensen handed her a white envelope with her name scribbled across the front.

So anxious that she forgot to even thank her, Evangelina ripped it open and perused the letter. Her heart almost stopped when she recognized Diome's handwriting.

Evangelina,

The devils caught me yesterday, brought me back to the Burning Bowels, and locked me in a cell after torturing me. I escaped and am now at room 703 in Horizon Hospital. I'll have to play hooky next week because I can't let the school know what happened. Just writing this letter to let you know where I am. I love you, as always.

Diome

Evangelina stared at the letter for a few moments, then turned on her heels and hurried in the direction of the hospital. It was only five blocks away from the school, but to Evangelina, it felt like five miles. Her heeled boots made the distance even harder to walk, but her concern for Diome made her forget the pain in her feet. He had been tortured. How badly was he injured? The letter indicated almost nothing about the seriousness of the situation. And worse, where had the devils abducted him? Would they come out and launch a search party to find him? What if the human world was no longer safe—for either of them?

Horizon Hospital had a high, vaulted ceiling, and was adorned with green stripes and pretty leaves. A fountain with a spherical glass ball was nestled in the middle of the lobby. However, Evangelina was in a hurry. She didn't have the heart to admire the decorations. She caught an ascending elevator, dashed in, and jabbed the button marked six.

When she arrived, she strode along the hallway, searching for the number 659. At last, she found it at the end of the corridor.

"Diome?" Evangelina rushed in. "Diome, are you all right?"

He was lying on the bed, his legs wrapped up like a mummy. Dried blood seeped from the bandages, dying them burgundy.

"Evangelina, you're here," he replied, slightly weaker than usual.

"Diome, I ... What happened?"

He smiled in a reassuring fashion. "Don't worry, I'll be all right. It takes devil skin a week to heal from burns. My parents told me that before. Just a second-degree burn on my legs."

"Just?" Evangelina asked, stunned by his optimism. "What in the world did they do to you? And how did you escape?"

"After we parted ways yesterday, I was wandering

in town. Then, I heard some footsteps and saw two devils behind me. They knocked me out, brought me back to the Burning Bowels, tied me to a stake, and tortured me. But I somehow survived, and when I woke up in a cell, I escaped and flew out of the Burning Bowels. I collapsed on the cliff above the entrance to the Burning Bowels, and when I woke up, I was in the hospital."

"Did the doctors notice anything unusual?" Evangelina pressed on.

"No. They only bandaged my wounds and brought me here. It was nice of them to bring my letter to Horizon High, though. I overheard two nurses talking about sending their daughters to school yesterday, so I wrote a letter and asked them to give it to the security guard and ask her to hand it to you."

"What a clever idea," Evangelina remarked. "I wouldn't have thought of it. Did the doctors ask you how you got hurt? What did you tell them?"

"That I burned myself by accident when boiling water and spilled it over my legs."

Evangelina nodded, though still concerned. "The human world isn't safe for you anymore. Where will you go after being discharged?"

Diome sighed, and his gaze betrayed sadness. "I don't know. There's no way I'd ever set foot back in the Burning Bowels. I'm a fugitive now. Are there any shelters in Horizon?"

Evangelina shrugged. "I have no idea. Maybe if you found a shop to sleep in ... "

"What shopkeeper would let a homeless boy in?" Diome asked.

Evangelina hung her head. "If it hadn't been for the debutante ball ... "

"That's in the past," Diome consoled her. "Don't dwell on it."

Evangelina remained silent for a while. "I'll find you an island to live on," she replied.

Diome contemplated the idea. "Well, why not? If it's not too much trouble. Anyway, I can't go back to the Burning Bowels or live on the streets. I'd get killed either way, sooner or later."

"I can't imagine what you went through in the Burning Bowels," murmured Evangelina. "Were you scared?"

"No. But Evangelina, when they were whipping and burning me, I thought of you. The only reason I'm still alive, the only reason I hadn't given in was because I needed you. I want to grow old with you, propose to you, see you walk down the aisle, trade vows with you, watch our baby age, and walk you through all the stages of life. The thought—losing so many incredible possibilities with you—was what kept me going, what made me stay strong."

A powerful surge of emotion washed over Evangelina. She felt a well of warm honey rise in her chest. Of course, they had always loved each other with all their hearts, but never did she know she meant that much to him. Moved by his words, Evangelina held his hand and kissed it.

"Diome, you mean the world to me too."

****

For the next week, Evangelina visited Diome in the hospital every day, bringing him fresh fruit, bread, snacks, and meals. She also promised to cover the medical bill, since Diome wouldn't be here if he hadn't been unwelcome in the Burning Bowels, and she felt responsible for that. Often she read books to him, fed him some school gossip, and told him stories. Evangelina knew love had created a strong bond between them, but she hadn't known how powerful it was until now. Diome didn't blame her for his accident. On the contrary, they only grew closer to each other. His face lit up every time she entered his room. Evangelina felt terrible for Diome's predicament. She couldn't help thinking he had sacrificed more in this relationship than she, becoming a total outcast among the devils and being homeless for two weeks. However, she was doing all she could to help, to make sure Diome wouldn't be all alone anymore.

One day at midnight, Evangelina snuck out of the house and spent an hour navigating the floating islands around hers. There were three adjacent to the island where she lived, which she didn't have to fly longer than a minute to reach. One was small, a random chunk of rocky land with some bare rocks stacked in the middle. Another had many slopes and a well on the hilltop, but the third one had a small forest that appeared uninhabited. Evangelina lit the darkness by summoning an orb of yellow light before proceeding. The dense trees gave off a sense of foreboding, but otherwise was safe enough. The sanctuary of the trees were enough to shield Diome. A river, some grottos, and white toadstools with blue polka-dots rested behind the trees, behind the thin veil of mist.

Fluttering from tree to tree and scouting for any signs of habitation, Evangelina wondered if this forest would suit Diome. It was more than a little cold in there, but he could build a fire to keep himself warm, couldn't he? And the most important thing now was for him to have a place to settle.

Just when Evangelina thought her day couldn't get better, she spotted a wooden tree house a few feet above her resting on a sturdy branch. She climbed up the rope ladder under it, and discovered it was much larger than it appeared from the outside. The abandoned tree house didn't belong to anyone It was empty, and nobody had lived there in ages, as evidenced by the weeds growing from the cracks in the floor. The walls were covered with streaks and stripes of rainwater—had it rained here yesterday? Yet despite the flaws, the tree house was big enough to fit a sleeping bag or two. It was damp and dark inside, but Evangelina dried the moist planks with her magic and did her best to make the tree house cozy.

Gazing down at the river below, Evangelina took a moment to appreciate how picturesque the little island was. Blossoms glittered at the foot of the giant trees, and above the river was a stone bridge. Under the pale moonlight that seeped through the canopy of leaves overhead, the undulating waves glittered eerily, mysteriously, as though beckoning to her.

This was the place. Evangelina dried the tree house with magic and gazed around it proudly. She hadn't spotted this island before, or perhaps, she had ruled it out due to the ominous woods in fear there were unknown dangers waiting inside. But now that she knew it was safe, she could ask Diome how he felt about her new discovery.

****

"What are you doing, Evangelina?" hissed Diome. "We're not supposed to be here. Or at least, I'm not. If the angels see me, I'm dead meat."

"Nonsense," said Evangelina. "Did you see any angels along the way? This island is much lower than the one I'm on. It's closer to the human world below, which makes it more convenient for you to go to school."

"Are you sure there's nobody around?" Diome asked, pursing his lips. "No angels?"

Evangelina shook her head as they plunged deeper into the forest. "I doubt it."

"You doubt it?"

"Look, I've been coming here every day after visiting you in the hospital for the past week. I think it's safe."

Six days had gone by since the night she had first set foot in this enigmatic forest. Diome had recovered and regained most of his strength. Evangelina understood his concerns about setting foot in the Land of Heavenly Dreams after the unpleasant experience at the ball. However, she hoped he wouldn't decline her offer, for living on the streets without a proper home could get him killed anytime.

"I'll show you something," Evangelina suggested. "Maybe you'll change your mind after seeing it."

The colossal columns of trees glided by them as they flew through the forest. The sky, shredded into little triangular, square, and rectangular fragments by the thick leaves overhead, watched them from above the trees. Shadows draped over their flying figures like large black cloaks. Evangelina turned right ahead and sighted the tree house. Under the sunlight, she could see that it was clad in moss and draped with ivy. Gesturing for Diome to climb up the creaky rope ladder, she made a mental note to fix the frayed edges.

"What do you think?" she asked, breathless, after clambering up after him.

Diome studied the tree house. "I like it." He smiled. "It's really pretty. And I love the little window."

"You don't look thrilled. What's the matter? What are you worrying about?" Evangelina asked, sensing the uneasiness in his eyes.

"Flying down to the human world. I'm scared the other angels will see me."

Evangelina contemplated that for a while. "I'll stop by here every morning and escort you back to your tree house after school. How's that?"

Diome frowned. "What if any angels see you? I'm already unwelcome among my people. I don't want the same to happen to you."

"Diome, I don't care what they think of me," Evangelina replied. "I'm not popular among the angels. My former classmates are longer in contact with me, and hardly anyone knows me now. It doesn't matter whether I'm an outcast or not. Because no matter what, I still have you, don't I?"

Diome's eyes shone with hope. "Really?"

"Really. From tomorrow on, we'll leave for school together."

"I can't believe this. You're all right with the idea of exposing how you're in alliance with a devil, and you're not the least scared about how the angels will punish you?"

Evangelina nodded, gazing earnestly into his eyes. "I'd do anything for you, Diome."

Diome wrapped his arms around her in a fierce hug. "If only you knew how perfect you are."

"I wish you didn't have to lose your home," whispered Evangelina. "The devils called you a traitor because they saw you killing Lenora to save me. They wouldn't have found out about us and kicked you out if—"

"I'm better off without them," remarked Diome. "You're worth more than a billion of them. And anyway, I'm proud to be with you, and I'm not afraid to let them know."

He pressed his lips to hers, and Evangelina lost herself in the pure bliss that enveloped her in a torrent of blissful sensations. She savored his lips, relishing the tingling sensation that crept down her spine. He was hers, and she was his. It was unquestionable, as certain as the sun and moon would rise every day and night. When they were holding each other, when she was in his proximity, she felt an unnamable surge of comfort. It was a powerful yet tender emotion words failed to describe. Affection, security, and an unexplainable wave of strength. The intense, ardent love Diome brought had overpowered her reason and charmed her heart. In the present, she saw, felt, and thought of only Diome. It was pure, pure euphoria.

When they leaned back to catch their breath, Evangelina saw her smile reflected on his face, tinted with a slight shyness.

"I'm glad I'm not alone," he told her. She echoed his sentiment.

In the tree house, they sat nestled against each other, watching the stray strands of sunlight streaming through the trees and hoping the peace would last forever. The sweet aroma of the wildflowers reminded them just how precious the moment was.

****

Later that afternoon, Evangelina went home and snuck out with a shrunken sleeping bag when her father was busy discussing work issues with a colleague. She flew to the island with the forest and tree house on it, glided through the trees, and spotted Diome waving to her.

"You can come in through the window," Diome told her. "Then you won't have to land on the ground."

Evangelina tried, but she was too big to fit in.

"Damn." She flew to the rope ladder, removing her wings and climbing into the tree house. "The window's too small."

"Well, that's a good thing," replied Diome. "Then nobody will fly in through the window all of a sudden and kill me."

Evangelina enlarged and smoothed out the

sleeping bag with his help. "But they could climb up the rope ladder," she pointed out. "What if we drag the entire ladder up into the tree house? Maybe that would be safer for you. Any angels who came would think it's an abandoned tree house with a broken ladder, and they'd leave you alone. Of course, they could blast the tree house apart with their magic, but I don't think any sane angel would do that unless they knew there's a devil in it. Let's face it, the chances of anyone blasting a tree house apart for no reason is pretty low."

Diome's eyes widened. "Do angels come here?"

Evangelina shrugged. "I think I spotted a few little angels playing on the rim of the island one day. But no worries, one of them said the woods were too creepy for her."

Diome nodded. "Good. We can't let them find us."

Evangelina fluffed his blanket. "I hope this is warm enough for the night."

"Definitely. I know I sound crazy, but I'd like to decorate the little space for a bit." Diome slapped a hand to his forehead. "Oh my gosh, I can't believe this ... "

Evangelina tilted her head. "What?"

"The rose you gave me. I put it in a vase by my bedside. I can't go back and get it."

Evangelina shrugged. "It's all right. I'll make you another."

She climbed down the rope ladder, flew over to a rose bush, and picked up a wilting rose. With her magic, she imbued life in the flower, and the shriveling brown petals soon became red and rosy.

"Here." Evangelina returned to the tree house. "What colors would you like?"

"Same as the one last time."

With a tap of her hand, the rose abandoned its

hearty red hue. A gradient of apple-green, ice-blue, and turquoise took over the petals.

"It's beautiful," murmured Diome, accepting the flower from her. "Evangelina, I love it. I wish I had something to give you, but I-I've got nothing."

"You've got everything to give," Evangelina consoled him. "In here." She gestured toward his heart. "I know you won't leave me, and that reassurance means more than anything. The greatest gift a person can give is love. And I'm really lucky to have all of it from you."

Diome smiled. "How do I tell the time, by the way? I don't have a clock, and my phone is already out of juice."

Evangelina peeked out the window. "When the sky lights up, I guess the sunshine will be enough to wake you up. It's not like you're surrounded by thick walls, is it? If you get up late for school, I'll make up an excuse for you. How does that sound?"

Diome chuckled. "I could play hooky. Wouldn't that be better?"

"But then I wouldn't get to see you in school," Evangelina replied. "I could come over to wake you up too. And we could fly down together and go to school. How does that sound?"

"Perfect. Let's try that tomorrow. You'd better go now. I'm worried your dad will be worried if you're gone for too long."

Evangelina nodded. "Good night, then. See you tomorrow morning."

Diome waved. She glanced over her shoulder at him one last time before descending the rope ladder and soaring into the distance.

****

The next morning, Evangelina left home thirty minutes earlier than usual. She glided over to the island with the forest, crisscrossed through the shadowy trees, and spotted Diome in the tree house.

"Morning." She climbed up the ladder.

"Hi, Evangelina. You're dressed in the colors of the sky today."

She was garbed in a white shawl, a blue blouse, gray trousers, and black kitten heels. "I didn't notice that until you mentioned it. You ready to sail the skies?"

Diome nodded. Evangelina knew he hadn't brought any textbooks to school since the day he ran away, but nobody cared or noticed. Between classes, she would lend him her books so that he could catch up with the lost progress. Fortunately, his grades were unaffected.

Draping her shawl over Diome's back so that nobody would see the black, leathery wings, Evangelina signaled for him to leave the tree house when she made sure the coast was clear.

"You can come down," she called, and he flapped his wings. The shawl dropped and landed on the stone bridge over the river.

"Sorry," Diome replied. "I'll go get it. I won't have to wear it after leaving the island, right?"

"No, but I'm afraid we'll run into some angels. What about this, I'll fly above you and try to cover your black wings?"

"Sounds like a plan," Diome replied. "Let's see it that'll work."

The two of them glided through the trees, through the shadows, and toward the light. When they reached the edge of the island, she jumped after Diome did, and they plummeted into the sea of clouds, soaring downward.

It was fortunate today was an especially cloudy day. Evangelina couldn't see five feet before her, for everything was blanketed by foggy swirls. Steering herself though the moist, warm clouds, she saw the green land rise to meet her. They made a safe landing and removed their wings, delighting in their success.

"We can do this every day from now on," Evangelina suggested.

"Definitely. I love flying in the clouds with you," Diome replied, his eyes sparkling. "There's something spectacular about soaring in the clouds, with all those floating islands above, around, and below us. It's dreamlike."

They arrived at school and headed to homeroom.

"I'm going to the bathroom for a bit to wash my hands," Evangelina told Diome. "Be back soon."

He nodded. "Can I borrow your chemistry textbook?"

"Sure." Evangelina handed him the book and left the classroom.

"Evangelina," someone piped up.

She spotted Camille and Merilee coming down the stairs. "Hey."

"How's Diome?" Camille asked. "Is he out of the hospital yet?"

Evangelina nodded. "Yesterday. He's better now."

"Is he all right? He looked really pale a while ago. And you too. What happened to you two?" Merilee asked, concerned.

"Can we help you two?" Camille asked. "If there's anything we can do, just let us know, okay? We'll do anything for you."

Evangelina wanted to confide in them, but it was impossible. Instead, she gave them a smile. "Thank you. You're great friends."

"Are you sure you don't need anything?" Merilee asked.

"It's all right. We're both going through a hard

time is all. He lost his father last month, and I lost my mother."

"I'm so sorry for your loss," murmured Merilee, sympathy brimming in her eyes.

Camille bowed her head. "Condolences. It's never easy to say goodbye to your family."

"Thank you," Evangelina replied. She felt a sudden surge of guilt for not being more open and honest with them earlier. Camille and Merilee would never judge her for whatever she told them. They were outgoing, supportive, and kind, and Evangelina wished she could reveal more, that she could share her big secret with them—that she was in fact an angel, and she was in love with a devil despite their tribal rivalry.

"Is there something else you'd like to tell us?" Camille asked, her voice gentler than ever. Apparently, she had seen the hesitation in Evangelina's eyes.

Evangelina shook her head. "I suppose I'm not ready yet."

For a fleeting moment, disappointment flitted across their faces.

"It's all right," said Camille. "We'll see you around, Evangelina."

"Good luck on everything," Merilee added.

Evangelina waved at them, and they headed over to the staircase, soon disappearing among a crowd of heads. With a heavy heart, she turned away from them and headed back to her classroom. As an angel, she was destined to be chained by secrets, unable to show the humans her true colors or confide in them details about her family and home. Diome was the sole exception, the only person she could be honest with. But then again, there was a rift between them nothing could bridge. Might a miracle dawn on them one day and bring them together forever, against all odds?

HERMIONE LEE

Chapter Fourteen

Priority
(Diome)

"Do you believe some devils, humans, and angels are born evil?" Diome asked Evangelina the next day at school. His mother's harsh words and the excruciating torture were still weighing on his heart.

Evangelina shook her head. "No. It's all about nurture, not nature."

The two of them were lying in Diome's tree house in the forest, gazing up at the leafy canopy. It was a tranquil little hideout, perfect for a recluse. Diome couldn't be more grateful for such an adorable little dwelling. She was more than a girlfriend to him after the tumultuous events they had gone through. She had done so much more than anyone else would have. They had risked their lives for each other innumerable times, and an unbreakable bond had been forged between them. It was something neither fire nor flood, neither blizzard nor storm could destroy. Rooted deeply in their hearts, it extended beyond the physical confines of their bodies and, like an umbrella, sheltered them from the trials and tribulations.

How many devils could have survived the torture? Every now and then, Diome wondered why fate had willed him to stay alive. It was as if some uncontrollable force wanted him to stay strong and resume his life. He thought of the people who were fortunate enough to survive catastrophes—the Plague, the Titanic, the Holocaust, and Chernobyl. Why did some people live to tell the tale, while others perished in the same calamity? Why was his heart still beating, his pulse still pumping?

The only explanation that crossed his mind was that fate—or the invisible hand that controlled life and death—somehow wanted him to stay alive. An unseen force, destiny, perhaps, was rooting for him and Evangelina. It was summoning all its might to keep them together. Evangelina's birthday party, his car accident, the debutante ball, and his dramatic escape from the Burning Bowels ... They could have lost their lives anytime, but to their great astonishment, they conquered all the hardships along the way.

Rolling onto his right, Diome gazed at Evangelina, who had her eyes fixed on the window in his tree house. The iridescent rays of the afternoon sun streamed through her platinum-blonde waves, giving off the impression of spun gold. How many peaceful days did they have in store for them? One? Two? Or none, perhaps? Diome thought of the day-to-day activities normal human couples would have. Going to the movies together, going on a camping trip, traveling and exploring new towns and cities ... But ever since the day he and Evangelina became a couple, disasters found them, burning down the possibility of them having an ordinary day together.

"When was the last time we had a quiet day?" Evangelina asked.

"We've had quiet days every now and then, but never did we have a peaceful day without having to worry about being caught or being ambushed."

Evangelina uttered a sigh. "It's not easy being us, huh?"

Diome glanced at her, uneasy. "You don't regret us getting together, do you?"

Evangelina shook her head and smiled, the melancholy on her face evaporating in an instant. "Not at all. Knowing you is the best thing that ever happened to me."

And Diome committed her words to his permanent memory, so that they could bring him light and hope even in his darkest hours and remind him someone loved him with all her heart.

****

Now that Diome had found a new place to settle, his spirits lifted. The tree house was far more luxurious than any refugee shelter. He considered himself the most fortunate devil in the world. Evangelina's friends Camille and Merilee were no longer concerned about him and Evangelina, for they had regained their usual joy. They sat with each other at lunch time and joked, and it was just like old times, as if nothing had ever transpired. Of course, they had no idea what either he or Evangelina had gone through. Diome wished he could confide in them, but he couldn't do so without revealing what he was. He and Evangelina were fortunate enough to remain incognito for two months, and he wasn't about to blow their cover.

"Christmas is coming!" exclaimed Merilee one day. "How are you guys planning to celebrate?"

"My family doesn't celebrate Christmas," Evangelina replied. "Do yours?"

Camille and Joey both nodded. "Ours do."

"Wish we had a Christmas dance this year," Merilee remarked with a groan. "The school had to cancel it because our budget got cut."

"Money problems," explained Camille. "Didn't we sell tons of chocolate bars last April? Where did that money go?"

"Into the Halloween dance, maybe," suggested Diome.

"It's still different," Merilee went on, pouting. "Halloween is Halloween, and Christmas is Christmas."

Lucky you, to only have to worry about the dance, thought Diome. The humans truly had no idea how fortunate they were. He would have traded places with anyone to have a mundane life with ordinary concerns— whether he appeared attractive enough, whether his grades were good enough to earn him a spot in a top university, and when the school held another dance or sports event. Instead, his life was plagued with fear, trepidation, and uncertainty. Every day, the looming terror of his demise grew more palpable than the previous. Even during the most tranquil days in his tree house, fleeting moments of panic would seize him. He jumped at the slightest noise, and on many blustery nights when the tree house creaked and moaned, he could never get enough sleep.

Diome never told Evangelina that, though. He wasn't in a position to bemoan his plight. Since he had nowhere to go, he could only stay in his tree house and be content with what he had. Evangelina had done her best to find him a safe sanctuary. Complaining about the wind and the creaking noises was beyond foolish. There were no better options at the moment, and it was either staying where he was or preparing himself for death.

The devils could have sieged him at Horizon High, but they didn't. Perhaps they decided pursuing a fugitive wasn't worth their time, and instead, they were planning a full-scale attack on the angels.

A full-scale attack on the angels. Every muscle in Diome's body froze. Could it be true? It was indeed bizarre the devils hadn't barged into Horizon High to kidnap him. Although they would risk exposing themselves to the humans, they could always conjure darkness and fool the humans into thinking it was a blackout and then grab him before escaping. Something about their silence wasn't right.

"What's the date, Camille?" Joey was asking her.

"December 22nd," replied Camille. "Last day of the term. Our school is weird in this way. Aren't students supposed to be free on the week of Christmas?"

Diome's eyes widened. It was his birthday. He had lost track of time during the past weeks that he had forgotten his birthday was coming. If only he and Evangelina could have a small celebration ... But to him, simply being alive was a luxury. He didn't dare expect anything from her. In fact, Diome wasn't even sure if he wanted to tell her, for she had done so much for him in the past weeks that he felt guilty for causing her so much trouble. He should make amends for everything, but how?

****

"What's wrong?" Evangelina asked after they left school. "You're extra quiet today."

Diome hesitated, then shook his head.

"Well, I won't make you tell me if you don't want to. I have to work on my English paper, anyway, so I'd better start working on that before thinking about anything."

"What's it about?" Diome asked.

"Edgar Allan Poe."

"Isn't he the guy who wrote *The Raven*?" Diome asked. "We studied his poem in eighth grade."

"That's him, yes. I'm guessing you know more about him than I do, so why don't we go to Sweet Nothings? You can help me get this report figured out if you like. I'll pay you."

"Oh, no, don't. I'm happy to help," replied Diome. A bubble of joy rose in him. This—a date with Evangelina—was the best birthday gift he could have asked for.

Evangelina beamed. "Great. Maybe that big

mystery of yours will escape your lips when we're working on my homework."

The two of them picked a window seat and ordered a steaming pot of peach tea. Outside, there was a light snowfall. Fluffy white flakes glided to the ground like tiny fairies. Diome shivered, grateful he had on a thick coat. Evangelina had made one for him yesterday with magic, complete with a scarf and black mittens.

"How do you like your new winter regalia?" Evangelina asked, nursing her cup of tea.

"It's very warm," replied Diome. "And I love the patterns."

Evangelina had sewn tiny snowflakes on his mittens and white skulls on his coat. The collar was furry and comfortable.

"I'm glad I finally started making clothes," said Evangelina, pleased with herself. "It wasn't as hard as I imagined. Everything's a lot quicker with magic. When I tap two pieces of fabric with my hands, they become one. Plus, embroidering things with magic is much quicker than one would assume. Anyway, we should start tackling my homework." She got out a notebook, ripped off a page, and began scrawling on her name and the date. "Which year was Poe born in? I forgot."

"1809. In Massachusetts."

Evangelina grinned, scribbling down the opening of her paper. "I knew I found the right person to ask. In what year did he die? And what was the cause of his death?"

"1849. There appears to be some controversy on how he died. It's a mystery."

Evangelina stopped writing. "He only lived for forty years. How sad. You'd think a great author like him would die a dignified death."

"He lived more than forty years, Evangelina.

People are still reading his works, still remembering him and celebrating his life. It's like he's still around."

Evangelina nodded. "That's an interesting point. Everyone will die one day, but if we make the most of our fleeting time in the world, our names will become immortal, like his. Not everyone can be remembered the way he's been, though. Do you think we will?"

Diome managed a smile. "If we end the rivalry between the angels and devils, of course."

A moment passed in silence as they both realized that was impossible.

"But I'm not very fond of the idea of being remembered posthumously," said Evangelina. "What good is that if I'm not alive to enjoy my fame and wealth?" She laughed, brightening the atmosphere. "How superficial of me," she added as an afterthought.

"Not superficial. Practical, I would say," commented Diome. "We all want to be recognized."

"From what I learned in class and read in the library, Poe didn't gain much recognition in his life. But when he died, he became some sort of literary hero. Is it better to be celebrated when you're alive but forgotten after death, or live a miserable life but be remembered by millions after you die?"

"Ah yes, a billionaire or a martyr," replied Diome, stroking his chin. "I don't know. Neither appeals to me. I just want an ordinary life. In geography, I heard one of the boys complaining to his friends about how boring yesterday was. I wish I could live a boring life like him. Why do people always want adventure and thrills?"

"Because they've never had a taste of what it's like to be different. And I don't mean 'different' the way Camille's sister has green hair."

"I know what you mean. You're talking about us. How we can never fit in with the humans. This is kind of different."

"Exactly. And same reason you want to live a boring life—because you never knew what it's like to live an ordinary life. As the saying goes, 'The grass is always greener on the other side.' All right, we've veered away from the topic. Let's get back to Poe."

Evangelina scribbled a few more lines, then stopped. "When we met at the flower shop on my first day in Horizon High, I wondered whether a sad story lies behind everything beautiful. Suppose it's the same with Poe. He lived a tragic life, but nowadays everyone glorifies his achievements without thinking about how much he went through."

"You're being more sensitive than usual today," Diome noticed. "Anything wrong?"

Evangelina shook her head. "Just nostalgic, I guess. Recalling our first conversation and all that. Reminds me of the events we've gone through. Quite a rocky journey, isn't it?"

Diome nodded. "But somehow, I don't regret it at all."

It was five when Evangelina finished her paper. The snow had slowed to a halt, and an idea bloomed in Diome's mind.

"Let's go home," Evangelina suggested. "Maybe we can talk in your tree house for a while."

"You're free or the evening, right? Could we do something special together?" Diome asked.

"Today? Why?"

Diome held his breath. "Well, today's my birthday."

Evangelina stared at him. "Really? Why didn't you tell me before?"

Diome lowered his gaze to his feet. "You're not mad, are you?"

"At the birthday boy? Not at all. Let's see, anything special around Horizon today? I think Merilee mentioned a Christmas fair in the town square. How about that?"

Diome perked up. "I'd love to go with you."

Evangelina beamed. "Then what are you waiting for?"

They paid the bill, headed out the cozy café, and made their way to the nearest bus stop.

"Let me see." Evangelina studied the bus routes on the faded poster. "Bus 2467."

Diome sat down, rubbing his hands. "Hope it's coming soon. Have you ever been to a fair before?"

"A few, yes. In the Land of Heavenly Dreams."

"I bet they were amazing," replied Diome. "The Land of Heavenly Dreams is just way superior to the Burning Bowels. You've got balls and fairs there."

"What's in the Burning Bowels, then?" Evangelina asked, sitting down beside Diome.

"Nothing but a lava ocean and tons of ugly, identical buildings. I don't want to think about the Burning Bowels."

Evangelina dropped her gaze to her lap. "Apologies."

Diome held her hand. "It's all right, Evangelina. No need to apologize. You must be curious, since you've never been there."

The bus arrived, and they got aboard.

"Are there any buses in the Burning Bowels?" Evangelina asked.

"No. They'd have to be able to fly across the lava ocean."

Evangelina giggled. "Tell you what, I had a dream about a flying tricycle yesterday. I was steering one, and you were sitting behind me."

Diome laughed at the absurdity, earning him a few glares from the senior citizens sitting across from them. "Sorry," he murmured to them. Then, to Evangelina, he said, "I wonder why you dreamed of flying tricycles."

Evangelina shrugged. "It's a mystery. I have loads of other things to worry about than a flying tricycle collapsing on me!"

They doubled over in a fit of silent giggles, just as the bus braked to an abrupt stop. The force almost made them topple over, which only made them laugh harder.

"Let's stop laughing," Diome reminded Evangelina as an old lady with a double chin glowered in their direction. He devoted his attention to the colorful buildings and tasteful signs along the streets, determined to avert Evangelina's eyes in case they both burst into laughter again.

When the bus reached the Horizon town square, the two of them hopped off.

"The old woman was ready to murder us." Evangelina shivered. "Well, we weren't very loud, were we?"

"No. But she was probably in a bad mood," replied Diome.

With a merry-go-round and countless stands, the Christmas fair was grander than he imagined. Framed by butter-yellow houses, the square was larger than the school gymnasium. Fairy lights and red-and-green pennant banners were strung overhead, forming a canopy of colors. Twilight was here, canvassing the skies in a charming blend of mauve and magenta.

"We came at the right time," Evangelina remarked.

Diome took a moment to appreciate her figure. With a lilac coat, a gray woolen hat, a furry white scarf, and long brown boots, she would put the cover models on all the fashion magazines to shame.

Steeped in yuletide festivity, jingling tunes issued from each stand. Christmas ornaments, baked snacks, and wrapping paper that came in all patterns and colors imaginable lined the stands. There were tiny glittering snowmen, Santa Clauses, and angels among the stacks of Christmas decorations. Diome felt a slight stab of disappointment, for there were no devils. The humans regarded devils as unholy creatures, so it would be unlikely for anyone to hang devil ornaments on Christmas trees.

They located a picnic table by an enormous, sinister snowman light. It was a unique snowman, he had to admit. Instead of a silly smile, this one had a frown. Perhaps it was someone's idea of a Christmas prank, he surmised. An early April Fools' Day joke.

Evangelina got them churros, pretzels, and corn dogs from a stand, and hot chocolate from another. Diome made a mental note to himself to pay her back for everything.

She returned with two steaming cups of hot cocoa and marshmallows.

"Next time, I should treat you to something nice," offered Diome. "You've been super generous for the past few weeks."

"No worries there," Evangelina replied. "Not meaning to brag here, but I do have a lot of pocket money to spare. I'll get you some birthday cake too."

Diome reddened. "It's all right. You've already done so much for me."

"You're worth it," Evangelina assured him. "Have you tried this corn dog, by the way? Let's share it."

Diome took a bite of the crunchy, savory snack. It was delicious. Never had he eaten a corn dog or visited a fair. This was a new first for him, a memorable experience. He was glad it was with Evangelina, with the most special person in his heart.

"Oh, look! That stand sells cotton candy!" Evangelina pointed at the vendor by the corn dogs. Like a little girl, she was more excited than he had ever seen her.

"Will you still be hungry after stuffing your stomach with so much food?" Diome quipped.

"I'll skip dinner." Evangelina's gaze traveled to an array of claw machines by the cotton candy stand. "What are those?"

"Claw machines," replied Diome.

"I've never seen those before," remarked Evangelina. "How do they work?"

"It's like an arcade game in which you have to manipulate the claw and try to get the prizes in the machine," Diome explained. He had seen the machines before in a few restaurants in Horizon, but he was hopeless at them.

"Prize? What prize? You get a prize for winning?" Evangelina's eyes were brighter than stars.

"Oh, yes. It varies, though. In some machines, there are stuffed animals, and in some others, candies or keychains. We can check them out after finishing our snacks."

They devoured the rest of the pretzels and churros and shared the corn dog together.

"Cheers." Diome brought his cup of cocoa to Evangelina's. "Thank you for everything tonight."

"It's not over yet," Evangelina replied. "The best is yet to come. I'll have to get a good look at those claw machines later."

"We can also look at the Christmas lights," Diome suggested.

Evangelina rested her chin on her palm, studying

the exhibition. "I see a snowman, a giant Christmas tree, some life-sized presents and snowflakes, and reindeer. It's magical, isn't it? I've never been to a fair like this before. The humans are ingenious, don't you agree?"

Diome nodded. "Imagine what they would say if they knew what we are."

Evangelina made a face. "I'm not very keen to contemplate that unfortunate situation. There are already hundreds of angels and devils who want us dead. I'd rather visualize what our future would be like if there were no prowling threats in our lives."

That was something Diome feared to imagine. Marrying Evangelina and starting a family with her. The idea sounded surreal. Too dreamlike, too abstract, and unreachable to be true. Like an iridescent bubble, beautiful yet fragile, divine yet vulnerable. All Diome craved was a serene day with Evangelina by his side. That itself would be the epitome of pure bliss.

"I'd love to have babies. Angel-devils, or devil-angels," Evangelina mused. "We could have all the normal experiences human families have. Watch the little ones take their first steps and say 'Mommy' and 'Daddy.'"

"If we relocated to the human world and severed our connections with the Land of Heavenly Dreams and the Burning Bowels, we might have that day," replied Diome, despite knowing how slim the chances were.

"Don't give up hope," Evangelina consoled him. "We need something to believe in."

"You say that as if it's realistic."

"Why can't it be?"

Ever the optimist, Evangelina always hoped for the best, no matter how unlikely it was. Diome knew he qualified as a pessimist in her eyes, but at least he was being sensible. He would never instill false hope in himself and convince himself he and Evangelina could have a bright, dazzling future with no hardships to overcome.

"Do you think people have faith because they believe in the power of believing, or is it because they need something to hold onto, a Linus Blanket of some sort?"

"Well, for complicated reasons, I guess." Evangelina ruffled her hair. "One, being hopeful gives you motivation to live and fight for a better outcome. Two, it's always good to have confidence and hope for the best. Three, like you said, everyone needs something to keep them going, right? A momentum in life to drive them forward."

"What I meant to ask was, do you truly think we can have a life together?" Diome asked. He wasn't challenging her positivity. Quite the contrary, he was curious what she thought of the current situation.

Evangelina thought for a while. "Things can change for the better anytime," she replied. "After all, the game's not over, is it?"

Diome blinked. "Now I am getting baffled. Do enlighten me, what does that mean?"

"We never know what will happen next. Maybe, just maybe, there will be a turn of events. Things will go in our way one day."

"Do you really think so?" Diome asked. He desired nothing better than to believe her words of reassurance, but hope was a dangerous thing to trust.

"It's hard to say," replied Evangelina. "Nobody can predict what comes next."

"Another invasion, maybe," grumbled Diome, deflating at that possibility.

"Let's talk about something else," Evangelina suggested. "It's your birthday, after all." She gasped and leapt to her feet. "Wait for me for a moment. I'll be back soon."

Diome twisted around to see where she went, only to see her vanish among the stands. He smiled in spite of himself. Evangelina was adorable. She must've wanted to surprise him.

After a few minutes, she returned, and she affirmed his assumption. In her hands was a yellow cupcake with rainbow sprinkles. A lit candle blazed atop the tiny cake, the flame swaying side-to-side.

"How did you get a lit candle?" Diome asked.

"Shh, don't tell anyone, but I lit it with my magic when nobody was around. Happy seventeenth! I wasn't sure if you'd like rainbow sprinkles, but I thought you'd like something more cheerful today."

Warmth flooded Diome's heart, and his eyes misted over. "Thank you so much."

"I wanted to get you a bigger cake, but they don't sell those here."

"I'll get you a cake next time on your birthday when I find a job," Diome promised her. "I don't want to owe you anything."

"You've sacrificed everything for me." Evangelina gazed at him profoundly. "You saved me on the ball, and you fled the Burning Bowels after being tortured. I wouldn't be here treating you to those snacks if you hadn't risked your life to save me. Now, don't think about it and make your birthday wishes. You can say two of them aloud, but keep the third one in your heart. It's a custom among the angels."

Diome closed his eyes. "One, I wish the rivalry between the devils and angels will end soon. Two, I hope we will get married in the future and have a perfect life as a wedded couple."

And the third one, I hope you will love me no

matter who I become, because I'd always do the same for you, Diome thought. He opened his eyes and blew the candle out.

Evangelina clapped. "Happiest of birthdays to you."

Diome shared half of the cupcake with Evangelina, and the two of them ate in silence for a while. This was the perfect day he had always yearned for. No battles, no invasions, no enemies. Only him and Evangelina, with nothing standing between them and pure, untainted happiness.

"It's the best birthday I've ever had." Diome devoured the rest of the cupcake. The lemon cream and sweet sprinkles complemented each other's flavor very well. He would have loved to get another, but he was too full.

"It's the least I can do for you," replied Evangelina. "After all, you'd never be an outcast among the devils if it hadn't been for me."

"True, but I wouldn't be the happiest devil in the world if I hadn't met you," Diome replied. "If I could start over again, I'd change nothing. All the decisions I made brought me to you, and that's the way I want. All right, no more soppy and sentimental talk on my birthday. We're going to get too emotional to celebrate."

Evangelina grinned. "No problem, birthday boy. You want to go see what those claw machines are all about?"

"Sure. You could try playing them. Maybe you're a natural. Who knows?"

They gathered their belongings and ambled over to the claw machines.

"Oh, look at those plush bears!" Evangelina gushed, pressing her face to the glass.

Red, purple, black, blue, green, and brown, the

bears gazed back at her with their beady eyes.

"Very cute," Diome remarked with a smile.

"How do you make those machines work?" Evangelina asked.

"You insert a quarter in the coin slot to activate it, move the joystick to the prize you want, and press the green button."

"Let me try it." Evangelina fed the machine a dollar, and out came a joyful tune. Positioning a hand on the joystick and the other on the button, she drove the claw to a black teddy bear and pressed the button. The claw reached down, seized the bear, but let go before she could move it to the prize slot.

"Damn," muttered Diome. "It's probably rigged."

"How do you know?" Evangelina asked. "I'm going to try again to prove you wrong," she added with an air of mischief.

"I've failed countless times."

Ignoring his reply, Evangelina stuffed another dollar into the machine. "This time, I'm not going to let go of the button. Let's see what happens."

"Good luck," Diome said.

To his surprise, the claw positioned itself over the black bear Evangelina had targeted, seized it, and moved to the prize slot.

"Ta-da!" Evangelina exclaimed. Her eyes were glowing with pride.

Diome applauded her and gave her a hug. "You did it!"

"Beginner's luck," she answered humbly. "Here, you can have the prize."

"Really? But I thought you liked it."

"Take it as a little birthday gift from me," Evangelina insisted.

Diome smiled. The bear was about five inches

tall, with shining black fur that melted under his fingers. "Thank you. This is the best birthday gift I've ever received."

Evangelina grinned. "You're very welcome. Let's go see the Christmas lights."

For the next hour, Diome immersed himself in the mesmerizing hues of the splendid lights. Bright crimson, amber, yellow, green, blue, violet, and pink lights dyed the evening in a vibrant spectrum of brilliant hues. They passed an arbor of glowing snowflakes that flaunted white, silver, and electric blue beams, their arms looped in each other's. The festive mood was contagious; it was a wonderland with vibrant, ethereal lights. Lost in a world of snowflakes, wreaths, garlands, snowmen, bells, presents, Christmas trees, floating ornaments, it was as if Diome had stepped into a fairytale.

"Fascinating, isn't it?" Evangelina murmured, breathless.

Diome noticed the ecstasy radiating from her, and a ripple of tenderness touched his heart as he realized he was the one who brought her such joy.

"Not as fascinating as you are," he whispered in her ear, earning him a kiss on the cheek.

****

That night, Diome returned to his tree house, his heart brimming with euphoria. Everything that transpired on this magical night kindled a flame of joy in his heart that would remain ablaze for hours, days, and weeks.

Evangelina had spotted a small, puffy cloud no bigger than her face on their way back and pocketed it. Now, she was patting it like a cat and making it solidify under her fingers.

"Evangelina, what are you doing with that cloud?" he asked.

"Wait and see," Evangelina answered. She

brought it to her lips and blew out a breath. Diome watched, astonished, as it began to shine. A warm yellow glow emitted from the cloud, and she set it on the floor of his tree house.

"What is that?" Diome asked.

"A cloud-shaped night light I created with magic," explained Evangelina.

Diome stroked the lamp. Like a ball of cotton, it was soft and fluffy, but hard and solid enough to stand on a surface.

"Like it?" Evangelina asked smugly.

"Love it," gushed Diome. "I don't know how to thank you, Evangelina. Words fail me."

"Trust me, I know," Evangelina assured him. "Have a good night, and I'll see you tomorrow."

They waved goodnight to each other, and she climbed out of the tree house. Diome escorted her retreating figure with his gaze, watching her thread her way through the lush forest. Among all the people—devils, humans, and angels—he knew, Evangelina was the kindest, purest, and sweetest.

Lying down in his sleeping bag, Diome gazed at the bright moon, recounting the merry conversations they had had today. The black plush bear and the cloud lamp by his pillow assured him everything tonight wasn't a dream, a product of his imagination. No, they would remain beside him forever, just like Evangelina and her love.

As his eyelids grew heavier, Diome drifted into a deep sleep. Soon, a nightmare took over his mind. In it, he was standing on a floating island, conflagration engulfing the Land of Heavenly Dreams in furious orange blazes. The scorching, smothering heat permeated his senses, making him dizzy and lightheaded.

Evangelina. Panic rose in him like a tide. Where

was she?

Diome took flight, circling every island in view as he yelled Evangelina's name, but nobody replied. He felt as if he were sinking into quicksand. The world he knew was collapsing. Evangelina was gone, and he had not an inkling where she could be.

A trio of devils zapped at a few angels flying away from the fire, and two of them plummeted downward, their tattered wings unable to hold their weight. Diome spotted a devil struck in the chest by an incandescent beam of white light and fall unconscious.

Stop, he wanted to shout, but his voice was gone. Or perhaps it was drowned out by the screams and shouts that rang clear in the air. There were more. More devils and angels, all dueling to the death. Rage blazed in their eyes, and sizzling heat reigned the air, clinging onto his senses.

This was the end. Never had Diome seen such a violent battle. Both sides were fighting to kill. Blood, flames, and destruction. Everywhere all at once.

Before Diome knew it, a silver arrow impaled his wings. A scream tore from his throat as he felt himself falling, falling, falling, his skin almost peeling from his flesh as gravity summoned all its power to devour him.

And then he jerked awake. A sheen of cold sweat made his body moist and clammy. Taking a deep breath, Diome sat up. His heart was still racing, as though he had been chased down a street by a group of gangsters moments ago. It was midnight, he supposed, as the moon was at the zenith of the sky.

For some reason, he felt ill. A sense of dread and anxiety clung to his heartstrings like sticky strands of gossamer. Diome leaned against the wall of his tree house, reviewing the details of his nightmare. It was just a lucid dream, right? It couldn't have implied anything.

He was no seer, and he didn't believe in superstitions. Nobody could foresee the future.

But what if a storm of chaos was brewing below him, below the Land of Heavenly Dreams? Diome's heart trembled at the possibility. The Burning Bowels. The devils. What if they were plotting something? Surely it wouldn't hurt for him to fly to the cave just to check on the devils, right? He'd be extra careful and hover above the clouds, using them as a veil to fog his existence.

Before Diome knew it, he was donning his wings and zooming out into the night. Was it foolish of him? Part of him criticized his rashness and recklessness. Evangelina had outdone herself to keep him alive. What if the angels or devils ambushed him and got him killed? No, he couldn't die from his own foolishness. He had to live for Evangelina, for their future. She was his priority, his sole concern.

But what if his dream was a sinister premonition? What if the devils decided to take their anger out on the angels and launch a full-scale attack on them?

It was dark, and there were more clouds than usual. The gauzy puffs cloaked his figure, masking his identity. He passed countless islands, many with houses and cabins, but all the angels were asleep. Like a ghost, he glided by them, by the soundless islands, a dark comet sailing through the night. As Diome spotted Horizon Park below, he flew in the direction of the Burning Bowels. When he reached the cliff, his intuition told him something was severely wrong.

A sea of black fire sizzled below him. The devils—hundreds of them—were carrying torches that sported dark flames.

"To the Land of Heavenly Dreams," one of them ordered. "We split into six troops. Tonight, we'll teach them the lesson we've been planning for weeks. Tonight, we will claim our victory and eradicate them. They're all sleeping now. Perfect time for a surprise assault."

Diome didn't have to hear more of the speech. His mind was already spinning. So this was it. This was why he had been nervous and restless the entire day. An innate part of him knew it, feared it, dreaded it, that the epic confrontation would come when he least expected.

Without wasting another second, Diome flapped his wings and ascended into the clouds. He had to find Evangelina. Her island was above his, with a beautiful white house. It shouldn't be difficult to find. All he had to do was to locate his forest, and then travel upward.

How could it be? Hours earlier, he and Evangelina had been indulging themselves and relishing in the revelry of the fair. But now, a war was imminent, and it was up to him to inform Evangelina of the devils' invasion.

What would he do if he found her? Elope with her? Try to escort her and her father to safety? Diome doubted whether her father would trust him. However, an emergency was pending. No matter whether they would believe him or not, Diome had to deliver the news.

Evangelina's island loomed into sight above and ahead of Diome. He flapped his wings to accelerate and flew straight to one of the upstairs windows. They were all identical, with white frames. Since the curtains were thankfully parted, he spotted Evangelina asleep in one of the rooms.

Diome knocked on the glass panel three times. "Evangelina!" he hissed. He was quivering from either coldness or terror—he had no idea which.

Evangelina shifted in her bed but didn't wake up.

Diome knocked on her window, this time louder than before, and her eyes opened. She leapt out of her covers and hurried over to him.

"Diome, what are you doing here?" she mouthed, panic written on her features.

"Open the window, I have to tell you something," Diome replied.

She did. "What is it? What happened?"

"The devils, they're coming. They're planning a mass-invasion on the Land of Heavenly Dreams, and—"

The door to Evangelina's room opened, and a strong figure emerged in the doorway, hands on hips.

A shiver crept down Diome's spine. He didn't need to look to know who it was.

HERMIONE LEE

Chapter Fifteen

The Evil Ones
(Evangelina)

"What is going on here?"

Evangelina gulped. Her father. A sense of horror dawned on her. Now that Diome was talking to her, now that he had seen them together ...

Diome was frozen to the spot. His lips parted, but no sound came out.

"What are you doing here?" Evangelina heard her father thunder at him. She flinched, as if his booming voice were a whip.

Diome blinked twice, as if fumbling for an explanation.

Her father rounded on her. "What are you doing, letting a devil in the house?"

Evangelina pressed her mouth into a thin line. "We ... "

All the words in her mind withered on her tongue. Could she talk herself and Diome out of this situation?

"I'll kill you!" her father growled, seizing the front of Diome's shirt. His eyes blazed with madness, with a terrifying lust for murder.

A blinding streak of white light escaped his fingers and zapped at Diome's heart. Evangelina screamed. Without hesitation, she raced up to Diome and stood in front of him.

"Get out of my way!" her father snapped, shoving her aside. "He—that intruder—mine to kill—"

"Stop!" Evangelina shrieked as a torrent of white-hot sparks zapped at Diome. "Dad, stop! That's my boyfriend you're trying to kill!"

Her father paused. The air between them solidified, thick with heavy tension. Diome's eyes widened, and he shook his head at Evangelina. He probably thought she had let it slip, but the truth was, Evangelina knew she could no longer hide their relationship. It was the only way to save Diome, the only way to tell her father he was no trespasser.

However, when Evangelina noticed her father's expression, she almost wished she had kept silent. A deathly pallor reigned his cheeks, and a mixture of horror and disgust worked its way into his eyes. His gaze drifted to Diome, and comprehension dawned on his face.

"Diome Lenoir?" He shook his head in disbelief. Evangelina could sense a storm of fury brewing within. "How dare you!" he whispered, fixing his gaze on his daughter. "How dare you!"

Before Evangelina knew it, a searing sensation flooded her body. He had slapped her across the face, flooring her.

"You nasty, wretched angel!" her father roared, seizing a fistful of her hair and yanking her to her feet. "You're a disgrace to the angels! You and that horrible devil—I—what would your mother say if she knew?"

He raised a hand to strike her again, but Diome leapt in front of her, shielding her from the blow. "Mr. Leclair—"

Her father whirled him out of the way. "It's none of your business," he growled. "Now, you listen to me, Evangelina Leclair, I won't sit here and tolerate your nonsense. If you end this relationship now, I will do you a favor and not mention this scandal to anyone. But if—"

"No." Evangelina crossed her arms with a defiant, unwavering expression.

Her father stiffened. "What did you say?" "I'm not leaving Diome," Evangelina declared, her hands balled into fists.

She felt a bizarre sense of calmness coursing through her veins. Everything was exposed, and she no longer had to worry about her father discovering their romance. In other words, her shackles had been removed, and she was free to be herself.

Her father let out a roar of frustration. "You filthy traitor! Get out of my house, you wicked demon-lover! I'm disowning you right this moment. You are no daughter of mine! You betrayed—"

"I didn't betray anyone," Evangelina replied serenely. "I never wanted to antagonize the devils. Since the first time you and Mom told me to kill Diome, I refused again and again, but neither of you listened. In fact, did you two ever care about what I thought or felt? Never. Dad, I'm your daughter, not your weapon. I'm an individual with my own opinions. Why should they matter any less than yours and Mom's?"

"Don't play clever with me," her father growled. "You ought to be ashamed of yourself. Have you ever stopped to think how ungrateful and disrespectful you are? Your mother and I raised you for seventeen years, and now you think you're better than—"

Evangelina fought back the urge to roll her eyes. "Again? Every time I make a valid point that contradicts yours, you call me out on being disrespectful and ungrateful. Those are two different topics. Just because my thoughts are different than yours doesn't mean I'm rude or rebellious. You need to stop imposing your beliefs on me and leave me alone!"

Her father's face was now whiter than paper. He opened his mouth to retort, but Diome cleared his throat.

"Mr. Leclair, everything can wait until the battle's over. The only reason I'm here in Evangelina's room is to warn her and you, if you're willing to believe me. The devils are launching an attack on the Land of Heavenly Dreams. A mass invasion that—"

"And you're behind it?" Evangelina's father cut across him.

"I'm not. I'm here to advise you two to run."

Evangelina's father snorted. "And why should my daughter and I believe you? How do we know it's not a dirty scheme of yours? You nasty, scummy devils are all liars and cheaters. Don't think I don't know what you're up to. You're here to lure me and Evangelina out, so that you and your evil clan can kill us. We won't fall for it!"

For the first time in her life, Evangelina desired nothing better to slap some sense into her father. How could he be so shallow-minded and hopelessly ignorant when Diome was warning them to run?

"Mr. Leclair," Diome continued, heat rising in his voice. "I could've killed you and Evangelina when you two were arguing earlier, but in case you haven't noticed, I didn't do anything. If I were here to lure you out and murder you, I would've killed you by now."

Evangelina's father snorted. "I don't believe a word that comes out of your dirty devil mouth. Why would you risk your life to come up here to warn us if your clan of devils hadn't sent you?"

"Because I love Evangelina, and since you're her father, I don't want either of you to die. My clan banished me from the Burning Bowels because I saved Evangelina's life during the devil invasion at the debutante ball."

"And I'm supposed to believe that?"

"Look, Dad," began Evangelina, losing her patience. "Diome's here to help us. It's a life-or-death situation we're dealing with now. If you don't believe him, fine, just stay. I'm going with him." She walked to her wardrobe and donned her white, feathery wings.

"You're not going anywhere," her father snarled, grabbing her by the elbow.

Evangelina jerked free of his grasp in a swift movement. Ignoring him, she turned to Diome, the devil she trusted with all her heart. "Where do we go?"

Diome held her hand. "To my island. We'll be safe there."

Jumping out of the window, they flapped their wings and took off.

"Evangelina Leclair!" her father hollered at the top of his lungs. "You come right back this instant, you hear me?"

But Evangelina and Diome were already gliding, dipping, and soaring through the gossamer clouds, far away from her home.

"Do you think he'll come after us?" Diome asked. "I hope he does."

Evangelina stared at him. "You've got to be insane."

"He'll be in danger if he stays at home."

Evangelina bit her lip. She glanced over her shoulder and spotted a black dot emerging from the window of her room. Her father. But the misty clouds between them shrouded her and Diome from his view.

"We live in a rural area in the Land of Heavenly Dreams, though," Evangelina began. "I don't think we'd get blown up if we stayed in my house. Come to think of it, it might be the safest place."

"I wouldn't take my chances," Diome replied. "And anyway, it's not as if your father would want me showing up in your room again. We're lucky he didn't assume we were up to something bad in your house."

Evangelina shrugged. "But he's not inside the house now."

"I still think we should hide in my tree house for a

while. You never know whether they'll attack the residential islands first or not."

Evangelina sighed. "I guess I can't argue with that. Sorry about the horrible words my father said. I know you meant well, and you were trying to save us."

Diome smiled. "The way you stood up to him like that, it blew my mind. You were so brave. But then again, why should I be surprised? From the first time I saw you, I knew how strong and independent you are, and that's one of the reasons why I adore you."

Evangelina blushed. Even though they were running for their lives—or, to be more precise, flying for their lives—he still had the power to melt her soul.

The forest loomed into sight, and Evangelina heaved a sigh of relief.

"Nobody's in it," observed Diome as they sailed through the trees and arrived at his tree house.

Clambering up the rope ladder, Evangelina spotted the night light she had gifted him yesterday, the plush bear and the colorful rose silhouetted against it. A smile lifted the corners of her lips.

A warm moisture filled Evangelina's eyes. "You kept every gift I gave you."

"They're my treasures," replied Diome.

The two of them sat against each other in silence, bathed in the darkness.

"What do we do next?" Evangelina murmured. "We can't go out. If my father goes around telling the angels about us, he'll turn us into fugitives. Right now, he doesn't believe in the invasion. The only thing that concerns him is our relationship. We'll be finished if the angels see us together."

"Sooner or later, he'll have to believe there's an invasion."

"Pretty absurd, isn't it? The devils are probably in

the Land of Heavenly Dreams now, and my dad's still fretting about us. Should we join the battle? I'm still mad at my dad, but I don't want him to die."

"They'll all turn their attention toward us if we show up. Don't forget, I'm still an outlaw among the devils." Diome sighed. "If only your father agreed to come with us."

"You tried your best to save us," Evangelina reminded him. "It's not your fault he didn't take you seriously."

Evangelina analyzed the situation for a moment. If she emerged onto the battlefield, which side would she take? Neither. All she wanted was a peaceful world with no violence or bloodshed. She and Diome were a neutral third party, refusing to take sides. It would be pointless for them to join the battle. Plus, something told her if Diome appeared before the devils, he wouldn't be as fortunate as last time. They wouldn't let him escape again, she was sure of it.

However, what about her father? Nothing condoned the terrible insults he had hurled at Diome, but he was her family. She couldn't abandon him. Perhaps if they dragged him to safety, that would be enough to convince him Diome cared about her happiness.

"Diome," started Evangelina. "I've got a plan."

"What is it?" he asked.

Evangelina took a deep breath. "We go to the battlefield, find my father, and bring him here."

"He won't come quietly," Diome replied. "First, it would take a miracle for him to not kill us at first glance."

"We could zap him unconscious and then drag him here," suggested Evangelina.

"As if he won't start accusing us of kidnapping him the moment he wakes up," Diome muttered.

"We're trying to save his life," Evangelina protested.

"Mark my words, he won't stop to consider that. He's dying to have a reason to murder me. I was lucky enough to make it out of your house alive, and I really don't want to tempt fate."

"Then I'll go alone," insisted Evangelina.

Diome exhaled. "Are you mad at me?"

Evangelina shook her head. "I can't blame you because my dad was the rude one. But I can't sit here, not knowing what's going on in the Land of Heavenly Dreams."

A curtain of silence fell upon the two of them as they gazed out at the moonlit trees, silver stars, and nocturnal cloudscape. Evangelina glanced down at the plush bear and trailed her long, pale fingers over its furry head. The Christmas fair was like a century ago. Back then, they were so immersed in the festive joy that the idea of a possible invasion never crossed their minds. But now, hours later, they were huddled in the tree house, leaning against each other to seek comfort and support.

"All right," murmured Diome after a long while.

Evangelina shifted her gaze to him. "All right what?"

"I'll come with you on that suicide mission to find your dad among the chaos. But could you give us five minutes?"

"Us?" Evangelina repeated.

Diome reached out the window and plucked of a few twigs from the tree the house was built on. Silver flowers dotted the tiny branches.

"Silvertrees," Evangelina explained. "They're the most common trees in the Land of Heavenly Dreams."

Diome didn't reply. He braided the twigs together, forming a crown. "Close your eyes," he whispered to Evangelina.

She did and felt a ring of branches land on her head.

Diome held her hand. "I finally have something to give you."

Evangelina felt the soft petals with her fingers. "It's priceless, Diome. Thank you."

"I wanted to give you something before we both set off to war," replied Diome, wrapping his arms around her.

"And one final kiss before we set off?" Evangelina asked.

Diome nodded. She pressed her lips to his, and all her unpleasant thoughts and worries melted into oblivion. A blissful sensation erupted in the depths of her bosom. Like spring roses, summer rain, autumn breezes, and winter sunshine, his ardent kiss reminded her of everything sweet and pleasant, of all the beauties and wonders in the world. She felt as if she were no longer inhabiting her body, but rather soaring through a universe of rainbows. Losing her sense of time, space, and identity, all Evangelina felt was a dizzying flood of euphoria. With her eyes closed, she could let her imagination roam. Where were they? In a vintage café on a street lined with buttery yellow lights? In a garden with flurries of floral fragrance dancing in the air? In a ballroom with towering walls, ornate carvings, and twirling couples attired in their finest? That was the mystery and romance of it, kissing Diome with her eyes closed. That way, she could create memories that never existed and store them in her memory as a keepsake whenever she missed his dark, brooding figure and soft, smooth hands.

When they pulled back for air, breathless, Evangelina was surprised to see her blazing emotions reflected on his face. Excitement, longing, and a dash of fear.

"I hate to say this, but should we go now?" Diome asked. "Your dad ... "

Reality washed over Evangelina, and she nodded urgently. "Let's go."

They clambered out of the tree house and soared into the night, Evangelina's white robe rippling and fluttering in the wind. Diome tightened the collar of his black coat around his neck, and Evangelina draped her hair around her shoulders as the chilly air seeped into her clothes. Ahead of them, the trees thinned, revealing the plethora of stars in the inky sky.

"Where do we go? Up?" Diome asked.

Evangelina nodded as she spotted a group of devils chasing three angels. Cries and shouts of fear and menace filled the air. Her heart sank. Where was her father? Had the devils caught him?

"Evangelina, does that look like your father?" Diome asked. He descended on a large island the size of a soccer field and pointed at an angel.

Before Evangelina could inspect him, someone pinned her to the ground.

"Got the little traitor!" the stranger shouted triumphantly.

"And I got the other!" another yelled.

"Get off me!" Evangelina struggled to escape, but her captor removed her wings. She bit at the rough hands and kicked herself free.

Beside her, an angel had taken off Diome's wings too, and he was doing his best to fight the angel off. Evangelina fired an incandescent streak of light at the angel's eyes and, seizing Diome's hand, she led him in the opposite direction, running for their lives.

"Stand still!" one of the angels hollered.

"There's a cliff ahead!" the other added. "You won't be able to fly, now that we've got your wings!"

To Evangelina's horror, they were right. She and Diome turned, only to see a group of angels making their way toward them in a siege. Had this been a scene from a movie, Evangelina would have found it dramatic and irresistible, but now, she was helpless. Behind her and Diome was a cliff, and below it an endless fall awaited them. Without their wings, they would no doubt die an excruciating death if they lost their balance and fell.

"What do you want?" Diome demanded.

Evangelina recognized a familiar figure among the crowd. Her father. He sauntered up to them, shaking his head. In his eyes there churned a sea of fury.

"Young lady, I'm very disappointed in you. Have you any idea what you've done?"

Evangelina crossed her arms. What was the worst thing her father could do to her? Kill her? She wasn't going down without a fight, and she might as well make it clear to him.

"I haven't done anything wrong, and I'm not ashamed. In fact, you should be the one who's ashamed—all of you." Evangelina glared down at the ever-growing number of bystanders—mostly angels, but several devils joined, drawn by their curiosity at the large gathering of angels.

Her father slapped her across the face. "You tried to elope with a devil, and if that's not humiliating enough, you're shaming the other angels for your behavior?"

"You traitor!" one of the bystanders shrieked.

"Devil-lover!"

"Why don't you drag yourself to the Burning Bowels and burn to death in there?"

The catcalls didn't faze Evangelina. She stood tall

and dignified by the cliff, gazing down at the angels like a regal queen regarding her subjects. Pride, satisfaction, and an odd sense of comfort wafted through her as she clutched Diome's hand—not because she was afraid, but rather due to the fact she knew it would upset them the most. She was irrevocably in love with Diome, and she wanted them all to know that. Never had she been prouder of being a rebellious non-conformist, of defying societal expectations and liberating herself from the handcuffs of the rivalry. It wasn't her fault, and it wasn't Diome's either. While all the angels and devils had let the hatred in history govern their minds and contaminate their hearts, she and Diome were different. They had achieved a spiritual dominance and risen above the petty animosity between the two clans. Their love had brought them to the top of the world. The conflicts, disputes, and battles appeared small, insignificant, and meaningless, paling in comparison to their desire for each other.

When the wave of insults dwindled, Evangelina spoke again. "You can call me whatever you want. It doesn't matter to me. But one day, you'll look back and realize how stupid and meaningless this is—brainwashing young angels and teaching them to hate devils, or worse, killing the innocent."

"Not a single devil is innocent!" an angel shrieked.

"I'm not here to debate with you," Evangelina cut in. "What difference is there between the angels and devils? None. You're the evil ones, all of you. Vigilantes who lie to yourself and think you're acting in the name of justice." She was now addressing not only the angels but also the devils. There were several gathered on the island before her, and even more hovering in the air, though still half-heartedly engaged in the battle. "Because of the rivalry, you feed young angels and devils—your sons and daughters—propaganda and make them supremacists. But have you ever stopped to think—?"

"Stop lying!" a devil bellowed. "You and your sanctimonious clan—"

"We're no better than each other," Evangelina interrupted her. "I'm not afraid to admit it. But we do share a lot in common. Right now, you're all gathered on this island, shaming an angel and a devil for loving each other, for being themselves. We're not hurting anyone, not killing anyone. Why can't you leave us alone?"

She raised her voice, colored with frustration. Why? She and Diome never wished either side any ill. They weren't forcing them to get along either. They wanted nothing but a quiet, serene life, one where they didn't have to fear for their lives every morning and worry about getting killed in their sleep every night. They were innocent in every way, two people who craved peace and simplicity. Surely anyone with a sense of decency would grant their humble wish, right? But then again, the angels and devils were too dense to see through the cocoon of bitter resentment they had woven around themselves. It was questionable whether they possessed even a minimal amount of decency. They derived pleasure from witnessing the death and destruction of the opposing clan. It was sick, perverse, and appalling, but nobody could change their minds.

Meanwhile, the angels and devils were still yelling and screaming nonsense at them.

"Enough!" Diome retaliated. "If you have an ounce of self-respect left, leave us alone!"

"You should be lucky we haven't decided to execute you yet!" one of the devils snarled.

"If you want to execute him, you'll have to execute me too," Evangelina declared. She was surprised to hear how detached she sounded. The idea of dying didn't bother her the least. After all, what was death compared to a life without love? Treason was a crime punishable by the death penalty. She knew that ever since she fell in love with Diome. It was absurd to execute anyone only because they were in a relationship with who society deemed the wrong partner. While the price of death might have been daunting for many angels, Evangelina couldn't care less. It was either liberty or death for her. It was her freedom to stay with Diome, and she would defend their romance with her life. Perhaps if she died on this cliff on this fateful night, she would be remembered as a hero several decades or centuries later. The unyielding warrior who sacrificed her life rather than abandon her true beliefs.

"Fine," her father snapped. His eyes no longer held the shock they did several minutes ago. Now, they were aglow with determination. "I will have Diome Lenoir dead before dawn, and as for you, Evangelina Leclair, you can leave the Land of Heavenly Dreams and never come back again."

She stared at her father, and a memory rose to her mind. The day he and her mother had called her to the living room and mentioned Diome Lenoir's name. They had instructed her to assassinate him. But in the end, she couldn't. Her family and her clan imposed their expectations on her, but he was the only boy who loved her because she was herself and nobody else. How could she betray someone who had stolen her heart, who had become a fragment of her soul? To eliminate him would mean destroying an indispensable part of herself. She would never be complete again.

"I'm sorry," Evangelina whispered, to herself, to him, and to her fellow angels. She was about to make a decision that would change her life forever.

"I'm sorry," she repeated herself, gazing into her

father's ocean eyes. "But I won't kill him."

Before he and the throng of bystanders could decipher her words, Evangelina fired a streak of white light at the angels holding her wings. She was going to retrieve them and elope with Diome forever. Never would the selfish, ignorant angels and devils control them again. If they couldn't leave her and Diome alone, she would force them to back off.

A battle erupted throughout the crowd, and everyone, angel and devil, sprang into action. Blinding beams and suffocating darkness reigned the clouds, equally determined to overpower the other. Sparks flew everywhere, glowing in the night, and a cacophony of battle cries echoed in Evangelina's ears. Paying no attention to the angels and devils around her, she wrestled and grappled with the angel, who was refusing to relinquish her wings.

Meanwhile, Diome was waging a war against the other angel who had stolen his wings. His opponent summoned a streak of light and flung it at his eyes, while Diome conjured a void of darkness that devoured it in no time.

"It's no use," snapped the angel who was fighting Evangelina. "Just give up. If you beg for mercy and admit you were wrong, they might banish you but still leave you alive."

"Why admit I'm wrong when I'm not?" Evangelina asked. She tossed a white flame at her and dived out of the way as a pink fireball came sailing at her.

"Very stubborn, aren't you?" The angel smirked. "Tonight, you either fall on the battlefield or survive the invasion and get executed afterwards. Either way, you'll die sooner or later. Why not surrender to them? It's much easier and faster."

"Because they're the ones who should surrender,"

Evangelina replied. "Death is a small price to pay for freedom."

And it was then that she realized it was all about freedom from the start. There were no actual dictators among the angels and devils, but in fact, the vigilantes played that very role. Like the moral police, they enforced their own opinions on others and resorted to violence when they failed. Smothering any different voices, all they cared about was making everyone the same, brainless slaves who lacked judgement and followed the majority like a herd of sheep. True freedom was a lie, an illusion in their realm. As much as the angels would deny it, they weren't free. The propaganda, the brainwashing, and the biased knowledge they gleaned from history classes were a testament to that. No, their minds were in captivity, their hearts locked in a prison of blind hatred.

Around Evangelina, the war escalated. The air grew hotter, the sizzling sparks, blazing fireballs, and occasional spells of darkness soaring between the fighters. White and burgundy blood stained the grass like splattered paint. Yet despite the chaos, Evangelina knew she could win this—with Diome by her side, nothing was impossible.

"I got my wings!" Diome shouted.

Evangelina glanced in his direction, just in time to see her father hurtling toward Diome and tackling him to the ground. A flash of silver seized her attention, and she gasped.

"No!"

Evangelina leapt in front of Diome, shielding his figure from the blade. Something colder than ice and sharper than needles sliced into her chest, and she grimaced. Pain exploded among her senses, an agony more than an agony needling through every nerve in her body. Someone screamed. Perhaps it was herself, her father, or Diome. Or perhaps it came from all three of them—she wasn't certain. Her eyes were squeezed shut, her face contorted in pain. But it was worth it, for the agony tearing her apart was nothing compared to what would have been the outcome if she hadn't intervened.

Evangelina heard mingled voices in the background. Some were calling her name, while others were mumbling words she couldn't comprehend. However, the only thing that mattered to her was the agony that clouded her mind and blocked every notion from her brain. When the soul-shredding pain in her reached a peak, numbness dulled Evangelina's senses. Her vision fuzzed, and darkness engulfed her vision, thieving her consciousness.

White, gray, and black hues bloomed before Evangelina's eyes when she came to. Someone was cradling her in his arms. That was the first thought that encountered her sluggish mind. She glanced up, resisting the heaviness in her eyelids.

"Evangelina ... " murmured her father. He was kneeling beside her, his eyes raw and red and tearful. "I'm so sorry. I never wanted to ... to ... "

Every ounce of his anger had evaporated, replaced by grief, remorse, and heartbreak.

"It's ... all right ... Dad ... " It took all of her remaining strength to manage a reply. Her chest was soaked with white blood, but it wasn't evident on her robe. She glanced up at Diome, at the boy holding her mangled body. He looked so distressed that she felt a tug on her heartstrings.

"Why?" Diome mumbled. Tears collected in his eyes. One trekked down the length of his cheek and plummeted onto a blade of grass, an eerily poignant scene. "Evangelina, why?"

She wanted to answer, but her strength was fading. A flash of colors passed her eyes, and Evangelina saw herself as a baby, swaddled in a purple blanket in her mother's arms. An illusion of her first day of school ensued, her blonde pigtails wiggling behind her as she bid her parents goodbye. She then saw her first day at Horizon High, Diome's mysterious yet alluring figure, the Halloween dance, and the beautiful first kiss they had so fondly shared.

And now, she was breathing her last in Diome's arms. What was she to say to him, the friend who was more than a friend, the boy she had allowed into her heart, the devil who had breathed meaning into her life and made it worth living?

"Diome ... " Evangelina whispered. "I-I love you."

She wished she could sit up and plant a final kiss of farewell on his velvety lips, but like a dying hourglass, the last of her stamina had seeped away. A gravitational pull toward sleep, toward oblivion fogged her consciousness. For the last time in her life, Evangelina exhaled. Closing her eyes, a floating sensation enveloped every fiber of her being. She was at peace.

Chapter Sixteen
Reconciliation
(Diome)

"Evangelina? Evangelina ... "

Diome couldn't believe this, couldn't believe how much pain was coursing through his body. The weight of the truth was unbearable. Evangelina had died for him, and he was left with nothing but her mangled form.

A soul-stabbing ache penetrated his body as a shuddering sob that wrenched his heart escaped his lips. He refused to accept the fact she was gone. Her ashen face, her closed eyes, her fading heat ... It was all a meticulous prank. Soon, she would wake up, wouldn't she?

The angels and devils around him were all in shock. Nobody moved a muscle, nobody uttered a word. Like him, they were still frozen in astonishment, like motionless mammoths sealed in ice for centuries. It was obvious they were more than flabbergasted at what they had beheld—how Evangelina had sacrificed her life for love, protecting a devil by flinging herself before him. She was too pure, too selfless, too virtuous, Diome always knew that. All along she had been protecting him—from the moment her father instructed her to murder him, from the moment she entered Horizon High, from the moment they first locked eyes in their homeroom on that fateful morning of her first day of school. Yet he had no way of predicting his destiny. The new girl in Horizon High whom he had adored and admired turned out to be his savior.

Diome recounted all their memories, all the golden recollections they shared. The Halloween dance, her confession afterward, their first kiss, his saving her life just in time on the disastrous debutante ball, the time when they traversed through the vast skies and sailed through the clouds like two shadows, all the affectionate moments that formed their epic romance ... But now, it had ended.

And worse, he was to blame for this. If it hadn't been for him, if his sinful clan of malevolent devils did not exist, she would still be alive. None of the angels would learn of her relationship with him. The war wouldn't have taken place, and Evangelina wouldn't have sacrificed herself for him. It was his fault. He killed her.

From the start, the universe was toying with their fates. Diome thought about the first play Evangelina had mentioned to him, the one that happened to be his favorite. *Romeo and Juliet.* An epiphany struck him like lightning. Could it be? Could the play have been a foreshadowing of their future? Was it a hint from fate, a warning that a poignant story about him and Evangelina was written in the stars? Their romance paralleled Romeo and Juliet's story. It was destined to fail from the start. How foolish and naïve they had been, assuming their love was strong enough to overpower the centuries-long rivalry? Before the mountain of history, they were nothing more than tiny specks of stardust. But both of them had believed their love was unstoppable. They had the audacity to continue dating, a bizarre faith that it could change the world. As long as their love for each other blazed like a strong, steady bonfire, they could burn down the barriers forcing them apart. With Evangelina standing beside him, everything was possible. But now, like an extinguished candle, she was gone for good.

Diome lost track of time, space, and everything. He was blind and deaf to his surroundings. Nothing in the world mattered to him anymore except the sobering fact the love of his life was dead, her empty shell of a body in his arms. He gazed at her serene countenance, at the bloody gash across her heart, at the deathly pallor in her skin. Evangelina was at peace. She had traded her heartbeat for his. For the past two-and-a-half months, she had been his sunshine, his world, his every emotion, the very purpose of his existence. Even until the end, she remained righteous, courageous, and true to herself.

Diome was still in denial. How could a person be alive and breathing one moment, and the next, snuffed out into nothingness? His eyes, his ears, his senses, they had joined forces to deceive him. Every fiber of his being rejected the possibility she was dead. No, like that time she woke up in his arms after the ball, she would again come around. He moved his hand to her wrist, waiting.

Nothing. As silent as the ocean at night. Her pulse no longer existed. Her heart had stopped.

Something in Diome tore, ripped, shredded, parted with his body. Indescribable agony clawed at his heartstrings. For a mad moment, he almost hoped one of the angels could shoot an arrow at his head or stab a knife into his heart. Then something else would pain him more than the excruciating agony that dug into his bones, burning his flesh with the intensity of a thousand hellfires. A second wave of tears rose to his eyes and flooded down his cheeks. To say his heart hurt would have been a drastic understatement. It was shattered like a glass vase dropped from a skyscraper, split into so many fragments he could never piece it back together. Tears plummeted from his eyes and landed on her body.

"Evangelina ... " he choked. "I love you too."

There were a thousand things he regretted at this moment. Not gifting her a promise ring, not being brave enough to court her earlier, not sneaking into her debutante ball the moment it started, like Romeo in the

Capulet's party, and inviting her to dance before the other angels did ... Self-hatred, scalding and sizzling, filled him to the brim. For most of his life, he had been a coward. And now, he felt nothing but remorse for his insecurities. He had let his fear of rejection and his sense of worthlessness dominate him and overwhelm his desire to pursue Evangelina. Gently, he laid her down before him. Breaking down in silence, he leaned his head beside hers. Perhaps he could die from heartbreak. Perhaps that would be for the best, a slant of hope in a tragic ending. He closed his eyes, begging, imploring darkness to sweep him away.

"Diome?"

That voice. Her. His eyes flew open, meeting a pair of bright blue ones.

Were they both dead? They couldn't both be alive, could they?

"Evangelina?" Diome asked, sitting up. He blinked away his tears, and the miracle before him cleared.

His beloved Evangelina was awake, revived by some celestial force. He cradled her again. To his great shock, the gash on her chest was healing.

"You ... ?"

A stray tear slid off his chin and landed on the other end of the gash. It became one with the wound. Diome watched her skin mend, the crimson cut fading away and within moments, vanishing without a trace.

A beat.

"Diome ... How did you do it?" Evangelina asked, her eyes wide.

The bystanders drew nearer, and many gasped.

"He resurrected her," one of the devils murmured, staring into space as if in a trance.

Evangelina's father approached her, wide-eyed.

"Evangelina? Is it really you? You're back?"

She nodded, smiled, and Diome felt a wave of warmth touch his heart.

"I am, Dad," she replied before he pulled her into an embrace.

The angels and devils, still at a loss, were more than astonished by the miracle they had beheld. Some whispered theories, some shed tears of joy, while others simply stared.

"But why?"

Diome smiled. "Devil tears," he explained. "They can revive dead angels. It must be. There's no other explanation for this miracle"

He was shocked when his mother joined them. "Devil tears?" she repeated.

A hush descended among the crowd.

"Never has a devil cried for an angel before," an older devil Diome recognized as their neighbor pointed out. "This could be a first for our kind."

"Our kinds," Diome corrected him.

"But what if there's more to it?" a young angel insisted. "There could be a lot of reasons. Love, sacrifice, and grief. What if it's a combination of all those factors?"

"What if it's a sign the angels and devils should reconcile?" Evangelina asked, looking at her father.

Diome held her closer to him, stroking her back. "Shh," he whispered in her ear. "Just relax."

Her father frowned. "Evangelina—"

"Diome just saved my life. I owe him one."

"Well, he owes you one—"

"Then nobody owes anyone. And it should've been this way for years. Dad, don't you understand? The rivalry between the angels and the devils hasn't done anyone any favors. It's harmful, shallow, and ridiculous. Think about how many deaths could have been avoided if everyone decided to get along. Nobody knew devil tears could resurrect dead angels until today." Evangelina glanced at the angel who had spoken earlier. "Or perhaps, like Aurora suggested, it's not that simple. Devil tears mixed with love, an act of sacrifice, remorse or grief strong enough to undo death, anything or everything. I don't know what the precise recipe is, but I do know it must be something powerful, something intense, something innocent and earth-shattering in equal measure. Something only peace can bring."

Her father was silent for a moment.

"Numbering the deaths of the countless fallen angels and devils isn't something anyone should focus on. Deaths are sad, yes, but it's all in the past."

"It's not in the past," an angel bellowed. "It's still affecting the living angels. Families are still grieving. The dead angels won't ever come back."

"I know, because I lost my mother last month," said Evangelina patiently. "But if the rivalry had ended much sooner, wouldn't they have discovered the effects of devil tears centuries ago? Wouldn't that have reduced the death toll on both sides? If peace had been restored earlier, a lot of bloodshed and battles could have been avoided. We can't change history. None of us can. But we can build a new history starting from now."

Diome's mother exhaled. "Call a truce, you mean?"

"More than that," Diome joined, backing Evangelina up. "We want this to stop. All of it. Forever."

Evangelina's father huffed. "We're not going to be allies with the devils."

"No," Evangelina chimed in. "And I don't expect any angels to. However, it's time we let it go. Nobody is required to befriend anyone else. But for the sake of the bigger picture, this has to end. The invasions, the fights, everything."

A devil crossed his arms. "If you're asking us to forgive and forget—"

"Not that either," Diome cut in. "Scars have been left, and damage has been done over the past years, decades, and centuries. I don't expect anyone, much less everyone, to forgive and forget and pretend nothing happened. What we're suggesting is a reset. A new beginning that starts from zero. No more hatred, no more battles. Just peace."

"You mean not having anything to do with the angels?" Evangelina's father questioned.

Diome mustered the courage to look him in the eyes. Though he was as stern and severe as before, Diome sensed his concession. "That's correct. No more provoking or initiating fights."

"This takes time," Diome's mother pointed out. "We should do it step-by-step. Gradualism is—"

"That's not a solution," Diome cut in. "It has to start now. A petition to the presidents of both sides would do. After what happened today, I believe it won't be hard to get enough signatures."

A buzz of conversation erupted among the bystanders. Diome tightened his grasp on Evangelina's hand, fearing he would lose her again. She squeezed his hand, and Diome smiled down at her despite the anxiety boiling in him.

"You did great," she whispered to him. "Everything will be fine now."

And Diome let himself believe her. It would take a miracle for the two sides to reconcile, but after tonight's events, he was convinced that, as impossible as it seemed, miracles could happen.

****

Three days after the battle, Presidents Albert

Leclair and Ebony Lenoir held two meetings—one in the Land of Heavenly Dream and the other in the Burning Bowels—that dictated the future of the angels and devils. A new law was enacted in both nations—neither side, angel or devil, was allowed to launch attacks on the other. It was a historical moment when the news of the presidents' pact disseminated throughout both lands. Tears were spilled, hugs were given, and relief enveloped the two lands as they rejoiced together in the promise of eternal peace. At long last, the centuries-long rivalry had ceased. The rift between the two clans was too deep and too wide to be bridged, but they were making an effort to fill it up with forgiveness and tolerance.

Angels and devils were now permitted to visit each other's lands if they so desired, but under the condition they bore no weapons and did not make any attempts to provoke a fight. Diome was overjoyed, for that meant he could visit Evangelina every day after school. The Land of Heavenly Dreams was a whimsical realm of utmost beauty, and he felt delighted to be there as a guest.

****

Today was December 31st, the last day of the year. Less than a week had passed since the enactment of the new law. Since there was no school that day, Diome and Evangelina flew to the Land of Heavenly Dreams and spent the entire day there. As the light breeze caressed his skin and hummed in his ears, currents of air enveloped his body in a cloak of coolness. On the floating island to his left, Diome spotted a few young, dark-haired angels frolicking without wings. Some of them shot white sparks at the ground, and a tiny blossom emerged from the blades of grass.

Diome came to the abrupt realization of how alike devils and angels were when they weren't wearing their wings. In fact, weren't they all wired the same? Every devil and angel had a heart, loved ones, a place they called home, and people they called family. They weren't as different from each other as they claimed to be.

"Let's go to that little island over there." Evangelina pointed at a small one a few feet below them. Dressed in a white angel robe, she looked like a goddess with a waterfall of silvery-blonde hair flapping behind her.

Diome nodded. "Sounds good."

The two of them dipped low and descended on the island. Not a single angel was in sight. A rippling carpet of velvety grass stretched before them. Pale blue flowers with delicate, quilted petals dotted the lawns.

Evangelina removed her wings, shrunk them, and put them in the pocket in her wide, billowy sleeve. She lay down on the grass, gazing up at the sky, and Diome followed. For a long minute, neither of them spoke. Diome relished the tranquility of the moment, thinking about all the moments and memories that built up to the ordinary but precious present. Never would he take another day with Evangelina for granted. Every breath of hers, every heartbeat in her was a gift. Once Diome knew the soul-shredding pain of losing her, he realized the significance of each unique moment they had.

"Finally, we can be together," Evangelina said. "I never thought I'd live to see this day."

"We made it possible," replied Diome, reaching out to hold her hand. He leaned closer to her and kissed her cheek.

"I only wish they saw sense earlier. We never were different from each other. If they realized that earlier, they could have prevented many deaths."

"Can you believe it? We're the ones who put an end to the enmity that lasted between the two clans for hundreds of years. How heroic, now that I come to think of it."

"A sublime feat for sure. You'd think the presidents would honor us with some kind of medal. There wouldn't have been a new enactment if it hadn't been for us. The discovery about devil tears and all that."

"Sign us up for the Nobel Prize for Chemistry," joked Diome, smiling. "We ought to win an award for our discovering the resurrection powers of devil tears."

"And the Nobel Peace Prize too," Evangelina replied, humoring his humorous suggestion. "We stopped more deaths from occurring. It's all been reset to zero. We can't undo the past, but we've created a new future. Maybe one day, little angels and devils will sit together, play, be friends, and fall in love."

"You're starting to sound like Martin Luther King, Jr.," remarked Diome, reminded of the historical figure he'd learned about in ninth grade. He had aspired to be a man of his stature and terminate the hatred between the angels and devils, and now, he couldn't believe he had fulfilled his dream. "In one of his speeches, he said he hopes one day black and white children can join hands and be sisters and brothers."

"I'm not a hero like him, but I am flattered. It'll take time, of course, for the angels and devils to truly reconcile and put aside their prejudices. But one day, the dawn of a new era will come. One day, maybe when our grandchildren's grandchildren are born, nobody will even know there once was a time the angels and devils were enemies."

Diome smiled. A month ago, he had been too terrified to imagine they would have a married life together, too terrified to map out the details of their future in fear the brighter the flame of hope in him blazed, the longer the embers of depression would last when their dreams wilted into dust. But now, they were free—the shackles of history had been destroyed. Their hands were no longer tied, their fates no longer bound by insurmountable challenges. Because they had watered their hopes with blood, sweat, and tears, their forbidden love was no longer a secret. Like a rose blessed by sunshine, it thrived and bloomed with every day that passed and would pass.

"See the stars, clouds, and shadows above?" Evangelina asked.

Diome nodded. It was almost twilight. The sky, a gradient of blue that transitioned into turquoise and green below them, was decked in its full splendor. A million stars littered the heavens, some dotting the fluffy puffs of shadowy clouds.

"I've always thought stars symbolized hope, since they're bright and sometimes unreachable. Clouds represent fate because they can be light or dark, resembling pleasure and pain. And as for shadows, they're the problems we must deal with. It's like a big metaphor for life, isn't it?"

"Or you could look at it this way. You are the stars, I am the shadows, and the clouds represent the obstacles forcing us apart. We've come such a long way. Ever since I realized what you were, I knew our relationship wouldn't be an easy one. All the insane events we went through only proved my guesses right. But they were worth it—if overcoming all those hurdles meant I could spend one more moment with you, I'd do it in a heartbeat."

Diome meant it with all his heart. If he could rewind the clock and start everything over, he would make the same choices that brought him to her. Every moment with Evangelina had been nothing but magical. It was she who had healed him, fixed his depressed, insecure self, and shown him the beauty and brightness of the world. Together, they had worked wonders and made miracles. She had imbued an infinity of colors, music, and joy in his lonely life. Because of her, he was no longer cursed to live in the Burning Bowels and shrink in the shadows. Although it had only been almost three months since he first met her, their names were engraved on each other's souls for the rest of eternity. Diome would rather live another day with her by his side than a century without knowing the beloved angel he proudly called his girlfriend.

"You know I'd do anything for you too," murmured Evangelina. "I love you, Diome."

"Forever?" he asked, seeking verbal reassurance. Under the starry sky, under the sapphire-blue canopy adorned with diamonds, everything was possible. Love could live forever and remain immortal if he so wished.

Evangelina smiled, her expression dreamy. "For as long as the stars shall remain, as long as the universe shall endure."

The End

Evernight Teen ®

www.evernightteen.com